BLOOD SPELLS

BLOOD SPELLS

ALICIA ELLIS

BLOOD SPELLS

This is a work of fiction. All characters, organizations, and events portrayed in this book are products of the imagination or are used fictitiously.

Copyright © 2021 by Alicia Ellis

Cover design by Sanja Gombar

Published by Figmented Ink in Atlanta
First Publication, April 2021
Trade Paperback ISBN: 978-1-939452-55-9

Library of Congress Control Number: 2021906283

*To Shelley and Barb,
for your wise counsel.*

CHAPTER ONE

I'd heard of people cutting their wrists, but I'd never seen it. Not until five minutes ago.

Now, I stood outside the master bedroom of my home, cell phone clutched in hand, my mouth pasty-dry from losing my breakfast in the bathroom sink. On the other side of this door, my stepmother Cora lay in a bathtub. A thick layer of blood filled the bottom of the basin.

My fingers fumbled as I dialed 9-1-1.

No ringing. The call didn't connect.

Stupid magical house.

I went to try again, but the screen had gone black and lifeless.

Phone held high, I ran into the family room, then the kitchen, searching for a spot with weaker magic. Magic trumped technology, and that rarely went well for phone calls in this house. The display flickered on and off. Near the back door, it lit up.

The call took an eternity to connect. During the wait, I tried not to think of Cora, her wrists slit halfway to the elbows, her body empty of blood, her knife discarded beside her.

"What's your emergency?" came a polite voice from the other end of the line.

"Cora . . ." My voice broke to pieces, and each shard stung my throat. "My stepmother is dead. I think she committed suicide."

"Are you sure she's dead?"

"I'm sure. There's . . . a lot of blood."

"What's your address?"

"6 Howell Lane."

"Your name?"

"Madison Cooper."

"Is the victim a blood-magic user?"

"Yes."

"A summoner?"

"Yes . . . I mean she used to be." What did that matter? She was dead.

"I'll send the Practitioners Bureau."

"She quit summoning."

"That's fine. When did you . . ." The woman said something else in her too-polite voice, but it didn't matter. It couldn't bring Cora back.

My phone beeped a warning that its power was almost depleted. I'd plugged it in last night, but it hadn't charged, thanks to the magic around here.

I disconnected the call and dialed Aunt Sara. I hadn't

talked to her for more than five minutes at a time since my father's death almost two years ago—she reminded me too much of him. And just like him, she'd know what to do in a crisis.

The phone flickered again. I raised it above my head, and the flickering stopped.

"Maddy?" she said when she picked up, her voice thick and low with half sleep. "It's early."

"Cora's dead," I whispered.

"What, honey?"

I reached my other hand above my head and hit the button to switch the phone's mode to speaker.

"She killed herself," I shouted upward toward the phone. "Cora's dead."

Aunt Sara's next words sounded more alert. "I'll be there in ten minutes—fifteen tops if I have trouble getting past the water line. Did you call the police?"

I nodded.

"Maddy?"

"Yes," I said. "They're on the way."

"Good. Stay on the phone with me. I'm getting in the car now."

I nodded again and dropped my arm before I realized what I was doing. The phone made a crackling sound, and the connection fizzled out. I considered calling her again, but it didn't matter. It couldn't bring Cora back.

I trudged to my room and slumped down on the bed. My hand went limp, and the phone dropped to my lap, screen bright, ringing. The caller ID announced my aunt calling back. I let it ring. I couldn't convince my numb fingers to reach for the phone. It stopped a second later, and the screen went black.

I was still sitting on the bed, staring at the wall, when my aunt arrived. My phone lay on the floor by my feet. And in the next room, Cora was still dead.

Still in her pajamas, Aunt Sara breezed into the room with her dark, kinky hair in a messy bun and her face fixed in determination. She crooked one hand under my back and laid me out on the bed.

"Sweet girl. I'm here. You can sleep if you want."

I rolled to my side, facing the wall, and curled into a fetal position.

"Can I get you anything?" she asked, her voice soft and smooth and sad.

"I want to be alone."

The click of the door told me when she'd left.

But I *didn't* want to be alone.

I rolled back over and reached for the pocketknife on my nightstand. My gaze slid from the small knife—with a blade carved from bone—to the closed door of my bedroom, to the analog clock beside the door.

I needed my mother. But as usual, time was an enemy. It had run out too quickly with my mom, then with my dad, and now with Cora. And with the Bureau on the way, I didn't even have time for a summoning. The dead would have to stay put for now.

More compact than the bone knife in the next room, which was covered in my stepmother's blood, *this* one was better suited for hiding. And that was what I needed to do with it, unless I wanted the Bureau to throw me in jail for illegal practice by a minor.

As I scanned the room for a safe place, I spotted a powder-blue envelope on the nightstand. On it, Cora's loopy script spelled my name. I held my breath as I lifted the blue envelope and flipped it over and over in my hand.

Her last words.

After I read this, I might never be able to reach Cora again. I could try to summon her, but it might not work. It never had with my dad. Maybe this was all I had left of her. I raised the envelope to my face and inhaled. Lavender. It smelled like her.

"Maddy?" My bedroom door opened, and Aunt Sara came in. Her head tilted to one side in that way people do when they pity you. I'd seen that motion a lot, starting the day my mother died. "You don't want to rest until the Bureau gets here?"

Three quick bangs on the front door cut off my answer. I tucked the knife into the back of my waistband, covered it with my shirt, and went out to meet the people who would take my stepmother away.

CHAPTER TWO

Aunt Sara tried to keep me in my room, but I refused. I would not hide like a coward while these people poked and prodded my stepmother. So my aunt ushered me into the family room and pushed me down on the couch before answering the door.

The knife rubbed against my spine, and I squirmed to shift it to one side.

Muffled voices came from the foyer, and soon my aunt returned with four other people, three men and a woman. She pointed to a thin man with his hair slicked back and a shorter man who lagged behind him. "This is the coroner and his assistant." Aunt Sara's voice was velvet-soft but not at all soothing.

I didn't meet the coroner's eyes. They gave solemn nods and, without a word, disappeared into the depths of Cora's bedroom.

"And these two are from the Practitioners Aid." Aunt

Sara gestured toward the remaining man and woman.

The woman, a tall blonde, cleared her throat and stared me straight in the eyes. "I'm Agent Tanner." She tilted her head toward the tall, broad man with her. "This is my partner, Agent Reyes."

Reyes dipped his head solemnly.

I stood, as if on command. They wore casual slacks and short-sleeved dress shirts—a blouse for her and a light sweater for him. The short sleeves were probably a job requirement. As far as the non-magic were concerned, long sleeves said you had something to hide—like cuts on your arms to draw blood for spells. Bare arms meant safe.

Despite the casual clothing, though, something in their demeanors felt formal. Maybe it was the erect postures, or the thin smiles that held no warmth.

I'd never seen a Bureau agent in person before, only fictional ones on television. Agent Reyes looked a lot like those: dark shirt and pants, shiny shoes, and a face devoid of feeling. He wore his hair a little longer than they did on television though—less military looking. It made him look more approachable, but not by much.

Agent Tanner kept her blond hair in a ponytail so tight I feared for her scalp. She quirked her lips in a way that might have been meant to pass for a smile—it didn't.

Neither of them carried weapons that I could see.

"And it's the Practitioners Bureau now," Agent Tanner added to my aunt. "Not the Practitioners Aid."

"Yes, of course. My mistake."

When Agent Reyes moved toward me, I fought the

instinct to shuffle away. Instead, I tilted my head back to look him in the eye.

"Did you touch the body?" He had a soft, round voice that resonated with empathy. His tone might have eased the tension in the room if it weren't for the knife that kept inching lower in my waistband, threatening to slip down my pant leg.

"No." It took every bit of my willpower not to adjust the knife.

"Take a seat." Tanner gestured toward the couch. "We'll be with you when we're done." She and her partner strode away to join the coroner, out of my view.

I dropped back onto the couch and adjusted the knife while pretending to scratch my back.

Aunt Sara sat beside me. "Do you need anything?"

I needed my stepmother back, but I couldn't have that so I shook my head.

Muffled voices reached us from inside Cora's room. I couldn't make out most of what they said, just snatches here and there. Words like *wasted blood* and *summoner*. Once, I caught a full sentence: "It's been years since she summoned."

When my father died, Cora had refused to summon him. I asked her once or twice, after failing on my own, but she insisted we should let him rest. His time here had ended, and we had to respect that. And if she wouldn't summon him, she wouldn't summon anyone. So she stopped. She kept using blood magic, but never for calling the dead. Not anymore.

So why kill herself? And why now, almost two years later?

Summoners committed suicide all the time—but after they quit?

Although I'd been too caught up in finding my stepmother dead to think about it before, now it struck me how strange a choice wrist-slitting was for a practitioner's suicide. We honored our blood, preserved it. Not only did it keep us alive from one second to the next, but it fed our magic. Summoners took sleeping pills or hung themselves.

They did not spill their blood all over the bathtub.

Aunt Sara smoothed my hair. I hadn't yet combed it this morning, and it was still in its wild, natural state of a mass of dark coils. Worry etched a line in her forehead. My dad had a line in that same spot, and more around his mouth when he smiled—a mouth shaped a lot like my aunt's.

My gut twisted. I'd avoided her for the past couple years because it tore my soul to be so close to my father's double when he remained so far away.

I turned my face so I wouldn't have to look at her. "I'm going to grab some air." I jumped to my feet and hurried to the front door.

The suffocating summer air engulfed me. But I still closed the door behind me to hint to Aunt Sara that I needed time alone. The alternative was to return inside, where I'd be surrounded by all those people who were here because of Cora.

Because Cora had died.

Because Cora had left me.

Because Cora had spilled all her blood in the bathtub, not thirty feet from where I slept.

Or maybe she hadn't.

"Bad day?" A male voice called my attention, and I focused on its owner. He was about my age—sixteen or so. Dark-blond hair. He used a hand to shade his face from the sun and stared at me with sympathetic brown eyes.

"Who are you?"

"Oh, sorry. I'm Marshall. My mom's a Bureau agent." He batted at the space in front of his face, scratched his nose, and then pointed at my front door. "We were in the car when she got the call. She told me to wait out here."

His voice was soft, lower than those of most boys my age and with a touch of hoarseness that I found soothing. It was the imperfection in his tone that made it comforting. In a screwed-up world, why should anything be perfect?

When several seconds passed, he added, "Is there anything I can do?" He swiped in front of his face again.

If the day didn't suck so much, I might have laughed. Instead, I slid down into a sitting position, back pressed against the front door. "You don't live in the community?" I toned it like a question, but the answer was clear.

Wordless, he sat cross-legged facing me. "How'd you guess?" He laughed and swiped at the air again.

"Leave them alone. I promise you'll stop noticing in a

few minutes."

"It's like they're attacking me."

I focused on the energy around us, which I mostly didn't notice after living most of my life inside the water line.

White-blue particles drifted upward, sparkling in the sunlight like miniature, weightless diamonds. They smelled simultaneously acrid and sweet—like burning rose petals. Swaying back and forth, sometimes circling one another, sometimes slowing, sometimes speeding up, but always moving upward.

They went out of their way to touch Marshall. They paused their dancing long enough to kiss his face on their way to the sky.

"You have magic blood." I said it as a statement rather than a question. I'd just met him, but the particles always knew the magic people from the nons. I attracted them too, but I didn't mind. I was used to their attention.

He nodded and swiped again. The bright lights swirled in a miniature tornado, kissed his hand, and continued upward.

"Relax." I stopped focusing on the magical energy and closed my eyes briefly to relax them from the strain. "I promise you'll start to like how it feels."

He fisted his hands at his sides and looked directly at me. He didn't say anything for a while—probably concentrating on not scratching—and I appreciated the quiet as much as I appreciated his voice. I liked his eyes too. Chocolate brown and deep, like I could get lost in them.

That would be nice—getting lost.

"Your mother and her partner are checking out my stepmother's body," I said after a while.

"I'm sorry." The fists at his sides loosened.

"Me too."

Marshall stared down at his forearm, scratched it, and then scratched his nose again.

"Is this your first time inside a water line?"

"I was inside the one in my hometown a couple times. But it's worse here."

"It's the ley line intersection." I leaned off my front door just enough to point behind me, in the direction of my house. "That way. Most magic communities are at the intersection of two ley lines. We've got three here."

My house faced away from the middle of the community, where the three ley lines—sources of magic embedded in the earth—met. In the distance, the particles floated out of the crack in the ground at the intersection and dispersed. There, they were dense. Since my house sat near the edge of the community, they were thinner here.

"You don't itch?"

"You get used to it. Plus, we're toward the edge of the water line, and it's weaker here. The folks who live in the center can't get electricity at all. We can get at least a little." The word *we* tasted wrong on my tongue. It was really just *me* now. I stared down at my hands and blinked a lot, holding the flood back.

There must have been a full minute of silence before Marshall spoke again. "It's okay to be sad."

I nodded, but I wasn't so sure. In my sixteen years of life, *sad* hadn't gotten me anything.

"Is there something I can do?"

"I just want to be alone."

He pushed himself to a standing position and, without looking back, walked to one of the cars in the driveway, a gray luxury sedan. He opened the door and slid into the passenger seat, leaving the door open behind him.

My chest felt tired and empty—and tired of being empty. I slumped against the front door, closed my eyes, and concentrated on not feeling. That was easier.

"You're going to be alone a lot, I'm guessing," Marshall said in a voice that was surprisingly familiar despite my first hearing it just minutes ago.

I opened my eyes to find him dropping down in front me again, a piece of paper and two pencils clutched in one hand. He set the page between us and drew two parallel vertical lines, with two horizontal ones crossing them. A tic-tac-toe board.

"We can be not-alone together." He gestured at the board. "We don't even have to talk."

He held out a pencil toward me. I stared at it for a couple seconds and then decided I had nothing to lose. I grabbed the pencil and marked an *X* in the middle of the lines.

He wrote an *O* right above.

I drew my next *X* in the upper left, next to his *O*. "Sometimes, I feel like I'm cursed."

I thought he hadn't heard me as he drew an *O* under

my first move, instead of blocking me. "Why?"

I could win now, by placing my *X* in the bottom right and creating a diagonal line of *X*s. Instead, I drew an *X* in the upper right. "I'm three parents down—Cora was my stepmother, and both my birth parents are dead."

"And that's somehow your fault?"

"I'm the connecting thread. You think that's coincidence?"

"I think it's really awful luck." Marshall drew an *O* in the bottom left, leaving my obvious winning move available. "My sister died. A couple years ago."

"I'm sorry."

"I think about it a lot. I wonder what I could have done differently—if I could have saved her."

I nodded as I placed my last *X* on our board, in the bottom right, finally winning the game. I knew that feeling of helplessness. That feeling of grasping at a life that could have been different and finding your hand full of air and nothing else.

Marshall drew another tic-tac-toe board below the first one and pushed the page toward me.

I pushed it back at him. "You go first."

He scratched his nose and then drew an *X* in the top-center section.

"Are you going to keep letting me win?"

He widened his eyes in mock offense. "Would I do a thing like that?"

"Oh, certainly not," I said, my expression solemn.

He laughed, and I cracked a grin. I liked being not-alone with him. It beat sitting here by myself, thinking of Cora's corpse being poked and prodded and packed into a body bag. My smile trembled and collapsed under its own weight.

The front door opened behind me, and I almost fell into the foyer. But strong hands caught my shoulder and righted me. Aunt Sara stared down at me, overflowing with pity. "I thought you might want company." She glanced at Marshall and then back at me. "But I see you found some."

Marshall hopped to his feet and grabbed my hand. His fingers were cool and soft despite the hot sun. He pulled me up and then held out his hand for my aunt to shake. "Marshall Tanner. My mom's one of the agents on this case."

"I see." She turned back to me and pointed to a line of sweat creeping down my temple. "Wouldn't you be more comfortable in your bedroom? Or you can wait in the car, if you like. I'll give you my keys to run the air conditioner."

"No."

But since I couldn't escape my aunt either way, outside seemed no less awful than inside.

I grabbed Marshall's hand and led him past Aunt Sara into the house. If I had to endure her and the Bureau and the coroner, he had to go with me. I liked how he looked at me—like it wasn't the end of the world, like he didn't think I would break.

Aunt Sara followed us to the family room. I released

Marshall and settled into a corner of the couch, legs tucked in front of me. Marshall hesitated for only a second and then sat beside me. Aunt Sara took the armchair on the other side of the coffee table.

"How are you feeling?" she asked me.

"Is that a serious question?"

She licked her lips, and her gaze wandered to Marshall's face before landing back on mine. "I could make you some tea."

"Sure." At least this way, she'd stop hovering.

"Would you like some?" she asked Marshall.

"No, I'm good. Thanks." He scrunched up his nose like he was trying not to scratch it. He hadn't scratched in a while, so that was an improvement.

Aunt Sara rose from the couch and hurried into the kitchen. When she hit the light switch, there was a soft click, and two gas lamps retrofitted to the walls flared to life. The electric bulbs overhead stayed dark, but the gas lamps were enough. Aunt Sara busied herself in the kitchen.

"Maddy?" she called no more than a minute later. She held up two mugs, one in each hand, and stood in the middle of the kitchen.

"Mm-hmm?"

"You don't have a microwave?"

"We used to have one, but it never worked anyway. I think Dad donated it."

"I don't know how you do it," she muttered, almost too low for me to hear.

"Tea kettle's in the cabinet above the sink, I think." I half stood so I could twist and point to the right cabinet.

"Got it." She grabbed the kettle and set it on the gas stove top.

When I sat again, Marshall was squinting down at the space between my back and the couch cushions.

"What?" I asked him.

"There's something . . ." He reached behind me and yanked the knife from my waistband.

I grabbed at it, but Marshall pulled it from my reach. He shot a glance at the door to Cora's bedroom—where the Bureau agents were—and then slipped it in his pocket.

"Give it back," I whispered.

"What are you doing with it? They'll arrest you."

I reached for his pocket. "Then let me hide it."

"No."

The firmness in his tone stopped me dead. "It's got nothing to do with you."

"Summoning kills people." He pointed to Cora's bedroom. "Every day." Something about his face went desperate. "Tell me you don't summon. You do other stuff. Other magic, right?"

I stopped reaching for the knife.

"You're not the only one who's lost someone to this."

"Who?" I asked, my voice softer. "Your sister?"

"She was four years older than me—just got her license. She got lost."

My chest ached for him. I'd performed summonings, so I knew how seductive death could be. The way it called to you and promised you peace and comfort, no more pain. Just quiet and warmth and bliss. Sometimes, people summoned and never ended the spells. They refused to break contact with that sensation, and they died in the middle of their summonings.

We called it *getting lost*.

"I'm sorry," I told him, "but that's not going to happen to me."

"Because you're careful? You haven't even trained."

If I stopped, I'd never see my mother again. And with Cora gone . . . I had more reason than ever for blood magic.

The tea kettle's shriek interrupted us before I could respond.

Marshall and I sat in complete silence, me glaring at him, and him pretending not to notice, until Aunt Sara joined us with two mugs of tea. She handed one to me and sipped from the other.

A thump from the depths of Cora's room startled me, and I lost my grip on the mug. It clattered to the hardwood floor but remained in one piece. A pool of light-brown liquid spread outward. I reached for the now-empty mug and set it upright on the table.

"I should clean that." I tried to push myself up to grab a towel, but Aunt Sara's gentle hand on my shoulder kept me in place.

"I'll get it." She grabbed a dish towel from the kitchen. When she returned, she stooped and soaked up the tea, waving my apologies aside.

The coroner and his assistant emerged from the bedroom. They carried between them a full body bag on a stretcher. Cora lay inside it, all zipped up in darkness. I couldn't look away as they made their way to the front door and exited. A voice inside my head screamed at me to follow them, to curl up next to Cora, to clutch her close to me, to keep the life I knew.

Instead, I fisted my hands in my lap and stayed put.

Agents Reyes and Tanner emerged from the bedroom and planted themselves on the other side of the coffee table.

Agent Tanner—Marshall's mother—quirked one blond eyebrow at him. "You're supposed to be *in the car*." She emphasized the last three words in a way that made it clear she meant for him to go back there.

"It got hot."

"It is not appropriate for you to be here."

"It's fine," I said. "I invited him."

She pressed her lips together but didn't argue.

"Do you want to tell us what happened?" Reyes said.

Aunt Sara moved to stand beside me and rested a hand on my shoulder. The weight of it kept me grounded. Otherwise, I might have floated away. Far away from here.

My tongue took up too much space in my mouth, but somehow I made it work. "When I woke up, her bedroom door was open. It's usually closed when she's away, and she was supposed to be gone another night. But she was . . ." I gestured behind him, to the master bedroom—from which they'd removed my stepmother's bloodless corpse.

"She committed suicide?" Agent Tanner asked.

"Looked that way." My voice sounded more bitter than I expected.

"Is that a suicide note?" She pointed at the sealed blue envelope on the coffee table, where I'd placed it when they arrived.

"I think so."

Agent Tanner grabbed it and tore the envelope open. I cringed. Cora's last words deserved more respect. She scanned the letter and then passed it to Reyes, who read it himself before folding it and sliding it back into the envelope.

I stretched my fingers toward the blue paper.

"It's evidence," Tanner said.

"It's addressed to me," I said.

"It's evidence in the death of a licensed practitioner. It belongs to the Bureau until we close this case."

"Then close it," I said, my voice rising. "It's mine! It's—"

My aunt patted my leg. "It's a suicide," she said. "Anyone can see that. Why would the case stay open?"

"It's not up to us, ma'am."

"Do you mind if I look around the house?" Agent Reyes asked, cutting into the conversation before I could rain down all manner of foul language.

"Why?" Aunt Sara asked. "You don't think it was suicide?" She continued to pat my leg, but it did nothing to soothe me.

"Perhaps. But regardless, it's standard practice to sweep a deceased practitioner's residence and remove all tools of her practice. We don't want them to end up in the hands of unlicensed novices." He paused and then added, "Sorry."

The two agents strode to the other side of the room and entered Cora's home office, separated from the family room by only an archway. Agent Reyes examined the tall bookshelves built into one wall. He removed two note-books and set them on the floor, for him to collect later I assumed.

Agent Tanner turned her attention to the desk and pulled out each drawer until she reached the bottom right. She yanked on the knob, but the drawer only clicked in response.

"This one is locked," she called, without glancing over at me. "What's in it?"

"That's where my dad kept his work stuff. He was a psychiatrist."

"You have a key?"

"No."

She turned to her partner. "We're going to have to break it open or take the desk with us."

"Really, Mom?" Marshall said. "Do you have to—" He clamped his mouth shut when she skewered him with a glance.

I bit my lip to keep from tearing up. It was just a desk, but my father had owned it as long as I'd been alive. Too much was changing, too fast.

While they searched the rest of the house, Aunt Sara brewed me a second cup of tea. She handed it to me and sat on the coffee table in front of my spot on the couch. Both my hands gripped the large tea mug, while steaming chamomile drifted upward from the brim.

Aunt Sara pried one of my hands from the mug and wrapped it in her own. She looked at me with kind brown eyes shaped like my dad's.

I stared down at my tea. It was easier.

She pulled in a long breath. "Do you want to talk?"

"You think she killed herself?"

My aunt's brow furrowed. "I'm sorry?"

"Do you think she killed herself?"

Cora and my dad had married mere months before he died. Cora and I hadn't gotten much of a chance to know each other by then, but she agreed to become my legal guardian anyway.

Even though she'd traveled for her work, she always left the fridge and emergency-cash drawer stocked. And when she was home, she made plans to spend time with me over dinner or a shopping trip. She wasn't exactly motherly, but kind and selfless. I liked her, and we had a comfortable arrangement.

I could have gone to live with Aunt Sara after my dad's accident. God knew she'd offered a hundred times. But this was my home.

When I sniffed the air, I still smelled the sandalwood scent of my dad's aftershave. Above my head, crown molding he'd carved himself lined the walls. So when he died, I stayed here with Cora. She could have sent me away, but she didn't.

I thought I could trust her. I thought I could love her.

Aunt Sara squeezed my hand. "You know Cora loved you, right?"

We sat in silence, with her staring at me like she feared I would break into a thousand pieces. Only I wasn't going to. This time, I would keep it together. Cora brought the number of my deceased parents to three.

Lucky number three. Third time's the charm.

A bitter laugh bubbled up in my chest, but I managed to stifle it. Instead, it came out like a mangled cough. Aunt Sara's forehead creased. I sucked my lower lip between my teeth and vowed to keep silent until I could maintain the proper amount of solemnity.

But when Aunt Sara opened her mouth to talk, I had to stop her from saying something touching and heartfelt—something that would make my resolve to keep it together shatter all over the hardwood floor.

"I'll miss her . . ."

I trailed off as the two agents returned from the back of the house. Before they could say anything, Reyes's phone rang.

He held up a finger at us, then drew the phone from his pocket. "Reyes." He paused while the person on the other end of the line spoke. "What about the request for further search?" For an instant, his brows rose upward. Then he caught me staring at him and resumed his placid expression. "Got it." He ended the call and turned to Aunt Sara and me. "We'll need to make a more thorough sweep of the house. It'll be better if you're not here for that."

"You need us to leave right now?" I asked.

"We can't do the sweep with you here. So yes, please go."

I glanced up at my aunt, already knowing the answer to my question. "Where should I go?"

"With me and your cousins. You want me to help you get your stuff?"

"No. I'll just grab a few things." I pushed myself off the couch and headed for my room.

Agent Tanner monitored my packing. She scrutinized every object I threw into the bag, so I had no chance to get my knife back from Marshall.

When I finished, I took a last glance around my bedroom. Dad and Cora had helped me paint the walls lavender on my fourteenth birthday, over two years ago, when I finally convinced them that a proper teenager couldn't live in a baby-pink room. I might never sleep in that bed again, with its deep-purple comforter Cora bought.

My old stuffed animals lined a shelf near the closet. I'd barely touched them in so long. On my way through the door, I grabbed a big pink penguin with a zipper down its back. Dad had won it for me at a theme park, and when I was a kid, I hid all my prized possessions in it.

I hefted my backpack onto my shoulder and rolled my suitcase into the family room. Marshall had disappeared, probably banished back to the car by his mother.

"One more thing," I said. In the kitchen, I grabbed the last forty bucks from the emergency-cash drawer.

Aunt Sara stood in the foyer waiting for me. Her mouth opened and closed a couple times before words came out. "Do you want to talk? If not to me, then . . ." She waved two business cards in my face. "Agent Reyes gave me this number for a grief counselor. He gave me his own number too, in case you think of anything else he should know about Cora."

I shrugged. "Let's just go." Blinking back tears, I said goodbye to the house I'd lived in for the past nine years— and the three people who'd lived here with me.

Outside, I dragged my bag across the small road in front of the house, and the bag's wheels bounced over each piece of gravel. Aunt Sara led me over a footpath through the yards of the neighbors across the street, and to the narrow road beyond. Her silver sedan sat in the middle of the road, where she'd abandoned it and walked.

"It stopped working," she said.

I nodded, even though it didn't require explanation. Inside the water line, sometimes cars just stopped.

Aunt Sara buckled me into the car and stuffed my suitcase in the trunk, as if I were a small child. I didn't protest. When she turned the key in the ignition, the car roared to life, and Aunt Sara let out a small but pleased squeal.

The clock on the car's dash read barely nine in the morning, and not only had I found a dead body, but I'd also spoken to the Bureau and packed my life into a bag with wheels.

Busy day.

A couple minutes later, she slowed the car as we

approached the water line—a moat that surrounded the community of blood-magic users. We could live wherever we wanted, inside or out. But blood magic worked better inside, and tech worked better outside.

Red water flowed through it in a never-ending circle, so deep that it looked almost black. The water line kept the magic signals from interfering too much with the electrical ones on the other side.

Sometimes, when heavy magic was in play nearby, it flowed so high and fast that it covered the narrow bridge leading across, waves lapping over the grass on either side. When it wasn't safe to cross, we simply waited until the water level sank again.

Today, it flowed barely beneath the bridge.

"It's fallen since I came across earlier this morning," Aunt Sara told me. "It was high before, almost over the top." She squeezed my hand and then released. "I would have waited for it to go lower if I hadn't been in such a hurry to see you."

As we crossed onto the bridge, the world became a shade grayer. The sun was still shining, but we left the particles of magic inside the water line. Although I didn't usually notice them, I always noticed their absence. Colors looked duller. And my skin felt cooler, exposed.

I leaned back in the seat, forced my eyes closed, and stayed that way until I heard the sound of Aunt Sara's garage door opening.

We'd arrived at my new home.

CHAPTER THREE

The four of us sat around the breakfast table one Sunday two months after Cora's death—me, Aunt Sara, and my cousins Ryan and Cassie. Six-year-old Ryan spooned marshmallows out of his cereal and ignored the rest of it, while Cassie jabbered on about tomorrow, her first day of eighth grade.

Cassie stared at me.

"I'm sorry. What?" I wasn't trying to ignore her. But Ryan had put cartoons on the television in the adjoining family room, and it felt like white noise against my eardrums.

We didn't have a TV at my old house because it wouldn't work well anyway. Here, I couldn't remember any one of them being home for more than a half hour without flipping the thing on. Over the noise of the cartoons, I had trouble focusing on the noise coming from Cassie.

It didn't help that Agent Reyes had finally informed me yesterday that they'd finished their search of my old house. I could go home. And that was all I wanted.

Cassie let out an exaggerated sigh. "I *said*, what's Pritchett like?"

My pleasant mood faltered, but I kept the happy expression plastered on my face. "It's good. I like it."

Like my mother, Cora had come from a practitioner family, so she'd ended up at Pritchett Academy. The school was a known gathering place for kids of the proper bloodlines, along with rich kids regardless of bloodline. Cora's connections in the administration, on top of my good grades, had gotten me a scholarship to go there.

At first, I'd had no interest in hanging with other blood-magic kids, who made up over half of the school's students, but it had been important to Cora that I go. "Magical and non-magical cooperation"—in her words— was essential to our world now.

On my first day, she introduced me to her cousin's daughter, Lauren. She and I became best friends, so it all worked out.

"If I get a scholarship, could I go next year?" Cassie asked her mom.

Aunt Sara grimaced. "You won't have anything in common with those rich kids."

"Maddy's not rich."

"No. But she's one of them for other reasons. Concentrate on your classes for now. We'll discuss high school later. Ryan—stop slurping your cereal, and put your bowl in the sink if you're done."

Ryan's eyes went so wide I could see the whites on all sides of his irises. "Is Maddy magic?"

"Only by blood, honey. It's nothing to worry about." Aunt Sara pointed at his cereal bowl, which he gripped so hard with trembling hands that milk had sloshed onto the table. "Sink please."

Ryan didn't rise from the chair but turned a pleading gaze toward me. "Do you have a soul, Maddy?"

"Of course I do. We're just like you. Most of us don't even practice." I pointed to the TV, still blasting on its highest volume, and then at the small chandelier over the kitchen counter. "See, your electricity still works. Nothing broke just because I'm around. That's not true either. None of it is."

"So you don't want to steal *my* soul?" he whispered, leaning forward in his seat.

"No, squirt. I'm good with the one I've got."

"And she couldn't if she wanted to," Aunt Sara added.

Ryan looked back and forth between us.

Aunt Sara raised her brows at me for confirmation. "Isn't that right?" she said in a tone that sounded more like an instruction than a question.

"Absolutely," I said. "It's impossible—not to mention illegal. Mostly we just use magic for blessings and to make small things more convenient. I promise. There's nothing to worry about."

Ryan leaned back in his chair, but his eyes remained a little too wide.

"So since there's no danger, I can go to Pritchett?" Cassie asked, seeing her opening. "What if I get a scholarship?"

Aunt Sara finally swept up Ryan's cereal bowl and placed it in the sink. "I said *later*."

"It could be cool," I said. "Sharing a school with you for a year before I head to college."

Aunt Sara shot me a discreet glare, so I changed the subject.

"Cool sweater," I said, pointing at the sheer, charcoal-colored sweater Cassie wore over a black camisole.

The dark clothing complemented her jet-black hair, which she wore pressed straight. Aunt Sara refused to let her dye it fire-engine red. As a compromise, my aunt let her darken it several shades from its natural dark brown and wear dark eyeliner, which Cassie never left the house without.

"Thanks." Cassie adjusted the sweater's wide collar to fall off one shoulder, revealing one amber-toned shoulder. "Found it at the thrift shop last weekend. You can borrow it if you want."

"I might do that." A ding of the doorbell made me push my chair back from the table. "Gotta go. That's my ride."

After Cora's death, we'd had to return her leased vehicle to the dealer. Aunt Sara couldn't afford to buy me one right now—especially since Cora's life insurance hadn't paid up after her death was declared a suicide. That officially left me car-less. I'd be bumming rides off my friends until I figured out how to earn enough for a used car.

Aunt Sara frowned at my bowl, still half full. "I thought we were spending the day together. Can we at least finish breakfast?"

"Can't. Gotta go."

After two months of anticipation, I finally had permission to return to my old house. I'd left most of my belongings there, but more importantly, I missed my home.

I lived with Aunt Sara now, but I still thought of this as *her* home. No way was I hanging out here all day when I could go back to the last place I remembered being truly happy—even if it was just for a few minutes to grab some of my stuff.

"Take something with you. Maybe a piece of fruit? Or I could pop a waffle in the toaster."

"I'm good. Just not that hungry. And Lauren's waiting."

"Does Lauren want a waffle?" Ryan's goofy grin filled up his little face. "She should come in and have waffles."

"I'm sure she's eaten already." I patted his head. "And find a girlfriend your own age." I grabbed my backpack, in case I needed to bring some things back with me, and headed toward the door.

When I yanked it open, my best friend Lauren stood on the porch, a wide smile on her face. "Hey."

"Hi, Lauren!" Ryan shouted from the table.

"Hey." Lauren peeked over my shoulder and waved.

"Don't encourage him." I squeezed her in a tight hug. "You look amazing, by the way."

After Cora's funeral, Lauren had taken off to spend the rest of the summer on the West Coast with her dad. She'd offered to cancel the trip and spend the time with me, but I insisted she go. No need for her to wallow in self-pity by my side—I handled that just fine on my own.

Lauren's mahogany skin now shone with the healthy glow of a new tan. She wore her locs in a large twist piled on top of her head, showing off the even tone of her long neck.

Even after I released the embrace, Lauren hung on for a few more seconds. "How are you?"

"Same as last time you asked. Fine. And you?"

"I'm good. It's not like she and I were close."

"You know that's not what I meant."

She nodded but didn't answer. I followed Lauren to her red convertible, which had its hard top open. I opened the door and slid in, while Lauren jumped over her door into her seat and then grinned at me. The car was only a few months old, and she still got a kick out of jumping into it.

"I missed you," I said. "Don't go away anymore."

"No time soon. I promise." She started the car, and the engine flipped over into a luxurious purr. "You sure you're ready to do this?"

"Definitely." Ever since I'd talked to Agent Reyes last night, all I could think about was going home.

"As you wish."

"So?" I asked as she backed the car out of the driveway. "How does it feel being back?"

"It's okay. A little weird with just me and Mom." She shrugged. "I like spending time with my dad, and the divorce didn't change that. I just wish he would've stayed here. It's like he moved all the way across the country to escape Mom, and it didn't even matter that it meant leaving me behind too."

"You know it's not like that. He—"

"Yeah, I know. New job. Fresh start. He still loves me. Blah, blah, blah." Lauren glanced at her fingers, which clutched the wheel in front of her. She let out a long breath and loosened her grip. "I just liked it the way it was before."

I knew the feeling.

"Enough about me. In exchange for my transportation services, you have to tell me how you really feel. And don't say *fine*."

I leaned my head back against the seat and, for just a second, imagined the two of us getting into a serious car accident. I would be mangled beyond all recognition, maybe even killed if I were lucky—and everyone would stop asking me *how I feel*.

"This sucks." I gritted my teeth because crying was not an option. Crying was for people who thought it would make them feel better, and I had no such delusions. "It sucks a lot, actually. But mostly I just feel numb. When Mom died, and then later Dad, I cried for like a month straight both times. And it still hurts, like a physical pain."

I cringed. "Like someone is reaching in and trying to tear out my heart—and succeeding. But it's not that way with Cora. I feel like . . . like I shouldn't have expected her to stay. Like I should have known better."

"You're not angry with her anymore—for killing herself?"

"*If* that's even what happened. It doesn't make sense. Why spill all that blood?" Although the Practitioners Bureau still considered Cora's death a suicide, I didn't buy it. I'd gone back and forth on the issue over the past two months. But in the end, I had to believe she wouldn't have wasted all that blood.

"She left a note, Maddy." Lauren's tone was honey poured over sugar—too sweet for the tongue. Like she was breaking bad news.

"A note I haven't seen. It has to be a fake."

Lauren nodded, but by the way her face screwed up, I could tell she felt conflicted. "I'll admit one thing—I don't understand why she'd do that with you in the house."

"I wasn't supposed to be."

"What do you mean?"

"Remember, I was at your place the night before. I told her I'd be there all night, watching movies. She said she'd be back in town the next day, and we'd meet for brunch and then go home together. We were going to . . ." Realization hit me like a head-on collision. "She didn't want me to find her. She wanted to keep me away from the house as long as possible."

Lauren was nodding, but she said nothing.

"No. That can't be right," I said, shaking my head. "Doesn't it seem weird to you? The way she died?"

"You mean suicide?"

"I mean slitting her wrists," I said.

She cocked an eyebrow at me and waited.

I shut my eyes and attempted to block out the remnants of last night's dream. I kept seeing Cora in the bathtub, head tipped backward, blood flowing from her wrists.

Of course, she hadn't been bleeding when I found her. She'd died hours earlier, before I got home. But in my dreams over the past two months, I had come home earlier. I heard a noise, dragged myself out of bed, and stumbled down the hallway.

I was still too late, but I arrived in time to see Cora's body still spilling its blood. It didn't form a shallow pool at the bottom of the basin either. Instead, it rose higher and higher, covering her tan skin inch by inch. Just when it seemed her body had emptied itself, the flow began anew. And despite the red pouring into the tub, her ivory silk nightgown remained pure, her auburn hair flowing around its low neckline.

I shook my head and pushed the dream to the back of my thoughts.

"She quit summoning," I continued. "Years ago. Don't you think it's weird that she killed herself *now*, after all this time? If she was going to do this, why wait?"

"Maybe she started again."

"That doesn't explain the blood."

"No idea about that. You're asking the wrong girl." Although Lauren and Cora were related, the magic came from Cora's other side of the family. Lauren didn't have a drop of magic blood in her body.

The suicide in general didn't baffle me much—just the details. When someone has touched death the way I did every time I summoned my mother, the fear of it went away. Death was no longer an unknown. In fact, there was something intoxicating about tapping into the other side. A sense of utter peace, flowing just beyond reach—something the living could never truly experience. I understood why summoners might want to fully give themselves over to that.

If I told Lauren that, she'd have me checked into the nearest mental institution.

Instead, I shook my head. "It doesn't matter anyway. Gone is gone."

As we approached the water line, towering churches stood among the shops and houses on either side of the road. The closer we got, the more frequently we spotted the churches.

Practitioners had successfully summoned all kinds—from saintly types loved by all, to serial killers and mass murderers. It put a kink in non-magic people's religious ideas that the good and bad suffered different fates after they died.

They fought for their beliefs by building each new church larger than the last one. Just before the water line, a brick church with white trim and a steeple reaching upward at least fifty feet took up one side of the entire block.

From a distance, the magic community looked like a white-blue cylinder that reached upward from the water's inner edge and disappeared into the atmosphere. But as we got closer, the cylinder came more into focus—a bright wall of shining particles that separated this side of the world from the other.

We slowed as we approached the bridge closest to my house. It stood in the church's shadow at this time of the morning, but the bright light of the particle wall cut the shadow short just beyond the bridge. The dark water flowed far beneath the bridge today, and we crossed over without having to wait.

On the other side, we drove right through the wall of light. Everything inside the water line looked as clear and bright as I remembered it.

I leaned forward in my seat.

"Excited?" Lauren asked me.

"You have no idea." I rolled the window down to let the particles in.

"How does it feel to be back?"

The energy of the ley lines tingled across my skin and settled into my bones, leaving a comforting warmth in my chest. "Even better than I thought it would."

The car made it all the way to the house without shutting down, and we stopped in the driveway of my one-story home. Its red shutters brightened up the gray stone exterior. It had been a while since the lawn had been mowed, but the grass wasn't yet long enough to be an eyesore. It looked perfect.

Inside, the house proved a lot less welcoming than the outside.

"What the hell . . ." Lauren gaped as we entered the family room.

"Exactly what I was thinking."

Sofa cushions lay on the floor around the bare frame of the couch. The cushion covers were unzipped, and the stuffing spilled out. I zipped one of the covers and tossed the cushion on the couch, while Lauren grabbed another. At least this way, we wouldn't trip over them.

"Do they do this for every suicide?" Lauren asked.

I glared at her.

She threw up her hands in surrender. "I mean *death*. Not suicide."

In the office space, the Bureau hadn't taken the locked desk like Agent Tanner had threatened, but they'd managed to unlock it or break the lock. The bottom-right drawer hung open, and its former contents—a stack of folders and papers—covered the desk and the floor nearby. Agent Reyes had selected two notebooks from the bookshelf while I was there, but the Bureau must have decided that wasn't enough. The shelves stood empty now, the books scattered throughout the room.

Lauren knelt and stacked some of the books and papers into neat piles. "Go check the rest of the house."

I spun and ran down the hall toward my room. Lauren followed more slowly. I peeked into Cora's as I passed.

The mattress and box spring had been pulled up, and both stood at an angle atop the bedframe, stuffing spilling from the torn mattress. Reyes hadn't been kidding when he said they would do a thorough sweep. In my room, as in Cora's, the mattresses and box spring had been removed from the frame. They now leaned against the wall.

This couldn't be a standard search.

I knew I should feel something. Lauren kept staring at me like she was waiting for the chance to glue me back together when I cracked. But my body was exhausted of feeling things. I couldn't deal with this right now.

I grabbed a few belongings to take to Aunt Sara's house. I'd been rotating through a sparse wardrobe lately, even after adding the few items Aunt Sara had bought me. In a few trips, I transferred about half my closet into Lauren's car.

"Did you see this?" Lauren asked as I grabbed the last few items I wanted for now. She waved me over to the threshold of Cora's room.

While many of my drawers had been left open, Cora's had been removed from her dresser. They sat piled in stacks on the floor, with some of their contents—socks, underwear, and workout clothing—spilling over the sides. The drawer on top of the pile had split, and the front barely remained attached to the sides, hanging askew on a single nail.

"Great," I said with a heavy dose of sarcasm. "I'll have to thank them for taking such great care with my home."

Lauren swept up a pile of clothes from the floor and

tossed them into an exposed drawer. "Seriously?" She gestured around the room with both hands. "They're dealing with an orphaned teenager who's lost everything except this house, and they treat it like it's trash. Who the hell do they think they are? We should call and complain."

"Lauren." I placed a hand on her arm. "It's fine."

She sucked in a breath and opened her mouth as though preparing to start another tirade.

"It's fine," I repeated. "We have to sell the place anyway. I need to let it go."

She pressed her lips together for a moment and then said, "You deserve better. That's all I'm saying."

"And I love you for it."

"At least they cleaned the bathroom though," she said. "Not a speck of blood anywhere."

"I'm sure. Practitioners don't leave blood lying around."

"But they'll leave everything else lying around, apparently."

It certainly seemed that way. What the hell had they been looking for?

CHAPTER FOUR

On the first day of school, I had no morning classes with Lauren. And by lunchtime, I itched for conversation outside of "How was your summer?" and "Do you have a pencil?" I'd also made up my mind to invest in some pencils.

With pasta piled high on my tray, I made my way out the cafeteria door and across the school's wide back lawn to a large tree. Lauren and I had eaten lunch there almost every day during sophomore year.

Like me, other upperclassmen grabbed their trays and headed to their favorite lunch spots. They filled the circular stone tables on the wide patio. Some sat on the curved benches, while others sat on the tables themselves and rested their feet on the benches.

About fifty yards away, an oak tree stood in front of a small, private bridge across the water line. Beyond the tree, a pale-blue translucent wall of sparkling light marked the edge of the magic community. The tree gave great shade at this time of day. And it was separated from most of the students by a large swath of grass, so it made a peaceful lunch spot. Right now, no one sat under it.

Another small wave of students shoved past me and sprawled on the grass in small clusters. Outer shirts, hats, and blazers came off, and sunglasses went on as the students relaxed and inhaled their lunches. A couple students stopped at a phone-charging station on the patio to my left.

I shifted my lunch tray to one arm and slipped my phone out of the open front pocket of my backpack. The battery was at eighty-nine percent, so I dropped it back into my bag. Last year, at this time of day, I would be charging my phone too. But now that I lived on the tech side of the water line, it faithfully took a charge every night.

I started across the grass to my tree. On the way, I passed Bryan Cary—who'd always rubbed me the wrong way. Maybe it was the way he dressed in high-end brands and a bored expression, like he was gracing everyone around him with his presence. But today, he didn't look so bored. He yanked items from his backpack and threw them on the grass and on the stone tabletop in front of him.

My path took me right past him, and curiosity got the better of me. "Lose something?"

He didn't look up but unzipped the front pocket of his

bag and felt around. Then he tossed the bag aside. "It's nothing."

If anyone knew that *it's nothing* meant *it's something*, it was me. I cocked my head toward his belongings scattered on the grass around him.

"I lost my watch."

I pointed down at his right hand, which wore a class ring sporting a diamond-like jewel. "You can afford a new one."

"It was a gift from Sheryl."

I shrugged. "So tell her you lost it."

"It's more complicated than that."

None of this was my business, but Lauren hadn't shown up yet, and I had nothing better to do.

"It's personal. So unless you can find it for me . . ." He gestured for me to go away.

Instinctively, I scanned his scattered possessions for the watch. Maybe I *could* find it for him—with a spell. To find the location of his watch, I'd have to give up the location of something else—which might mean losing my homework or my keys or something like that.

But I'd make that exchange for the right price. Bryan and I could probably help each other out. I still needed a car, after all, and maybe a new bone knife—I hadn't seen mine since that day I found Cora.

"Maybe I can," I said.

His eyes narrowed.

"And you're going to pay me to do it."

"Why the hell would I do that?"

"It seems important. And *personal.*" I made air quotes around that last word. "But maybe I'm wrong." I turned back toward my lunch spot and took a large step in that direction.

Bryan jumped to his feet. "Hold up. What makes you so sure you can find it?"

"You interested or not?"

"How much are we talking about?"

"How much is it worth to you?"

"I don't know. A hundred bucks."

I knew a shop that would sell blood-magic tools to minors. After I bought a new knife, I could find Bryan's watch and do all the summoning I wanted. But I'd need at least two hundred to get a good one. "Make it two."

He stared at me in silence—probably trying to figure out whether keeping his girlfriend was worth that much. "Okay," he said finally, "but I need it back in a week. Any longer than that, and I'll run out of excuses for not wearing it."

"Payment up front."

Grumbling under his breath, he snatched a wallet from among his belongings and handed me two crisp hundred-dollar bills.

I couldn't remember the last time I'd held this much cash in my hands. I folded it neatly and stuck it in my pocket. "What does the watch look like?"

"It's platinum with my name engraved on the back."

"Where did you have it last?"

"If I knew that, I would have found it already. For two

hundred, you can figure that out on your own." His gaze landed on something behind me.

I turned to find Sheryl, Bryan's girlfriend, waving as she approached. His best friend Walt walked beside her.

Blonde and smiley, Sheryl hurried toward us. I didn't consider us friends—not close ones anyway—but at a small prep school like this one, everybody knew everybody. She and I had been lab partners in freshman Biology, and she nearly fainted when we dissected a frog. I ended up doing most of the cutting, and she was friendly to me ever since.

"If it isn't my favorite hero," she said when she got close enough. She shoved some of Bryan's junk aside and placed her lunch tray on the table, then slid into her seat. "You eating with us?"

"No, but next time. Thanks." I waved goodbye and headed to the tree that had been my original target.

When I reached it, I settled onto the grass, facing the tech side of school. On the magic side, just across the bridge and beyond the glittering wall, the smaller of Pritchett's two main buildings held a few low-tech classes —art, history, and some others. The sound of rushing water set a pleasant, familiar background while leaves rustled against each other above me. For a moment, I almost felt content, but guilt shoved that feeling aside before it could get too comfortable.

I was supposed to be in mourning.

A history textbook hit the ground beside me, and I

looked up to find Marshall Tanner standing over me. He dropped down onto the grass next to his book.

"Hey." I sat up straighter. "I didn't think I'd ever see you again."

"Sorry to disappoint. I go here now. Transferred over the summer." He pointed to the goosebumps on my forearms. "Aren't you cold?"

I stiffened to avoid shivering as a breeze skated across my skin. My cuts were high enough on my arms that even short sleeves covered them, and I preferred it that way. Short sleeves meant safe, and safe meant beyond suspicion.

"You want my sweatshirt?" He started to shrug out of it, but I shook my head.

"No, I'm good. But I know what you can do for me—return my knife." I pasted a scowl on my face, but it didn't stick. Despite the whole knife-stealing incident, I liked the guy. He had a calming way about him, and it didn't hurt that he was nice to look at.

"Nope." He unwrapped a chicken sandwich in his lap and took a large bite of it.

I waited for him to explain *why* he wasn't returning it, but nothing else came. "I use it to summon my mom. She's dead." Emotional blackmail—I had no shame.

He stopped chewing and swallowed his food. "You can't bring her back with a knife."

"That's exactly what I can do."

"But you can't *really*. You're alive, and she's . . . not.

Summoning doesn't change that. Why not live the life you have?"

"Because I don't have to. That's why I have the knife."

"*Had* the knife." He took another huge bite of food and then offered the sandwich to me.

I ignored him. "So let me get this straight. You trespass on my property the day my stepmother dies, steal my very expensive bone knife, and then invade my lunch spot."

"Your powers of observation are impressive. If it makes you feel any better, I tossed that thing in a dumpster weeks ago."

"How would that make me feel better?" I realized I'd shouted, and then lowered my voice to a loud whisper. "Tell me you're kidding."

He shrugged. "It's probably crushed by a garbage compactor by now."

"That thing cost me a hundred eighty dollars."

"I suggest you stop spending your money on things that end up in the dumpster." He flashed a hint of a smile before taking his next bite.

A curse word tingled on the tip of my tongue, and I seriously considered snatching the sandwich from his hand and chucking it into the water line. Lauren showed up before I could make up my mind.

She set her tray on the ground and then sat cross-legged. "Who's this?" She tilted her head toward Marshall and then added, in a loud whisper, "He's cute."

I couldn't argue with her on that. Marshall's dark-blond hair was shorter than when I'd last seen him and combed back from his face. Dimples showed on both cheeks when he smiled.

I answered his grin with a scowl. "This is Marshall."

"Oh, right," Lauren said. "You're the guy who took her knife. The devil himself."

"I may have mentioned it once or twice," I said, my tone sandpaper dry.

"Or more," Lauren said. "Your mom was one of the agents on the case, right?" As she spoke, she reached into her backpack and withdrew a planner with a retractable pen hooked to the spiral-ringed binding.

Marshall nodded.

"Why did they destroy the place?" Lauren asked, flipping her planner open to today's date. "Tossed all the clothes around and even slit open a mattress."

"Is that normal for a so-called practitioner suicide?" I added.

"I honestly don't know. My mom doesn't usually drag me along on her cases. Do you know what they were looking for?"

"Practitioner tools—that's what they told me," I said. "To make sure unlicensed users don't end up with them." I glared at Marshall to let him know I hadn't forgotten our argument.

He flashed me a wide smile, dimples and all.

Lauren was writing something in her planner, pressing down hard on the page, her lips fixed in a frown.

"What's up?" I asked her.

She clicked the pen to retract the ink and then placed

it on top of the planner. "I feel like there's more to this whole search thing. You said they were about to leave. They were finished. And then one of them gets a call, and they spend the next two months pulling up floorboards, turning drawers upside down, and tossing mattresses. That can't be normal."

The three of us were silent as we mulled it over.

"I wish I knew what was going on, but all this is new to me. My mom used to be a regular-old cop before we moved here. I get the feeling she was trying to change everything at once—job, house, city."

"Because your sister died?" Lauren asked, her voice low.

He nodded. "It's been two years, but my folks were still sad all the time. We'd go somewhere—the two of them and me and my brother—and I know they'd wish my sister was there too. They could see her at the restaurants we went to. They could see her everywhere in our house. It was sad for them."

"But not for you," I said as more of a statement than a question.

"For me, it was like I was still close to her. I liked that she was everywhere."

I nodded because I knew exactly how that felt. Aunt Sara's home felt so sterile. I hadn't made any memories there, and I didn't want to.

"What was her name?" Lauren asked. "Your sister."

"You don't have to talk about it if you don't want to," I said.

"Her name was Kayla." Marshall gave us a smile that felt simultaneously sad and sincere. "It makes me feel better to talk about her. It's like I can keep her memory alive by introducing her to more people."

"I like that," Lauren said. She picked up the pen again, clicked it, and wrote something in her planner.

"Did you just write that down?" Marshall asked, peering at the page.

"It seems like good advice. Deep stuff." She tucked the planner and pen back into her bag.

"I wish I'd done something for her when she was alive. Maybe I could have convinced her to stop summoning. But this is what I have now—her memory. So I'm doing the best I can for her now that she's gone."

"You could summon her." Inconvenient as it was, I couldn't call words back into my big, fat mouth when I spoke before turning my brain on.

Lauren glared at me, and I looked down at my hands to avoid her judgment.

"Speaking of which," she said, "are you getting a new knife?"

"First chance I get." I spoke softly, gaze still on my hands as if my fingers were the most fascinating thing on the planet.

Marshall went solemn. "How can you still want to summon when you see what it does to people?"

For about the thousandth time since Cora's death, I pictured her in that bathtub full of blood—like it was burned on the back of my eyelids. "I don't summon that much, and I don't do it for kicks."

"Of course you don't," Lauren said. "But your mom isn't the only reason you do magic. You enjoy it."

"It's useful. But it's not like I'm addicted."

"Isn't it?" Stone-faced, Marshall stared at me until I looked up and met his eyes.

"No. And Cora didn't summon at all—not anymore. That's not what killed her."

If he doubted my answer, he had the grace to keep it to himself. Finally, a point in his favor other than his good looks and charm.

My phone vibrated the front pocket of my backpack, and I withdrew it to check the caller ID: Agent Reyes. I showed the display to Lauren and Marshall, hopped to my feet, and moved away from them to take the call in private. "Hello."

"Maddy, I got your voicemail. What can I do for you?"

I'd called him the day before, after Lauren and I saw my old house. Partly, I'd wanted to complain about the state in which the Bureau had left my home, but I also wanted to know if they would finally return Cora's note. They'd cleared out of the house, so that meant their investigation was over.

"The house is a disaster." I hesitated, then added, "Did you find what you were looking for?"

"I'm not prepared to discuss that with you."

"So you *were* looking for something in particular?"

"As I told you, it was a standard search to remove practitioner tools—like the one young Mr. Tanner slid into his pocket."

My entire body went numb. He'd seen that? When I sensed the phone slipping from my palm, I fumbled and gripped it harder.

"Madison?"

"I'm . . . I'm here."

"There's little that I miss, especially at my own crime scenes. Lucky for you, a bone knife concealed in your living room doesn't prove you're practicing underage—although it certainly suggests it. I can't arrest you without more evidence, and I don't want to. You've been through enough. But I suggest you stop whatever blood magic you may or may not be doing, before you get yourself in trouble. Do you understand?"

"Yes, sir."

"Now, if you don't mind, I have to—"

"The note Cora left for me. Are you done with it?"

"We're hanging onto it."

"Until when?"

"You'll be lucky to get it back at all."

"But it was addressed to me. It was for me." The restraint seeped out of me. I wanted to scream at him, to demand it back. The *last* note Cora had written me sat in the Bureau's files somewhere. For them it was just another document. For me, it was the last connection to the life I'd lost.

"I'm sorry, Maddy, but I have to go. Call me—"

"Wait! Can you at least read it to me?"

He hesitated before answering. "Unfortunately, I don't think it would be appropriate to share evidence. Call me if you happen to find anything else of Cora's related to blood magic. You have my number." Without waiting for my response, he disconnected.

CHAPTER FIVE

My Physics class got more boring each day, and Thursday was no exception. I paid attention for the first ten minutes, while Ms. Parker rambled on about mass and acceleration. After I had enough of that, I held my phone in my lap, hidden by my desk, and sent a text message to Agent Reyes.

He hadn't responded to my last two texts, but this time he did: *I still can't release the note.*

My knuckles turned white around the phone, but I resisted the urge to chuck it against the wall.

"Madison." Ms. Parker's voice pulled my attention to her face, which leaned over my desk. "Is your phone more interesting than this class?"

My irritation with Reyes got the better of me, and words popped out before I could stop them. "Is that a serious question?"

My classmates tittered at this, until Ms. Parker

silenced them with a glare. "Go to the principal's office. Tell him you're not to come to my class if you don't plan to pay attention."

Without argument, I stuffed my schoolwork into my bag and headed to the office. The receptionist's desk stood empty, so Ms. Louise must have stepped out. I arrived just in time to see Principal Spencer's back as he led two men into his inner office.

"Shouldn't you go to your representative at the Bureau with this?" Mr. Spencer asked in a soft, diplomatic tone.

"Cora went to the Bureau, and she's dead now," said the taller of the two men. "Coincidence or not, this third death proves she was onto something."

I froze. They hadn't seen me yet, and until they did, they'd keep talking.

"What do you expect me—" Mr. Spencer closed the door, cutting off the rest of his words.

But the latch didn't click, and the door popped open a crack.

I strained to hear more of the conversation. My doubts about Cora's so-called suicide grew every day, and these men seemed to be the only other people in the world willing to admit there was more to her story than appearances suggested. The taller man wore a long-sleeved shirt with a high collar, warmer than necessary for this early in autumn. I guessed he was a practitioner— hiding his scars.

Maybe he'd known Cora. Maybe she'd been involved in something. Maybe he'd been involved in it too.

"I still have a few trusted contacts inside," Mr. Spencer said, his voice muffled by the door. "I could ask around."

"Only people you trust," the taller man said. "Only members of the Aid. Not the new people."

"Everything is a conspiracy with you," added another voice. I didn't recognize this one, but I assumed it came from the shorter stranger who'd just entered the room.

"Not everything," the tall man said. "But the Bureau—I don't trust it. The government didn't spend almost twenty years trying to get their hands on the Practitioners Aid just to *help* the magic community. They didn't bankrupt the Aid and then pull off that takeover just to *play nice* with us. We were doing just fine on our own. They wanted to watch us, and the Aid was their way in."

"Please keep your voice down," Mr. Spencer said, his words barely audible through the door.

"We gave them their water lines," the man continued, his volume only a fraction lower. "We keep to ourselves inside them. And the war continues."

"No one's at war. And believe it or not, I have a school to run here. My time is valuable."

"Of course," the tall man said. He paused, and I imagined him trying to collect himself on the other side of that door. "Cora is the issue." His voice was calmer now, but tight like a rubber band preparing to snap. "She stopped summoning. So how do you explain her suicide?"

"We don't know that she stopped," the shorter stranger said.

"Of course we know it!" The tall one got so loud that I

flinched away from the door. "She spoke against it every time the subject came up. Tell me honestly that you never heard her say she'd stopped."

"Please, gentlemen," Mr. Spencer said. "Keep your voices down."

"May I help you, Miss Cooper?" Ms. Louise's voice rang out behind me. She reached around me and pushed the door shut.

Heat crept across my cheeks.

Ms. Louise brushed her wispy white hair back and set her lined face into a glare. She slid behind the reception desk and crooked a finger at me, motioning me away from the door.

I made my expression casual—as if I hadn't just heard three men discussing that my stepmother's death might be murder. "Ms. Parker kicked me out of class for using my phone."

"Sit." She jabbed a finger toward a chair in the corner.

I slumped into the seat and stared at Mr. Spencer's closed door. For the next five minutes, I twisted my fingers together in my lap. Although I strained my ears, I couldn't make out a word they said on the other side.

When the two men exited the inner room, neither spared me a glance. And why would they? They didn't know me or how much their conversation affected me. The tall one's face flamed red as he stomped across the room, his fists clenched at his sides. Whatever he'd been after in this conversation, he hadn't gotten it.

The shorter man lagged behind him, shaking his head

in exaggerated disbelief. He had the palest eyes I'd ever seen—almost eerie looking. As the tall man's footsteps slammed away down the hall, the shorter one turned to Mr. Spencer and clasped him on the shoulder. "It's good to see you, even under these circumstances."

"Same to you."

"Looks like you've got a hair there." The man removed a stray gray hair from Spencer's short-sleeved dress shirt. "No worries." He stuck his hands in his pockets and sauntered away. "Take care of yourself."

"And you as well." Mr. Spencer waved me into his inner sanctum. "Have a seat in here, Miss Cooper."

Mr. Spencer led me into his office and shut the door. Next to his young face, the gray at the temples of his dark hair gave him a distinguished look. He wore one of his trademark bow ties.

He'd decorated the space like an old, traditional library. Mahogany wood panels covered the walls, matching a desk that must have taken four men to heft in here. An oversized bookcase occupied the entire far wall.

Behind the principal's leather office chair, the Pritchett family crest hung on the wall—an adorned shield that held at its center a bone knife representing magic users and a rose representing non-magic. The rose's long, thorny stem wrapped around the knife blade in way that suggested an embrace.

"What was that about?" I asked. "I heard Cora's name."

Mr. Spencer cleared his throat. Stalling perhaps? He cleared it a second time before answering. "My colleagues knew your stepmother and simply needed to vent about her death."

"One of them thought the Bureau had something to do with it. Who was that guy?"

"Rick Hale." Spencer leaned back in his chair and steepled his fingers. "The Bureau pulled his license a year ago for failing his psych exams, long before your stepmother's death. I take everything he says with a grain of salt—a very large one." He let out a slow breath. "Your stepmother was a good student, but I remember her mostly because of her . . . strong personality. Once she put her mind to something, she never let it go—rules or no rules." His lips curled into a soft smile. "Not unlike you."

"Do you think—"

"Your stepmother committed suicide, Maddy."

Since I had the attention of a long-time practitioner with contacts at the Bureau, I finally asked the question that had plagued me over the past two months. "Doesn't the risk of suicide go down if someone quits summoning?"

"Maddy—"

"Please," I whispered. "I need to know."

His gaze drifted up to the ceiling before landing back on me. "It depends on your school of thought. Some believe summoners commit suicide because they've been in touch with the afterlife, and they're not frightened of it. Death is an easy escape from the trials of life. Given that, a retired summoner would be just as likely to kill himself as an active one."

So there was nothing odd or special about Cora's death. That tall man who'd just been here seemed to believe the same thing I did—that it didn't add up. But perhaps I was desperate, and he was delusional, and we were both just wrong.

"But," Mr. Spencer continued, "there's another school of thought that the channel between life and death has an addictive quality. Summoners commit suicide because they want to be on the other side permanently, because they can't resist the pull into the Deep. If that's the case, and it's an addiction, then I suppose retired summoners would make up only a small percentage of those suicides. After all, they are in recovery—actively fighting their addiction."

"What do you believe?" I asked.

He hesitated. "Until now, I've never heard of a retired summoner killing herself."

Neither had I. "Did you know her wrists were slit?"

He sat up straighter in his seat. "That wasn't in any of the public reports."

"I found her. Trust me on this."

"I'm sorry that happened to you." Before I could press the matter further, he changed the subject. "I understand you were using your phone in class."

"But what about—"

"I'm sorry, Maddy, but there's no more guidance I can give you on that subject." He placed his hands flat on his desk and leaned forward. "It's important to recognize that these conspiracy theories about Cora, the Bureau, and really anything magic-related—they are among the reasons there is so much fear in the non-magic community. Sometimes, things are as simple as they appear, and we should leave them at that." He steepled his fingers again. "Let's discuss what happened in your class today."

I pressed my lips together long enough to calm the frustration welling in my chest. When I had it back under control, I said, "I was trying to get a Bureau agent to return Cora's note." I wasn't above playing on the man's sympathies to get out of trouble.

His expression transformed from stern to sympathetic. "I'm not going to give you detention today—only a warning. Next time, it'll be detention. And make sure to ask Ms. Parker what you missed in class."

I trudged from the office more concerned about what I'd heard than about the threat of future detention. The man I'd seen in Mr. Spencer's office might have been paranoid, but that didn't mean he was wrong.

CHAPTER SIX

"Are you sure you don't want to come home and rest?" Aunt Sara asked over the phone that afternoon.

The school day had ended, and I'd called her from the parking lot on the school's tech side to tell her I would be home late. I didn't tell her what I'd be doing—shopping for a new bone knife.

"I'm sure," I said.

"How was school? This is the first time you've been around so many people since . . ."

"Since Cora died. Yeah, I know. It was—"

"Fine?" She pushed the word out like a sigh, and I couldn't blame her for it. As much as she was tired of hearing how *fine* I was, I was just as tired of saying it.

"I should be home in time for dinner. See you later." I hung up before she could extend the conversation.

I leaned against Lauren's car to wait for my friend. In

the distance, the white-blue wall marking the water line extended upward behind the main school building. The individual particles weren't visible from here, but they still gave off a sense of movement—a solid, translucent wall that danced forever upward. It created a moving canvas on which the stone facade of the school building was painted. Occasionally, a larger particle would catch the light just right and reflect a bright white flash.

I shielded my eyes as I waited for Lauren to exit the building. She skipped down the front steps and pointed a small remote at her car. The convertible top whirred open, and the locks clicked inside. I opened the door and climbed in.

Lauren jumped over the driver's door and landed beside me. "Where to?"

"East Square. You're in a great mood."

"You always keep me out of your blood magic. Marshall—a complete stranger—knows more about what you do in your spare time than I do. But now you're taking me to buy a bone knife. It's exciting."

"Summoning isn't exactly a team sport."

She lowered her voice to an ominous level. "But now you need me, so I get to experience the forbidden world of underage magic."

"Technically, I only need your car."

She slapped me on the shoulder. "Don't be a jerk."

"Okay. Okay." I dodged when she went to slap me again. "I need you."

"Damn straight." She started the car and drove toward

the parking lot's exit, which would take us past the front steps. "Isn't that Marshall?" She pointed at a boy standing in front of the school, toying with his phone.

"Don't stop," I told her. "Don't stop. Don't stop." The last thing I needed was a lecture about my magic use.

Grinning, Lauren stopped the car right in front of him. "You have a ride?"

"Yeah," he said. "Actually . . . I'm not sure. My brother drove me to school today because my car's in the shop. He should have been here by now to pick me up."

"Can we drop you somewhere?"

"Have I ever told you I hate you," I whispered, barely moving my lips.

"What?" Marshall asked me.

"Maddy was just agreeing that we should give you a ride."

"I hate you," I muttered.

"Where are you headed?" she asked him.

Marshall gave Lauren his address, and she looked it up on her phone.

"Perfect. This isn't far from where we're going. Get in." She gestured for me to get out so he could climb into the backseat of her two-door car.

I was reaching for the door handle when Marshall put his hand on the door to stop me. "You don't have to do that. I'll climb over." He scrambled over the car door and into the backseat.

"I can tell we're going to be friends." Lauren grinned at me.

"I think I feel sick," I said, complete with a dramatic eye roll.

We left the parking lot and headed east, away from the wall of light. A few minutes later, we hit the highway, music blasting so loud that passengers in cars we passed turned to stare.

The wind that whipped around us at highway speed gave some relief to the heat of the day. Soon, I found myself smiling and shouting along with the song on the radio. Beside me, Lauren did the same, while Marshall's hands pounded out the beat on the back of my seat.

A colorful billboard raised high above us caught my eye:

Want to say goodbye?
We can contact your deceased loved ones.
Increase your manhood for an additional fee.

I guffawed and pointed up at it. Marshall chuckled, but then turned grim as we passed a small white church. Its entire highway-facing side had been painted with huge blue lettering:

Death is for the dead. Repent.

The tapping on the back of my seat ceased, and the mood in the car got heavier.

"What exactly is your problem with blood magic?"

Lauren asked, half turning toward Marshall before returning her gaze to the road.

"I have zero problem with blood magic. Just summoning."

"Okay, so what's your problem with summoning? Is it a religious issue?"

"Nothing like that. It's just not safe. Magic always comes at a price, right? And usually that price is the opposite of what's gained. So logically, the cost of bringing the dead back even for a moment . . ." He didn't finish, but the weight of his words settled on my shoulders and bit deep.

"The cost of a life is a life," Lauren finished for him.

"Exactly. It's not always physical—like with my sister. But it's hope, love, the spark of living. It's dwelling in death instead of living for what's left."

I felt his eyes on the back of my head, but I locked my jaw and refused to respond.

Ten minutes later, we veered onto an exit ramp for East Square, a hip shopping district. I didn't get to this area of town much, but I loved it. It had a laid-back attitude, with people strolling instead of rushing. I leaned forward in my seat as Lauren took the few turns that brought us into the neighborhood.

"We're not dropping off Marshall first?" I asked.

Marshall had judged me enough in the short time I'd known him. I could only imagine what he'd say when he watched me buy a new bone knife—after he'd disposed of the last one.

"No, this is cool," he said. "No one will be home

anyway. My folks usually don't get in until late, and who knows where my brother is."

I chewed my lower lip while I searched my brain for a reason to drop him off anyway, but I came up blank.

"You think they've added any new shops?" Lauren said. "I haven't been here in ages—almost five months, I think."

"There's a new music shop." Marshall leaned forward, so we could see him, and pointed to my right. "Mostly indie stuff. The owners are cool. They love giving recommendations."

"So exactly how rich are you?" I asked him.

Lauren shot me a glare. "You can't just ask people that."

"What makes you think I'm rich?"

"You go to Pritchett, first of all."

"So do you."

"I'm on scholarship." I twisted in my seat to look at him and ticked off more reasons on my fingertips. "You live near East Square—swanky. You wear designer brands. Both you and your brother have your own cars. And I'm guessing they're nice cars too." I paused to give him an opportunity to contradict me. He didn't. "And I'm also guessing you have a million-dollar trust fund."

His mouth twisted into a mock frown. "You think it's only a million? I've never asked, but I may have to talk to my dad about that."

Lauren muffled a laugh, and I glared at her.

She drove around the outer streets of the neighborhood to search for parking. Pedestrians ruled this place, ambling across the roads without regard to traffic laws.

Lauren crept around them for ten minutes until Marshall spotted a parallel space on the street. We parked and hopped out of the vehicle.

Shops, bars, and restaurants lined the narrow roads. Many had their doors propped open and played music to entice people. I slowed as we approached a shop with tinted windows and the words *Practitioner Paraphernalia* in neon lights above the door. A redhead in her early twenties sat behind the counter, staring down at her phone.

"This is it," I said.

Marshall stopped walking, still ten feet from the entrance. "This is why you dragged me here?"

"Nobody dragged you. I tried to drop you home first."

"I'm not going in there."

"You're just going to stand outside while we shop?"

He crossed his arms over his chest. "If I go in there, it looks like I support your summoning. And I don't. You should quit. So yeah, I'm gonna wait here."

"You could have just said *yes* and left it at that," I muttered under my breath as I led Lauren into the shop.

A glass sales counter faced the door. Inside, it displayed rows of knives and bowls made of bone, sometimes mixed with porcelain, some etched with words in different languages or shapes derived from Wiccan or Judeo-Christian symbols. The words and symbols could be used as intentions. Having them fixed on a knife or bowl saved a practitioner from needing to redraw them every time.

Someday, I'd love to own some of those fancier articles, but right now, I needed the bare minimum.

Susan, the redhead behind the counter, glanced up at me and smiled. "Maddy. What's up?" She wore a long-sleeved shirt in black. Several pendants adorned her neck on chains in various colored metals, each one representing a different religion: a crucifix, a star of David, a cross, a pentacle, a star and crescent, and one more I didn't recognize. The pendants tinkled softly as she set her phone aside.

"I need a new knife," I said.

It was illegal for me to practice, and just as illegal for any shop to sell me practitioner tools. Susan worked here part-time between her college classes. Like me, she found the law *flexible*, given the right circumstances.

I scanned the glass display for something suitable.

"You're staring," Susan said.

I glanced up from the display to find her facing Lauren.

"I'm sorry." Lauren pointed at Susan's forearms, which were covered in the dark cloth of her shirt. "Do you practice?"

"That's kind of personal." Although her words suggested offense, Susan's sly smile said she liked the question.

My guess was that Susan didn't practice at all—or at least not enough to have scars down her arms. But she wanted to *look* like she did. She liked the infamy. And that was fine by me. It was that same rebellious streak that made her sell me practitioner tools despite the laws against it.

Lauren pointed at the pendants hanging around Susan's neck. "Why do you wear those?"

"I'm not indecisive, if that's what you mean," Susan said, her hand lightly touching the chains. She propped her elbows on the glass counter and leaned forward so Lauren could get a closer look. "I believe in all faiths. They all hold truth. We wouldn't be able to do what we do unless God—or whoever—allowed it. Despite what non-magic people think, we are not ungodly. We just don't limit ourselves."

Lauren was nodding, but her attention had already shifted to the items displayed inside the counter beneath Susan's elbows.

"How much is that?" Wide-eyed, Lauren pointed at a large knife with a double-edged blade.

Susan unlocked the display case and withdrew the knife, along with the red velvet pillow it was displayed on. She set both on the counter. "This athamé is for display only. We don't have a license to sell blades six inches or longer."

"You need a special license for that?"

"To sell them and to buy them, yes. The licensing requirement is meant to reduce the opportunity to perform sacrificial spells. Shorter blade, less lethal—that's the thinking behind it anyway."

Lauren traced her fingertips along the handle, shiny black and shapely, curved to fit into the wielder's hand.

Reverently, her fingertips brushed the surface before they pulled back.

"It's a stupid restriction," I said. "Bureaucratic nonsense—makes lawmakers and their constituents feel safer."

As Susan put the big knife back in the case, I pointed at a white pocketknife with the lowest price tag—eighty bucks. "How about that one?"

She placed the one I'd chosen on the countertop so I could examine it more closely. The bone blade flipped open and closed easily, and it was small enough to hide in a pocket. No adornment covered the handle, but that was what I expected for the low price. I frowned as I brushed my fingers across the blade. These things were nearly impossible to sharpen without the right tools, and I cringed at the thought of trying to cut myself with a blunt knife.

"It's too dull." I pointed at another one, similar in appearance but with a hundred-dollar price tag.

Susan extracted it and placed it on the counter.

I examined the new knife for a few minutes, then set it back on the counter and nodded.

"That'll be two hundred bucks," she said. Double the price. She'd pocket the extra in return for not checking my identification.

I slipped her the two bills Bryan had given me. She packed the knife into a custom box, which she slipped into an opaque black plastic bag and passed across the counter. My fingers tingled as they touched the bag.

Already, I felt the anticipation of seeing my mother and Cora again.

I made a point to look extra cheery when we stepped out of the shop and rejoined Marshall. I even put a little skip in my step and pasted a smile on my face, but he was too busy talking on his phone to notice.

An older couple—a bald man and a gray-haired woman—detoured to give us a wide berth in front of the shop. The woman's gaze locked on my plastic bag, while her husband gripped her elbow and pulled her along.

Marshall's attention flicked briefly to them. With his ear pressed to the phone, he shimmied one arm out of his hoodie, switched the phone to the opposite hand, and then slipped out of the hoodie entirely to reveal both bare arms. He tossed it over one shoulder.

"I don't know, Mom. I shouldn't be too late." His tone was taut like a tightrope, fraying at the edges. He took a couple steps away from Lauren and me and rotated his body away from us. "It's a safe neighborhood. Only a couple miles from the house." He paused and then added, "Don't worry, Mom. I'm with friends, and I'm safe." Another pause. "Okay. Love you too." He disconnected with a long sigh and turned to find both Lauren and me staring at him.

"Everything okay?" Lauren asked, one eyebrow curved upward.

"My folks can be a little protective." His gaze landed on the black bag in my hand. "You got what you needed?" His tone conveyed more distaste than I'd ever heard compressed into a sentence that short.

"Yes, I did." I gave him a cheery smile. "Thanks for asking."

"I'm trying to understand. I know talking to your mom is important, but all this calling-the-dead stuff is asking for trouble. You know what it does to people."

"You mean people like my stepmother?" I pushed more than a hint of annoyance into my voice.

"I don't want to fight with you."

"That's a nice change."

Marshall had the grace to look wounded.

And against my better judgment, I didn't like the look on him. "Sorry. I don't want to fight either."

Without meaning to, I reached out and touched his shoulder. He reacted by grabbing my hand and squeezing it. A warm thrill tingled at my fingertips even after he released me.

"We should get out of here," I said. "It's almost dinnertime."

"Or we could stay and shop. Plenty of places to eat here." Marshall gestured to the narrow street around him. He pressed his palms together in a praying gesture. "Please don't make me go home. My folks are driving me nuts. They want to know every detail about Pritchett, and they've been interrogating me all week."

"Why do they let you go there?" Lauren asked.

"It was part of the deal. I would move, and they would ease up a bit."

"So why did *you* want to go to Pritchett," I asked, "since you have issues with magic?"

"I don't have *issues with magic*." He made air quotes as he parroted my words back to me. "I have issues with summoning. Magic is cool. It's spiritual. It's personal." He gestured toward my bag. "It should not be used to yank the dead back from their eternal peace."

I scowled but said nothing.

"I have to get started on my homework," Lauren said, "and Maddy needs to be home in time for dinner."

Marshall turned to me, palms pressed together in pleading once again.

"I can have dinner with my aunt any day."

"But your aunt wants you—" Lauren started.

I glared at her, and she snapped her mouth shut.

"Can your homework wait?" Marshall asked her. "It's only week one. I've barely even got any."

Lauren set her backpack on the ground, unzipped it, and withdrew her planner. "I have to be home by six thirty, so as long as I drop Marshall home by six o'clock, I should be good." She snapped her planner closed and deposited it back into her bag.

"Great." Marshall pointed back the way we'd come. "Didn't we pass a taco place?"

He led the way. I tucked my brand-new knife into my backpack and followed.

CHAPTER SEVEN

At one minute until six o'clock, Lauren pulled her red convertible in the circular drive in front of Marshall's house. She checked the clock on her dash and gave one precise nod. "Here you go," she said, putting the car into park.

I opened the door and got out so Marshall could get out from behind me.

He didn't move.

Lauren twisted in her seat to look at him.

"Could you guys come in for a bit?"

"What's up?" I asked.

He pulled his phone out of his pocket and showed us the display. It showed two missed calls and four missed text messages. "I've been ignoring my parents' calls."

Lauren slipped her phone from the front pocket of her bag and flashed its display at us. "Look at that. No messages of any kind." She looked at Marshall's phone again and sighed. "At least they care enough to worry."

Since we were comparing phones, I checked mine too. One text message from Aunt Sara: *Let's talk when you get home.* I showed it to Marshall and Lauren and then stuffed the phone back into my bag.

"Your parents care," Marshall said to Lauren. "But that doesn't require constant contact."

She huffed.

"My dad's probably still at the office, but my mom's gonna be pissed. She can't yell if I have friends with me."

Lauren checked the clock again, which now read six o'clock exactly.

"I promise it won't be long." He held up his hand with fingers spread. "Five minutes tops."

Lauren opened her car door and climbed out. "Friends look out for each other—or else what are they for?"

Marshall offered her a weak smile and pushed himself out of the backseat to exit the car on my side.

We crossed the stone pavers of the circular driveway and approached what could only be called a mansion. The building stretched out forty feet on either side of us, and another forty feet upward. Its whitewashed brick facade felt both rich and understated. Less understated was the pair of two-person-wide columns that reached upward from the porch to the roofline. A short stone staircase led us to the bright-blue door between the columns.

Marshall fumbled with his keys for a few seconds before unlocking the door and pushing it open. He stepped aside for Lauren and me to enter and then shut and locked the door behind us.

"Marshall?" came a familiar female voice. "I'm in my office."

"I have friends with me," Marshall called back, gesturing for us to follow him toward the voice.

The cream-colored floor beneath our feet spread out across a two-story foyer with a massive chandelier hanging overhead. Another pair of columns marked the way into what looked like a formal sitting room. Who needed a whole room for sitting, anyway? On either side of the columns stood a matching pair of spiral staircases, just in case someone needed variety in methods for getting up and down the stairs.

We turned right from the foyer. Marshall led us over the stone floor made up of large square tiles to a pair of French doors. The doors stood open.

Inside the room, Agent Tanner sat behind a wide desk with a dark wooden top supported on metal legs. To her left, a colorful array of crumbling paperback books—with faded titles and broken bindings—filled two tall book-cases. Although multiple stacks of paper and a laptop computer sat on her desk, Agent Tanner was not working. She was staring at Marshall, her face expressionless.

Marshall cleared his throat and pointed at Lauren. "I wanted you to meet my friends. This is Lauren." He gestured toward me. "And you remember Maddy."

Agent Tanner squinted at me for a moment before nodding in recognition. "Madison Cooper?"

"That's me."

She offered us a smile that was more pleasant than anything I'd seen on the day we first met. She had straight white teeth framed by smile lines that suggested she actually made that face pretty often. "It's nice to meet you both —outside of my official capacity." The expression disappeared as she turned back to Marshall. "It's after six. I called you. I know your father called you too."

My face warmed on Marshall's behalf, and I lowered my gaze. It landed on a small book on the desktop, whose faded binding read *Blessings and Curses*. A book on blood magic? I'd never seen one before. It took every ounce of my self-control not to snatch the book off the desk.

"It's not even dark out," Marshall said.

She raised one eyebrow to an impressive height. "Are you unable to return calls before dark?"

"You said be home before dark, and I am."

Agent Tanner licked her lips, and her gaze slid across Lauren and me before landing back on Marshall. "We'll discuss this later. You can show your friends out now." The smile was back on her face. "It was lovely to meet you ladies. I'm sorry it wasn't under better circumstances."

"Nice to meet you too," I said.

Lauren mumbled something I couldn't understand and then put a firm hand on my back to shove me in the direction of the front door. Marshall closed the French doors to the office and followed us.

"Sorry about that." He opened the front door and ushered us out.

Lauren gave him a quick hug. "Call me later if you want. My number's in the school directory. We can talk about how much parents suck." She looked at me and bit her lower lip.

"It's cool," I said. "Add me to the call. I can complain about my aunt."

"Thanks for coming in, you guys. I owe you one."

"No problem. We'll see you tomorrow." Lauren grabbed my wrist and tugged me toward the car. "I'm behind schedule."

Fifteen minutes later, Lauren stopped her car at the curb in front of my aunt's house. I unlocked the car door and hesitated.

"You okay?" she asked.

"Fine," I said. The word came out as if driven by autopilot, but after it was out there, I realized I meant it. "I'm actually fine. Thank you for driving." I gave Lauren a quick hug. "Call me when you get home."

Even though we were running a little behind her schedule, Lauren remained in the driveway until I'd unlocked the front door of the house. I went straight for the stairs that led to my bedroom, but Aunt Sara's voice stopped me.

"Maddy?" she called from the kitchen. "Can we talk?"

I glanced toward the stairway and then at Aunt Sara. There was nothing I wanted to do right now more than flop into bed—still in my clothes—and drift off to sleep while my good mood held. I couldn't remember the last time I'd had a good night's sleep. A night without tossing and turning, without thinking about the Bureau and Cora, without staring at the ceiling and realizing I was still alone. Just like yesterday and the day before, and just like the day that would begin when I woke.

Tonight, maybe I'd have nice dreams. Or if I was lucky, maybe no dreams at all.

"I made apple pie," Aunt Sara added.

I hadn't noticed it at first, but now the strong, distinctive scent of baked apples and cinnamon filled my senses. My stomach rumbled. Marshall, Lauren, and I had planned to stop and grab food, but we'd had such a good time shopping that we hadn't gotten around to it. On second thought, there was nothing I wanted more than some apple pie—followed by flopping into bed in my clothes. I joined her in the kitchen.

The pie sat beside the stove top, covered in golden crust. Aunt Sara grabbed two plates and cut us each a piece. Then we settled together at the kitchen table. I sighed, contented, as I swallowed the first bite.

After what must have been a full minute of silence, she said, "You missed dinner."

"Sorry."

She frowned when I didn't offer more. "I know it must be different—living here with the three of us. My style of parenting is probably a bit different from Cora's."

I snorted. "Yes. A lot different." Cora's style—if you could call it that—was more like an older sister than a parent. When she was around, she indulged me rather than disciplining me. She trusted me, gave me a ton of responsibility, and expected me to live up to it. Aunt Sara, on the other hand, wanted me to check in every two minutes.

"Cora never had children, and unfortunately, your dad died before she had much chance to experience being a parent to you."

I stuck another forkful of pie into my mouth.

"You're almost an adult now. You probably feel like you don't need parental guidance, since you've managed just fine on your own. But I don't think you're quite mature enough to make all your decisions. And it's my job to look out for you—because I love you."

I'd heard some variation of this speech from her at least twice over the summer. I figured the quickest way to wrap it up was to agree. "I get it," I said.

"How are you doing with being back at school?"

I shrugged and stuffed another forkful of pie in my mouth. I didn't want to think about my troubles right now.

"It must bring back a lot of memories about Cora," she added.

An image filled my head—Cora in the bathtub, blood pooled around her. The pie in my mouth suddenly felt desert dry. I choked it down. There went my good mood. "I keep telling myself—suicide or not—she's with Dad, and I've got no reason to be sad for her."

Aunt Sara covered my hand with hers. "But you can be sad for *you*."

I shook my head. "What's the point?" My voice caught

in my throat, and I silently cursed myself for it. My family had left me. Even when I summoned them, our time together could be no more than a few minutes. They would go away again, always, and shedding tears wouldn't change that.

When I glanced up at Aunt Sara, she stared at me with my father's eyes. Right now, they swirled with love and compassion, but it only made me hate them more. My father wasn't coming back, and neither were the rest of them.

I yanked my hand from hers and pushed my chair back. "I'm tired," I said, my voice flat. "I'm going to bed now."

Aunt Sara let me leave without objection. But I made the mistake of turning back for a final glance before I reached the stairway. She still stared at me, sadness filling those brown eyes.

I took the stairs two at a time.

CHAPTER EIGHT

Aunt Sara insisted on driving me to school the next morning. I considered ignoring what she wanted and calling Lauren to pick me up. But that would have been awkward for all of us. So after Cassie's and Ryan's carpools arrived to grab them, I slid into the passenger seat of my aunt's car.

She flashed me a winning smile that made me squirm.

"I appreciate your making an effort this morning," she said. "It's good we can spend time together."

I wasn't so much making an effort as I was trying to avoid conflict. Did that count as effort?

"We should talk about your old house," she said.

I stiffened. "What about it?"

"Now that the Bureau has released it, we should spruce it up a bit and put it on the market. We can't afford the upkeep of two homes."

"It's paid for, and it barely uses any electricity."

"But I'll still have to pay taxes and insurance on it. Why do that when we don't need it?"

"Who says we don't need it?" Panic rose inside me like a tsunami threatening to crash down on what little was left of life. And it showed in the way my voice went all high and squeaky.

My aunt's tone softened. "Just think about it, okay? We won't do anything until you're ready, but we may need to cut back on some things in the meantime."

I breathed deeply and tried to calm my racing heart. When we reached a red light, Aunt Sara tapped her fingers against the steering wheel, and I could tell she was trying to think of something to talk about.

"Thanks for giving me a ride to school today." It was a stupid thing to say, and I felt stupid saying it. We both knew she'd insisted on driving me, even though I had other options.

But her shoulders relaxed anyway. "You're welcome." Out of nowhere, Aunt Sara burst out laughing. "I remember the first time I drove your dad to school. It was his first day in high school—my junior year. We didn't go to Pritchett, of course. I'm not sure Pritchett even existed at the time, and we didn't have the money or the blood for it."

I stared at her, wordless, waiting to see where this little tangent would go.

She shot me a quick glance, licked her lips, and forged ahead. "Anyway, David was ready to go early, sitting in the kitchen with his backpack on the table. He had this swagger in his steps on the way to the car. On the trip, I asked him if he wanted me to point him to the school office so he could finalize his schedule. He told me no, he had it under control. And he did." She squeezed my shoulder. "Kind of like you. Complete control on the surface."

That was how I remembered him too. Organized, efficient, calm in the knowledge that everything was in order.

"Halfway to school," my aunt continued, "David unzipped his bag and moved all his notebooks around. I asked him what he was doing, and he said he wanted to make sure he hadn't forgotten anything."

I was still trying to figure out the point of this story.

"I left him alone about it. But a few minutes later, he did it again. Unzipped it, moved his books around, zipped it. And then once more when I pulled into the school lot. My best friend Karen was waiting for me by my assigned parking space. Let me tell you—Karen was stunning. Deep-olive skin and dark hair that she always wore up to show off her amazing cheekbones. David went all wide-eyed for only a split second. Then he jumped out of the car and ran into the building without a word—and without his backpack."

I covered my eyes with my hands, as if that could somehow save the younger version of my dad from embarrassment. "What a dork."

"Yeah, but he was *our* dork." She squeezed my shoulder. "You look like him. You know?"

"Really?" I'd always thought I looked like my mom.

She moved her right hand from the wheel to point at

my face. "Around the nose and mouth. It's nice." She patted my hand. "Like he's still here." She sucked in a deep breath and added. "You're like him in so many ways. Cool on the surface, but underneath . . ." She shook her head and left the rest unspoken.

Aunt Sara turned left into the long driveway that led up to the tech-side school entrance. Today, a large banner hung above, tied to a tall tree on each side of the two-lane driveway: *Happy Founders Day: Celebrating Magical Cooperation.*

"What's that about?" Aunt Sara asked, peering upward as we drove under the sign.

"It's the anniversary of the school's founding. Also, the anniversary of our water line."

"That's a cool coincidence."

"Not a coincidence." I stared out the window, but I could feel her eyes on the side of my head.

"Maddy? I'd like to learn more about you, and that means more about your school and blood-magic history and whatever else is part of your life."

I turned to her, planning to say something snappy about how there was no point. I'd be off to college in less than two years, and she didn't have to try so hard to bond with me. But the look on her face cut through my resolve and split it in two.

"You know the magic wave?" I asked.

"Of course. It was awful. I'm still not sure why they did that."

"It wasn't on purpose—like the news reported. It wasn't an attack."

"Then what was it?" As the driveway in front of us veered left and uphill, Aunt Sara slowed. She inclined her head toward me to let me know she was listening.

"It was an accident, and the story goes back further than you think." I paused to consider how far back to go. "In some small town in the middle of nowhere, a bunch of non-magic people got together. Eight people, I think. They just found out one of their neighbors was a magic family. They showed up with bats and tire irons. I don't think they meant to hurt anyone, but it got out of hand. The whole magic family died. A couple and their two-year-old son."

"That's awful! Why wasn't it in the news?"

"It was local news, but no one outside that little town heard much about it. Except magic communities. We talk about what really happened."

"It's terrible, but what does that have to do with the magic wave and the water line?"

"Magic communities around the country scheduled a blessing. Exactly one week after the murders, they were all going to perform a spell to mourn and bless the souls of the dead. There'd never been anything like that—a spell performed simultaneously by hundreds of people, maybe thousands. And since magic trumps tech . . . you know the rest. The magic killed electricity all over the continent. Knocked down planes. Caused industrial accidents. Only the oceans stopped it from spreading around the world."

"The magic wave."

"Right. It cracked the ley lines open further, and the water lines were added to contain the energy. They don't do as well as oceans, but the spells on them make them strong enough to do some good."

Aunt Sara blinked several times.

"The truth is more complicated than non-magic people want you to believe. Anyway, the Pritchetts filed the school's formation papers exactly two years after our water line was established. They wanted the anniversaries to be the same, so they could celebrate magical cooperation every year on the date."

"How do you know all this?"

"Word of mouth mostly. Talk among blood-magic families." I gestured up to the school, whose buildings were coming into view as we crested the long hill. "But also Founders Day. I think they're trying their best to counteract all the bad information out there about blood magic." I grinned. "In fact, I bet you someone will try to tell you the entire story before you can leave school grounds."

She gave a short laugh that came from her chest and filled the entire car. Not long and loud and embarrassing like my mom's laugh, or soft and sweet like Cora's. But it was nice anyway. Awkward and real and relatable— complete with a snort. I liked it.

By the time we pulled into the parking lot, I'd decided I didn't mind having Aunt Sara drive me. When she put the car in park, we stared at each other in awkward silence, my hand on the door handle.

"Thanks," I said before I climbed out.

Principal Spencer got out of a nearby vehicle on her side. Along with blue slacks, he wore a blue-and-white striped button-down with short sleeves. His blue-and-yellow polka-dotted bow tie should not have matched but somehow did anyway. A pin-back button attached to the shirt read in white letters on a yellow background: Ask Me About Founders Day.

Aunt Sara rolled down the window and waved. "Principal Spencer, it's good to see you."

"Happy Founders Day, Ms. Cooper! How are you?"

"I'm lovely," she said. "Thank you."

"Maddy." He waved to me. "How are you feeling?"

"I'm good," I said. And I meant it.

"I trust I won't have to assign you to detention anytime soon."

"I should go get ready for class." I hefted my backpack on my shoulder, but I'd only taken a few steps when Aunt Sara's words stopped me.

"Hold on, Maddy." She added to the principal, "Detention?"

"Yes. I assumed Maddy would have told you I had to give her a warning."

I shot a desperate glance toward the school building.

"Apparently not," my aunt said. "Would you mind giving me a moment with my niece?"

Mr. Spencer took several steps away but still hovered nearby, greeting another parent.

Aunt Sara's glare pinned me in place. "What was the warning for?"

"Using my phone in class," I mumbled.

"You know better than that. Things are hard right now, but you need to keep doing well here if you want to keep your scholarship."

"I was just trying to get the note back."

Her forehead crinkled.

"Cora's suicide note." I used air quotes when I said the word *suicide*. "The Bureau still has it."

"I'm sorry. I didn't realize."

I shrugged. "Can I go now? I promise to stay out of trouble."

"Yes. I'll see you later. Dinner?"

Mr. Spencer appeared again, as if out of nowhere. "It looks like you two have settled your differences. And that's wonderful. After all, today is the day we celebrate cooperation of the magical with the non-magical—just like you two!"

"See you later." I raced up the front steps to the main school building.

"Do you know about Founders Day?" Mr. Spencer asked my aunt behind me.

"I win the bet," I shouted over my shoulder.

Aunt Sara's laugh followed me into the building as Mr. Spencer launched into the entire Founders Day story.

I had time before class, so I ducked into a restroom on

the third floor, at the far end of the hall. Lucky for me, it was empty. Bryan had already paid me to find his watch, so it was time to hold up my end of the bargain.

Someone who didn't know any better could easily mistake a Pritchett restroom for one in a high-end hotel or department store. Tile floors and counters accented the stone walls and ceiling. And a wooden door marked the entry to each individual stall.

The school was kind enough to keep an armchair in the far corner, opposite the last stall. I never understood the purpose of chairs in restrooms. Maybe it had something to do with girls always going to the restroom in groups. Regardless, this one came in handy.

I grabbed it, tilted it so that its feet stuck into the grooves of the tile floor, and jammed its back under the handle of the door. It wouldn't hold if someone stressed it, but it would make a noisy warning.

I dropped my backpack on the counter and pulled out two items: my new knife and a school map that administration had sent with class registration materials over the summer. I spread out the map on the counter. It showed a deconstructed view of the main building, including the annex that held the school theater, each of the three levels separated out and clearly visible.

If my luck held, Bryan's watch would be in this building rather than one of the school's smaller structures —or off campus somewhere. If not, I'd need a new map to complete this finding.

Since my brand-new knife had spent who-knew-how-long being handled by customers of the shop where I'd bought it, I scrubbed it with soap and water until I felt satisfied I wouldn't infect myself with anything.

Gritting my teeth, I pressed the blade into the flesh on the underside of my upper arm, where my short sleeves would hide the cut. My skin split, and blood sprang up around the blade.

The restroom door banged against the chair, and I jumped, almost cutting myself too deeply. Outside, someone banged on the door.

"Let me in. I have to go!" came a female voice.

I groaned and snatched a paper towel to press under my arm—to hide the cut and stop the flow of blood. Then I dragged the chair away from the door.

"Let me in!" the voice called again, just as a girl with long dark hair tumbled into the restroom. She shot me a glare and headed for the nearest stall.

I sat on the high bathroom counter and let my legs swing above the floor while I waited for the girl to finish her business. The toilet flushed, and she stepped out, eyeing me suspiciously. I smiled at her and hummed to myself as she washed her hands for a half second and then fled the restroom. Apparently, I'd succeeded in creeping her out, and now I had the restroom to myself again. I wedged the chair back under the door handle.

Before I could get started, my phone rang. It was Lauren.

"What's up?" I answered.

"How was the drive with your aunt?"

"I survived. And it wasn't terrible, actually. Are you on campus?"

"Yeah. Where are you?"

"In our restroom." I didn't have to tell her which one. She and I often met in here to have private conversations, since other students preferred the restrooms on the lower floors. "I'm about to do a spell."

"Can I watch?"

I hesitated. Lauren and I had been friends for two years, since the beginning of freshman year. And in that time, she'd never watched me do blood magic. No one had.

"Please," she said before I could say no. "I won't get in the way. Promise."

"Okay, but I'm starting in about thirty seconds, and I don't want to stop once I start. So get your ass up here."

I moved the chair from the door again, and Lauren burst into the restroom a couple minutes later, short of breath. I must have underestimated how much she wanted to see this spell.

"I should warn you that this won't be nearly as exciting as you expect. A finding is pretty basic." I wedged the chair back under the door. "I'll need quiet though."

"Basic to you, maybe." Lauren slid her butt onto the countertop and pulled her legs up in front of her. "Show me some magic." She mimed zipping her lips closed, locking them, and then tossing the imaginary key over her shoulder.

Time to get started.

In just those few minutes, the blood in my wound had started to clot. I pulled both sides of the cut apart to start the blood flowing again.

Lauren cringed.

"Sorry," I told her. "A loss of blood. It's a sacrifice required for all magic."

"I know, but *ew*."

I hadn't grabbed any paper to write my intention on. But by now, I was tired of the interruptions, so I didn't bother digging through my backpack. Instead, I ran my bloody fingers across the mirror to write the word I needed: *watch*.

Eyes narrowed at the mirror, I focused on my intention.

My new cut stung and warmed, as if hit by a handful of warm needles. The magical energy had found me, and now it was time to channel it. I lifted the map under my arm and squeezed a drop of blood onto it.

The droplet landed on a rectangle representing the third-floor bathroom on the east side of the building—where I was now. The blood soaked into the map, leaving a deep-red stain with soft edges.

Lauren trembled, arms hugging herself, hands running up and down her upper arms. Although she stayed put, her neck craned toward the map.

"You can talk now," I told her, still keeping my concentration split between the intention and the map in front of me.

I'd barely gotten the words out when she jumped off the counter and moved closer. "What's happening?"

"Nothing yet. The blood should show me where the watch is." I frowned at the map. "I hope."

In truth, I didn't know whether this would work. I was guessing Bryan had lost his watch on the tech side of school, outside the water line. I'd never seen Bryan hang out on the magic side, after all. If I performed the spell from inside the water line—on the magic side—my magic would be stronger but the water line would block the spell from locating anything outside of it.

Basically, my options were limited, but I was keeping my fingers crossed.

"How do you know this stuff?" Lauren asked. "I mean, it's illegal for people to teach you, right? Or sell you books on it?"

"The girl who sold me the knife talks about spells sometimes—if I pay her. And I know a shop that takes cash to let me hang out and eavesdrop. I can't buy anything there though." While I spoke, I kept my gaze glued to the map and the intention clear in my mind. "Less talking," I told Lauren.

The spot of blood jerked into motion. Lauren squealed and clutched my arm. I kept my cool on the outside, but on the inside, excitement flooded every nerve ending.

On the map, the blood crept away from the bathroom. It left a red trail in its wake, which faded to pink, and then back to the ivory color of the map's background. It flowed straight downward from the third floor to the second. There, it hooked a sharp left and headed to the west side of the building. With every millimeter it crawled, the red spot grew fainter and fainter, and my stomach tensed. If it disappeared before it reached its goal, I'd have to try the spell from somewhere else—closer to the object I was looking for. And in that case, I'd have to pay for the spell twice.

In the annex, the blood—now little more than faint pink—slid into the AV room and settled against one wall there. It stopped moving and, a second later, faded to nothing.

"It's in the AV room." I straightened up and grinned at Lauren.

"And the price?" she asked.

My grin faded. "I'll lose something." I folded up the map, cleaned my knife, and shoved them both back into my bag.

Despite my relief at having located the watch that I'd already been paid to find—and spent that payment already—a weight of nervous anticipation settled in my chest.

Energy was a fixed thing that could not be created or destroyed, and just like any other energy, blood magic always came at a price—of the same type and magnitude as the spell. In this case, I'd found something, so I could expect to lose something.

If I was lucky, it would be something I didn't care about. A hair band or an old stuffed animal. But I'd asked for something important to me—after all, the watch had gotten me a new bone knife—so more likely, I wouldn't appreciate the price when the time for payment came.

I pulled out my phone and dialed Bryan's number.

"I found it," I told him before he got out so much as a *hello*. "It's in the AV room."

He cursed.

"Are you in the AV club?" I couldn't remember seeing him at any school performances working the equipment.

"No."

"So you don't have a key to get in there?"

A pause, then, "No."

My curiosity wouldn't let it drop. "Then why is your watch in there?"

"If I tell you, can you get it back?"

Expensive audio-visual equipment filled that room, and because the school allowed members of the community to use the attached theater, they kept the room locked. I didn't have a key, but I could probably snag one from the school office. "I can get it."

"I was making out with this girl who's in the club, and the watch kept getting caught in her hair. I took it off. I must have forgotten to grab it before I left."

"What about Sheryl? Are you guys breaking up?"

"No. She doesn't know, so don't repeat any of this. Please."

Suddenly, I liked Bryan a lot less. "Why don't you call the girl you were making out with and have her get it for you?" I made no effort to hide the scorn from my tone.

"She stopped talking to me when I told her it was over. I'll pay you another twenty to get it back for me."

I hesitated. "I can get it."

"Thanks. I really appreciate—"

"For another forty bucks." The fact that he was such a jerk made it a lot easier on my conscience to squeeze him for money.

"Fine." He cursed again and disconnected.

CHAPTER NINE

By lunchtime, I'd come up with a plan to snatch the keys for the AV room, and I headed to the principal's office. Ms. Louise kept a complete set of school keys in her desk. I just needed to distract her long enough to grab them.

It wasn't so much of a *plan* as it was a *goal,* but I'd figure out the *how* part of the plan once I got in the office.

A high-pitched shriek quickened my steps before I reached the office doorway, and I darted inside.

Mr. Spencer lay on the floor of the reception area, his eyes rolled back in his head to show little more than their whites. His body trembled on the ground. Ms. Louise's chair slammed into the file cabinet behind her as she jumped to her feet.

I was closer to him though. "Call nine-one-one," I shouted as I ran toward the principal.

I'd read something about trying to get someone who's seizing on his side, so he doesn't choke if he vomits. But Mr. Spencer rocked so violently that I couldn't get a grip on him to roll him that way. He continued to tremble, and every few seconds, his head thunked against the floor. I cringed at each impact.

Ms. Louise's voice barely registered, but she'd made the call. Seconds later, she got off the phone and hurried over to lend support.

"Your jacket." I nodded toward Ms. Louise's pink blazer, which sported a white-and-yellow Founders Day button just like Mr. Spencer's. "Push it under his head."

She let go of Spencer long enough to strip off the jacket and tuck it under his head, revealing her bare arms. Now, when his skull hit the floor, at least it had some padding. The metal of Ms. Louise's button clicked as Mr. Spencer's head jostled it.

Thunk. Thunk. Click.

I wanted to do more, but I didn't know what. This couldn't be happening.

"Please stop," I whispered to him.

"I don't know what happened." Ms. Louise's voice had gone shrill and staccato. "He looked stressed. I finally convinced him to talk to me."

Thunk. Thunk. Click.

"Do you think it was stress?" she asked, her tone still frantic. "Does stress do that?"

I didn't know, so I didn't answer.

I barely knew Mr. Spencer, but I knew his easy smile and his soft voice and his bow ties. I knew how he cared about all his students. And I knew I didn't want to come to school tomorrow and pass this office and know he'd died here, while I watched. While I was so close. While I was helpless.

Again.

Thunk.

Finally, Mr. Spencer stopped moving and lay there—looking like death. Eyes closed, skin pale and damp with sweat. When I pressed my hand to his chest, his heart still beat—so fast—beneath my fingertips.

It had been only a few days since I'd last seen him, yet somehow, he seemed thinner. Pasty-white skin looked almost translucent and sagged into the grooves under his cheekbones. Darkened skin beneath his eyes spoke of little sleep, and the gray around his temples had spread across the sides of his hair.

My breath came in shallow pants, and I concentrated on trying to get it regular again. The last thing we needed was for the paramedics to have to deal with a hyperventilating teenager in addition to everything else.

"Principal Spencer," I whispered, my voice hoarse. "Can you hear me?"

Ms. Louise released him and sagged beside me.

"Did they say how long until the ambulance gets here?" I asked.

"They're on their way. Any minute."

Mr. Spencer groaned and squirmed. His shuddering

moan clutched at my heart and twisted. No more people dying on my watch. I'd met my quota—and then some.

It was official—I was cursed. I should move to a deserted island where the only beings that could die around me were fish and really big spiders. Without even thinking about it, I clasped my principal's hand in mine and pressed both our hands to my chest. It should have been weird—I couldn't recall ever even making physical contact with him before—but it wasn't. Not with his life in doubt.

Pounding footsteps echoed down the hall, and two paramedics burst into the room. One of them dragged me to my feet. With precision timing, they checked his vitals and then hefted the principal onto a gurney. They strapped him down and steered him for the doorway.

A small crowd of students had gathered just outside the reception area, but the paramedics remained unfazed.

"Out of the way," one of them shouted, and the crowd parted at his command.

The two men jogged through the school's front doors, under yet another unreasonably large banner proclaiming in loud lettering that it was Founders Day.

The paramedics moved easily, as if they rolled a full-grown man between them while they did their sprints on a daily basis—which maybe they did. They looked like they knew what they were doing, and that gave me hope they could save him. They had to save him.

I shouldered my way past other students and into the hall to get out of the limelight. The hovering students took that as their cue to disperse, some following the paramedics out the doors and others loitering in the hall.

Outside, the siren roared up and wailed until the ambulance left my earshot.

I leaned against the wall beyond the office and tried to steady my breathing. My lungs had other ideas. I pulled in long breaths, one after another, but the hallway spun around me. I bent over and put my hands on my knees.

"You okay?" asked a male voice, but I waved him away, and whoever it was left me alone.

A hand landed on my shoulder, and I jumped, my elbow clanging against a locker.

"Hey, hey. Maddy, it's me."

I tore my gaze from the floor up to Marshall's brown eyes and then propelled myself at him. He wrapped his arms around me and pressed me close, cradled me with my arms locked in the narrow space between us.

When I released him, he pressed a hand to my back and led me to the school's lawn, which stretched between the tech and magic sides of campus. We kept walking, past the lunch tables, until we left the noise behind. It was just us and the trees and the wall of twinkling light.

Marshall pulled me onto the grass beside him. "Let me guess. You were somehow involved in what just happened with Principal Spencer." When I shot him a questioning glance, he added, "School gossip is faster than the speed of light."

"Right." I offered him a bitter laugh. "I was the one who found him on the floor. Of course. Because who else at this school is a corpse magnet?" He opened his mouth to deny it—to tell me that the truth wasn't the truth, but I didn't let him. "This has something to do with Cora."

His lips tightened.

"What?" I asked him.

He didn't answer right away.

"*What?*"

"You're seeing conspiracies where there are none. Cora committed suicide because she was a summoner."

"A *retired* summoner."

"Once a summoner, always a summoner. Nobody quits."

I certainly couldn't imagine quitting, but maybe Cora had been stronger than me.

"No one murdered her," he said, "and no one tried to kill Principal Spencer either. He had a seizure. Not every bad thing that happens is magical."

"None of this adds up. Why would she kill herself two years after quitting? And just yesterday, I overheard Principal Spencer debating her *suicide*." I made air quotes around the word. "And now this . . . It's too much coincidence."

"You were there. You found her."

"You think I don't know that?" I shuddered as the image came back to me. So much red filling the bathtub, splattered across the wall. I would never forget it.

"I mean you were at the scene of the suicide—or the crime, if that's what it was. Did you see anything suspicious?"

The image still filled my vision, so my answer came easily. "No. The knife was right there, so it must have been hers. But why would she?" It took Marshall's hand on my shoulder before I realized I'd shouted that last part. "It doesn't make any sense," I added, more quietly.

"Maybe you should skip afternoon classes. I'm sure Ms. Louise would give you a pass."

I waved away his concern. The principal's illness could be a coincidence—just health issues, like Marshall said. I could think of only one way to be sure. "I need to talk with the two men who came to see him about Cora. They know more than we do."

Marshall said nothing, but his expression said plenty.

"You think I'm crazy?"

"Of course not."

"But you think I should drop it?"

"I think your grief is stopping you from seeing things clearly."

"And that's where you come in?" Against my will, annoyance vibrated through my words. "I'm being irrational, and you're going to step in and save the day?"

"That's not what I said." By the way he drew out each word, I could tell he was working hard to hold back what he really wanted to say. He thought this was all in my head.

"But it's what you meant," I said.

He said nothing.

"No one's asking you to tag along. You told me your

concerns, so your conscience is clear." I jumped to my feet and turned to stalk away, but he grabbed my sleeve.

"Maybe it's not my conscience I'm worried about."

I shook him off and hurried back to the school building. One way or another, I was going to figure out what the hell was going on.

CHAPTER TEN

After the final bell released us from school for the weekend, I threw my notebook and textbook in my bag and hurried to the classroom door. Over the noise of students gathering their books, our instructor shouted something about weekend homework assignments. I cut off one of my classmates in our joint bid to reach the doorway first.

My last class of the day was Spanish, which was held on the magic side of school. But I had research to do, and I needed to be on the tech side for that. When I hit the hallway, I hurried past locker banks separated by wall-mounted gas lamps. All students had lockers on the tech side, but some who had a lot of classes on this side opted to have secondary lockers over here. This building was a smaller structure than the main one on the other side, so it didn't take me long to reach the front door.

I headed across the lawn at a pace that alternated every

few steps between a fast walk and a short jog. My sneakers skimmed over the manicured grass and kicked up fresh clippings.

The air smelled fresher on this side—it always did. Maybe because there were fewer cars. Or maybe it was just my imagination. And when I breathed deeply with the effort of keeping this pace, the sweet, smoky aroma of flowers tickled my senses—the scent of magical energy.

I hurried over the bridge without looking down at the water that flowed far beneath it. As soon as I hit solid ground on the other side, I dropped my backpack on the ground and pulled out my phone.

The website for the Practitioners Bureau loaded quickly enough, but it was a mess of text and images all on top of one another. Not optimized for use on a phone screen. It would look better on a large monitor, with everything spread out where it belonged.

I snatched my bag up from the ground and headed for the school library. Since I was among the first students coming back from the magic side of school, I'd beaten the crowd, and the lunch area stood empty. I passed the big oak where I ate lunch, the stone tables where most other upperclassmen ate, and the charging station on my way to the doors of the main building.

A few minutes later, I dropped onto a chair in front of one of the library computers. The librarian, a twenty-something brunette with her hair pulled into a ponytail, glanced up at me and then back to the book in her hands.

I opened a web browser on the computer and pointed it toward the Practitioners Bureau's website.

The Bureau required blood-magic practitioners to have licenses. Judging from the conversation I'd overhead in Principal Spencer's office a few days ago, the two men who'd visited him were both licensed, or had been at some point. And licenses were public record. That made my job easy—find those men on the Bureau's website, and I'd find their addresses there too.

And then I could talk to them myself.

In the middle of a column on the far right of the web page, a blue link read *Check license status*. Perfect.

After sixteen years, it was about time something went right for me.

I clicked the link. The page took too long to load, and I leaned forward in my seat as outlines of a sidebar and images popped up one at a time. I bounced my leg impatiently as the page finished loading.

Enter license number, it read.

"I don't know their license numbers," I said to the display.

The librarian shushed me.

I'd spoken too soon about something finally going right for me. Back to the status quo.

I had a name for one of the two men—Rick Hale. So I scanned the top and side sections of the web page for a link that would let me search for a licensee by name. I found links for applying for a license, applying for the Bureau's training course, reporting unlicensed magic, etcetera, etcetera. But nothing that looked like it would help me.

My phone buzzed. I fumbled to unzip the small front pocket of my backpack and felt around for the phone, my gaze still glued to the computer screen. I checked the caller ID before answering—Lauren.

"I'm in the library," I said, my voice a hushed whisper.

"Okay . . . Why are you there instead of the parking lot? We're supposed to meet by my car."

"I'm proving Cora didn't kill herself."

A long sigh and then, "How?"

"Rick Hale." I'd given Lauren the whole story about my eavesdropping already. "He's that former practitioner who was in Principal Spencer's office yesterday—the one with licensing issues. He knows something. If I find him, maybe I can get him to tell me."

"Don't move. I'll be there in two minutes."

"You can't change my mind on this."

"Just don't move."

She hung up, and I returned my attention to the computer screen.

I navigated away from the Bureau's website and to my favorite search engine. In the search box, I typed the words *Rick Hale blood magic license suspended*.

Again, the web page stalled, and it took every ounce of my self-control not to hit the monitor. For all the tuition parents paid to send their kids here, you'd think Pritchett could afford a decent internet connection. My search results filled the screen, but none of them looked useful.

Just web pages in which those words happened to all appear near one another.

I slammed my hands against the keyboard, and the librarian shushed me again. I shushed her back. When she gave me a glare sharper than a papercut, I ducked my head, turned back to the screen, and tried to breathe more quietly.

I'd given up on the search engine and was back on the Bureau's website when Lauren walked into the library, Marshall close on her heels.

"Hey." She threw her bag on the floor behind me and dropped into the chair at my side.

Marshall shifted from one foot to the other. "Lauren offered me a ride home. Hope that's okay."

"I guess I can survive that." I liked Marshall's company most of the time, so I'd try not to hold his summoning-hatred against him.

"She also filled me in on this Rick Hale person. I hope that's okay."

"It's going to have to be. Isn't it?"

Lauren jabbed a finger at my computer screen.

I held up both hands before she could say anything. "I'm doing this." I saved the librarian the trouble of shushing us by grabbing my bag and heading for the door. The computer was useless anyway.

Lauren's and Marshall's footsteps whispered on the plush carpet behind me. The two of them caught up with me in the hallway, and Lauren grabbed my shoulder.

"You are not being realistic." She said the words so

deliberately that I wondered how long she'd wanted to say this. "Cora committed suicide. Stop torturing yourself."

I shrugged her off. "How would you feel if you'd been murdered, and no one investigated it? Everyone just assumed you'd killed yourself?"

"There are so many things wrong with that sentence. I don't even know where to start."

We reached my locker, and I spun the combination lock and then slammed the door open so hard it clanged against the one next to it.

Lauren slipped between me and the locker so I couldn't ignore her. "Maddy, you need to let her go."

I spun to glare at Marshall, who stood quietly behind me. "You agree with her?"

He stared down at his shoes.

I glared at Lauren until she sidestepped out of my way. "What if I can prove it to you?" I grabbed a few books from my locker and stuffed them into my bag.

"You can't," she said.

"What if *we* can prove she killed herself?" Marshall asked. "Then will you accept it?"

"You can't," I said.

"So we look into it," he said. "And we accept whatever we find."

"We'll do anything you need us to do. But you promise to quit if we prove it was suicide?" Lauren added.

"I don't know about *anything*," Marshall said. "Within reason."

I traced a letter *X* over my heart. "Cross my heart."

Lauren nodded toward my phone, which I still had clutched in one hand from when she'd called me a few minutes ago. "Did you check the white pages?"

"Of course I did." I hadn't.

I set my backpack on the floor, turned on the phone's display, and searched for *Richard Hale white pages*. The first result that came up was for a Richard Hale who was twenty-two years old. Not my guy. But the second result was a forty-three-year-old. I touched the screen to select the entry—and there it was.

I turned the phone toward Lauren and grinned. "Found it."

"You're welcome."

I stuck my tongue out at her while I entered Hale's address into my phone's map application. The screen displayed a route from school to his house. I grinned up at Lauren. "Only a thirteen-minute drive."

"Good," she said. "I have to be home by six."

"Of course you do. All that homework's not going to do itself."

She stuck her tongue out at me.

"Just so we're clear," Marshall said, "when this Hale guy turns out to be a crackpot, we're done with this."

"At least until I get another lead. Even if he doesn't know anything—that doesn't prove Cora killed herself." In two long jerks, I zipped my bag closed. "Let's go."

CHAPTER ELEVEN

"Why don't we just ask him straight out what he knows about Cora?" I asked as we climbed out of Lauren's car. In one hand, I held my phone with the directions to Hale's house displayed on the screen.

Lauren and I had been arguing about how to approach Hale for the entire car ride. In the backseat, Marshall had kept mostly quiet.

The car stopped on its own about a half mile inside the water line. Rick Hale lived close to the center of the community. We hadn't expected to make it all the way there, but we'd hoped to get closer than this. We were still a mile away, which meant we had a long walk ahead of us.

"He could lie," Lauren pointed out. "Or give us some nonsense that he believes is the truth—regardless of whether it actually is. Principal Spencer said he failed his Bureau psych exams. That's *exams*—plural. How do we know anything he says is reliable?"

"I'm with Maddy on this one," Marshall said. "We definitely won't get the truth if we don't ask for it."

I let out an exaggerated gasp. "Did Marshall just agree with me?"

His face went blank and solemn, and he raised his right hand as if taking an oath. "I swear to you that I will agree with you every single time you're right." He cracked a crooked grin. "Rare as that may be." His grin fell as he scratched the back of one hand and then the back of the other.

"Stop scratching." I slapped his hands away from his skin. "Try to relax." My phone's display flickered, threatening to give out. I squinted at the map on its screen. "Give me a second to memorize the directions, in case my phone gives out."

Lauren peered over my shoulder and made a couple *mm-hmm* sounds. "I've got it." She tapped her temple.

"Show-off." I turned off the display and tucked the phone into my backpack.

"We walk the rest of the way?" Marshall asked. "How far?"

"About a mile," Lauren said.

"Then let's go." Marshall passed Lauren and me, continuing down the road in the direction we'd been driving.

Lauren caught up to him, grabbed him by the shoulders, and pointed him toward the row of houses across the road. "We walk across lawns here." She crossed the road and pointed at a narrow footpath that extended back from the front of one ranch house's lawn.

Nearly every house here had some kind of path worked into the lawn. It was one of the things I missed about living here: the sense of community. The sense of being welcome. The sense of being home.

I remembered the directions for the first five minutes or so of the fast walk. After that, I slowed and Lauren quietly walked past me and led the way. Twenty minutes later, she stopped walking, and Marshall and I stopped at her side.

She pointed down the road. "It's the fourth one on the right."

Marshall grabbed my sleeve as I moved to pass him. "Are you sure about this? I'm starting to think it's a bad idea. We don't know anything about this guy."

"So we find out." I shook him off. "Stop trying to save me. I don't need it, and I don't want it."

"We all agreed to this," Lauren said. "You can wait here like a coward if you want."

I didn't look back, but her footsteps followed me, and Marshall's scrambled behind her.

I let them catch up on the front porch of a brick ranch house with faded blue shutters. Tall, uneven grass surrounded the porch and threatened to claim the cement walkway between it and the road. I rang the doorbell as Marshall joined Lauren and me on the porch. Ten seconds later, when no one had answered, I banged my fist against the red door.

"Just in case the doorbell doesn't work," I explained.

"Or maybe it does," Lauren said, "and you're just annoying the crap out of the guy before he can get to the door." She gave me a sarcastic thumbs-up with both hands. "Great job."

The door flew open, revealing one of the men I'd seen in the principal's office last Friday. He'd looked tall next to Mr. Spencer, but I hadn't realized *how* tall.

Hale stared downward at the three of us—even Marshall, who was threatening six feet. Today, Hale's disheveled brown hair spiked upward on the right and lay flat on the left. The long-sleeved button-down shirt he wore hung crookedly on his thin frame. He'd skipped a button, so the bottom of the shirt extended farther on one side than the other. But it was his eyes that stood out, in their lack of expression. He scanned our faces, his gaze neither welcoming nor unwelcoming.

My mouth hung half open. I couldn't read the guy, so I didn't know what to say—how to make him give me the information I wanted—*needed*.

Lauren recovered quickly enough. "Mr. Hale?"

No response.

Lauren pasted a stiff smile on her face. "Are you Richard Hale?"

The man's eyes narrowed. At first, I thought he would say nothing, and we would continue to stand there fumbling.

"Who's asking?"

"My name is Lauren Evans. And these are my friends Maddy and Marshall." She grabbed my arm and pulled me forward. "Maddy overheard you talking to our principal at Pritchett Academy yesterday."

He gripped the side of the door tighter.

I couldn't have him slamming it in our faces, so I stuck my foot in the doorway. "Cora was my stepmother."

Hale's lips pursed. He opened the door and stepped aside, ushering the three of us through. He led the way through the undecorated foyer. Only a stack of papers on a small side table occupied the space. The living room was more of the same, surrounded by bare walls with a single gas lamp mounted high on each wall. The couch, stuffed armchair, and wooden coffee table all held additional stacks of paper.

"Have a seat." He pointed to the couch without looking at it. When we didn't move, he glanced in that direction, then mumbled something under his breath. Folders and documents littered the couch, in what looked like complete disarray. "Give me a second." He swept up an armful of papers and dumped the stacks beside a pair of scissors on his desk. "There you go."

He'd managed to clear two of the three couch cushions. The third still held a stack of papers. Lauren and I sat in the now-empty spots, while Marshall lifted documents from the chair and set them on the floor before settling down himself.

Across from us, a large corkboard covered the wall.

Tacked on it were photographs, notes, and newspaper clippings. It felt rude to stare, but I couldn't help noticing that most of the clippings held some mention of blood magic or the Practitioners Bureau.

Hale stood in front of us, on the other side of the paper-littered coffee table, his arms crossed over his chest. "How old are you?"

"How old do we need to be for you to answer our questions?" I asked. When he didn't answer, or even move, I said, "Would you believe me if I said twenty-three?"

"Would you believe me if I said I was the king of America?"

"So that's a no then," Lauren confirmed. "We're students at Pritchett."

"High schoolers." He sat at his desk, shaking his head. "What the hell do you want with me?" His jaw tightened, and he added, "Excuse my language. I'm not used to keeping kids around."

"Yeah, well, we're not middle schoolers," I said. "Say whatever the hell you want."

Hale smiled, the first clear facial expression we'd gotten out of him. I relaxed and eased back on the couch. He uncrossed his arms and let them fall to the surface of his desk. "What do you already know about Cora's death?"

"I found her body." I tried my best not to picture it again. No crimson on white. No blood covering the bottom of the bathtub. And definitely no stepmother lying cold and dead, her hands and feet sticky and red.

It turned out that the death of parents wasn't the sort of thing I got better at with practice.

Lauren and Marshall exchanged silent glances, and I pretended not to notice.

"Is that all you know?" Hale asked.

"She killed herself," Marshall said. "We know that too."

Hale shifted his posture in a way that angled his back toward Marshall. "I'm talking to this one." He nodded toward me.

"Maddy," I said.

"Doesn't matter." He waved a dismissive hand. "Cora was here the week before she died."

I sat up straighter.

"She was at the Bureau renewing her license when she heard me asking tough questions—about a magic-related death that everyone assumed was a good, old-fashioned, non-magic sickness. She hunted me down and showed up on my doorstep, just like you three."

"Is that what all this is about?" I gestured toward the scattered piles of papers around the room.

"For the most part, no. There's a lot more going on at the Bureau than meets the eye. I'm writing a book about it. A sort of exposé."

"Tell me about the death everyone thought was non-magic," I said. "The one Cora wanted to know about."

Hale pointed to his corkboard display. "See that clipping near the upper right?"

I stood to examine it more closely.

"A little more to the left," he said.

I followed his direction and removed a thumbtack from a short printout of an obituary. "Sam Schneider," I said, reading the page. According to the obituary, Sam had died of malnutrition, and his death had followed only a week after his brother's. "It says his half brother died only a week earlier. Did he die the same way?"

"Nope." One side of Hale's mouth quirked up into a wry smile. "Murder." He drew a finger across his neck. "Throat slit. Medical examiner said the wound could not have been self-inflicted."

"Maybe Sam lost the will to take care of himself after his brother died," Marshall offered.

"The two weren't close. The murdered half brother was non-magical and resented his brother for his abilities." Hale's gaze flicked to Marshall. "Would you stop that!"

Marshall froze, his hand mid-scratch at his nose.

"You can feel them, right?" Hale continued, his tone overweight with no small amount of annoyance.

"Yes." The word came out like a growl.

"And they itch?"

"Obviously."

"Imagine they don't."

Marshall glared at him. "We're playing make-believe now?"

"Magic is not just about the body. It is also about the mind. That's why we draw intentions. So imagine they don't itch—the only reason they do is that you are fighting them. Imagine the universe is one energy, rather than uncountable different energies. This magical energy belongs to you, as does your arm or your leg. Own it. Accept it."

For a moment, the room stood silent. Not silent with a constant hum in the background the way it occasionally got outside the water line—but truly, calmly silent except for the soft sounds of four people breathing.

Slowly, the skepticism leaked from Marshall's face, leaving relief in its wake.

Hale returned his attention to me as if the exchange with Marshall had never happened. "Cora investigated Sam Schneider's murder, and someone killed her for it. Simple."

"But *you're* still alive," Marshall said. "Why kill Cora and not you? Seems you'd be a higher-priority target, since you were the one spreading the theory around in the first place."

"I don't know the answer to that. Maybe I didn't push the right buttons, and Cora did."

"Maybe." Marshall leaned forward and looked as though he wanted to say more, but his phone dinged. His jaw tightened as he reached into his pocket to grab it. Straight-faced he read the display and then started furiously tapping at the screen to type a response.

With my own phone, I snapped a photo of the obituary in my hand. I returned it to the corkboard and snapped photos of the other articles up there too, before returning to my spot on the couch.

Lauren had been silent through most of this, but now she said, "You're a conspiracy theorist."

A muscle twitched in Hale's jaw. "I see the truth when others refuse to. I don't trust what I'm told without question."

"Great. I have to get home, and I think we're done here." Marshall tucked his phone back into his pocket and grabbed a loose sheet of paper from a stack on the floor. He ripped off a corner of it, lifted a pen from the floor, and scribbled something on it. Then he stood and shoved the torn paper at Hale. "This is my number. Call me if you come up with something useful." Without waiting for Lauren or me to agree that it was time to leave, Marshall walked toward the foyer.

Lauren jumped to her feet and followed. She jerked her head toward the door, urging me to do the same.

"Is there anything else you can tell us?" I asked, hoping for a reason to stay.

"About Cora? No. About the Bureau . . ."

Reluctantly, I stood and offered Hale an apologetic shrug.

Wordlessly, the three of us started our walk back to the car. We were five minutes into the walk when I realized I no longer had my phone on me.

"Hold up. I must have left my phone inside."

"I'll get it," Marshall said, but I had already turned around and was jogging back the way we'd come.

"I'll be right back," I called over my shoulder.

Hale answered the door more quickly this time. "Where are your friends?"

"Waiting for me." I paused to catch my breath. "Sorry, but I think I forgot my phone." I pointed behind him, and he stepped aside.

He'd closed the front door behind me before it occurred to me that this was probably a bad idea. I was alone in this man's house. I didn't know him. The only thing I knew about him was that he wore long sleeves in hot weather and couldn't pass psych exams.

With my heart working its way up to a stampede, I hurried to the couch where I'd been sitting. My phone sat nestled between the couch cushions. Just as I snatched it up, the doorbell rang. Probably Marshall, having second thoughts about my coming in here alone—not that I could blame him. I heard the door open beyond my view, and then Hale's voice.

"Mike, I wasn't expecting—" He stopped with a startled choking sound.

The adrenaline swimming around inside me had been trying to decide whether I was crazy for being in this house. It suddenly made up its mind and went into overdrive. I froze.

"Whatever this is about," Hale said, a tremor in his voice, "we can talk about it."

I didn't know what was happening right now, but I knew it was bad. I scanned the room for an escape route. It was a small house, and from my spot in the living room

I could see almost the entire first floor. Only the foyer was hidden. No exit.

I spun to scan the kitchen behind me, and my heart sank when I found no back door. The corkboard hung next to a closet with sliding accordion doors. I could hide in there if I needed to.

"Let's get out of the doorway," said a soft voice that struck a vaguely familiar chord.

"In the living room?" Hale's voice shook, but I couldn't miss how loud it had gotten. A warning?

As quickly and quietly as I could, I slid the closet doors open to reveal unused washer and dryer sockets, plus a large wooden rack for drying wet clothes. I scrambled inside next to the rack and then slid the doors shut. I pressed myself against the wall of the closet. The rack looked rickety, and if I touched it, I had no idea how much noise it would make or whether it would outright fall over.

There were no handles on this side of the closet, so I couldn't get the doors all the way closed. A narrow gap extended vertically between them. I tucked myself into the corner of the closet and held my breath as footsteps entered the room.

Hale passed across my line of sight, in the crack between the doors. He walked backward, his movements stiff and his gaze locked on the man with him.

"I'm sorry about this, Rick," said the other man. This time, I recognized his voice—the shorter man from Principal Spencer's office. I hadn't gotten his name at the time, but Hale had just called him Mike.

The man moved toward Hale only enough that his bare arm stretched into my field of view. In his hand, he held a knife with a long, white blade, pointed at Richard Hale.

CHAPTER TWELVE

"What is this about?" Hale asked. Fear sliced his words short—almost as sharp as that knife.

Mike flicked the blade upward. "It's about blood. Always."

"Whatever you're doing, I'm sure there's another way. You don't want to kill me."

"I don't. I'm sorry about this. Believe me, I am."

"You—"

"If you're stalling, it won't do you any good." Mike's other hand came into view, and it gestured to the stacks of paper around the room. "What do you have on me?"

"N-nothing. What should I have?"

"What do you have on Cora?"

When Hale hesitated, Mike held the knife up higher.

If I were positioned closer to the middle of the closet, I might have had an angle to see his face. I started to inch behind the clothing rack beside me, but my shoulder brushed it. The rack flexed and made a high, threatening creak. I froze and silently begged it to stay upright.

Hale pointed to the clippings he'd shown me on the corkboard. "It's almost nothing."

"Grab it. We're leaving."

Hale took a step toward the board—and then darted for his desk. He swiped up the scissors and lunged back at Mike.

In one smooth motion, Mike drew the blade across his own forearm. Hale froze in place. His arm remained in the air, stuck in a motionless downward arc.

"Hand me the scissors."

Tension tightened every muscle of Hale's body. His jaw locked, and his eyes bulged. Trembling, he lowered his arm and extended the scissors toward Mike, handles first. Mike relieved him of them and stuck them in his pocket.

I watched the exchange, hardly breathing. I'd never seen blood magic used against someone like that.

"I'm going to release you, but if you try that again, I won't be so kind."

Hale stood stiff and unresponsive.

"There. That's better. Yes?"

Hale's body sagged in place. "Where are we going?" he asked, his voice quiet, defeated.

"No questions. Let's not make this harder than it has to be."

"If this is about the cancer, there's still time. Don't give up on medicine."

My phone buzzed in my hand, and my heart tried to

catapult from my chest. Really? All those times I couldn't make calls inside the water line, and *now* my phone wanted to work. I scrambled to send the call to voicemail before the men beyond the closet door heard it. Luckily, I hadn't switched the thing off vibrate when classes ended. I was officially the *worst* on the planet at hiding from a potential murderer, but the universe was on my side today after all.

That was a nice change.

I'd just switched the phone to silent when its screen lit up as another call came through. The caller ID announced Lauren—not good. How long had I been away from my friends? Ten minutes? She'd let me into a strange man's house, and I'd disappeared. She'd be freaking out.

My phone's display flickered and died.

"Doctors are useless," Mike said on the other side of my entirely-too-thin closet doors. "But I'm not going to die. I said, let's go."

Hale stood straighter and shook his head. "Don't do this. You're not a killer."

"No, I'm not."

There was a knock at the door—a loud one. Between the growing knot in my chest and the fact that I'd been holding my breath, I almost shouted at the unexpected noise. That had to be Lauren and Marshall at the door. Not good. The opposite of good.

"You expecting someone?" Mike's arm shifted direction as he rotated halfway toward the door.

Hale's face stayed cool. "Sometimes high school kids

stop by after school, trying to get me to support their athletics." He waved a hand in a motion that felt overly dramatic. "That sort of thing."

"Ignore it. We'll wait for them to leave."

"And then what?"

Mike didn't answer.

Someone knocked again, this time pounding multiple times in succession.

"Answer it. And be smart. Neither of us wants some kid to get hurt."

They shuffled from the room—an awkward dance where Mike's knife hand waved Hale past him, while Hale walked stiffly, his body bending away from the blade. As they moved, the flat of the knife faced toward me. It was among the fancier ones I'd seen, with a symbol etched on the blade itself. That explained why Mike had been able to freeze Hale without drawing an intention.

I heard the front door open, and then Marshall's voice. "Where's—"

"Now's a bad time." Hale cut him off before he could say more.

"Where's—" he started again.

Hale's voice was louder this time, more forceful. "It's not a good time. Come back later."

Sounds of shuffling followed, and my whole body itched to jump out of the closet and run to my friends. Maybe between the three of us and Hale, we could overpower Mike . . . But he had a knife. Someone could get hurt. With my luck, someone *would* get hurt.

I gritted my teeth and stayed put.

"We're going in there," Lauren said.

As quietly as I could, I pushed the closet doors open and inched around the clothing rack. On tiptoes, I hurried from the room and peeked into the foyer, breath tight in my throat. Both men had their backs to me, facing the door.

Lauren spotted me, and her eyes went wide. She opened her mouth to say something, but I waved frantically until she snapped it shut.

I drew a finger to my lips, miming silence, and then waved her away. I ducked back into the living room and pressed my back against the wall, so I was out of view but still within earshot.

"What did you do to Maddy?" Marshall's voice had gone deep and gruff. He was working himself into a fury.

Lauren stopped him from saying more. "He didn't do anything to *me*." She emphasized the word *me*. "We just had a little misunderstanding."

"Yes." Hale caught on quickly. "I'm sorry about earlier, *Maddy*," he said to Lauren. "I really should watch my language around kids. Come back later, and I'll make a donation."

"We're sorry to bother you," Lauren said. Her voice was smooth, like melted butter. I'd have to compliment her lying skills later. "Marshall, let's get out of here?" After a second, she added, "Let's go. Everything's fine."

The door closed. I hurried back into my closet and tried to pull the doors closed. Once again, I couldn't get rid of the small slit between them. The two men didn't follow me, and the space between the closet doors revealed nothing but the empty living room. For minutes the house lay deadly quiet from where I sat. After what seemed like infinite time, the front door opened and then closed again.

I counted out the seconds of two full minutes—long enough for the men to be long gone. Then I opened the closet, dodged the rickety clothing rack, and ran into the foyer at top speed. I pulled the front door open and ran smack into Lauren.

She squeezed me in a tight hug. "You're okay." When our embrace ended, she slapped me on the shoulder. "What the hell was that about? You almost gave Marshall a heart attack."

"Me?" Marshall said. "You weren't much better."

She glared at him. "I was the picture of calm."

"She's been humming to herself for the past five minutes," he said.

"She does that when she's nervous. But I'm fine. That other guy was named Mike. I think he was the one from Principal Spencer's office. He had a knife. I hid when I saw what was happening, and Hale covered for me." I'd spat the words out in a tumble of consonants and vowels, and now I paused to catch my breath.

"They took off that way," Lauren said, pointing to a path through the lawn across the street.

"Let's get out of here," I said. "If they come back, we don't want to be around."

We headed back to Lauren's car at a fast walk. Lauren led the way, half running ahead of Marshall and me, while Marshall kept begging her to slow down and stay together.

"Can you speed up?" he said to me. "Let's catch up with her."

I obeyed without objection, mostly because the faster I got to the edge of the community, the sooner my phone would start working reliably again. Finally, a few minutes into our walk, my phone's screen lit up and stayed solid. I dialed Agent Reyes. The call rang twice and then abruptly stopped. The display went dark. I sped up to a short jog, passing both Marshall and Lauren. The phone came back on.

This time, he picked up on the fourth ring.

"Reyes," he said.

"We just saw Richard Hale get kidnapped by a practitioner named Mike. I didn't get a last name, but I think he's involved with the Bureau. We came to Hale's house to talk about Cora. We were on our way out when Mike barged in. They talked, and Mike threatened him with a knife. They took off."

"Slow down, Maddy. When did this happen?"

"Five minutes ago!"

"Hold on." Muffled voices spoke in the background, and then Reyes returned to the phone. "I have someone going out there to look into it. Please tell me you're not still there."

"No. We're getting as far away from there as possible."

"Tell me what happened. Take it one step at a time. Who are you with, and why did you go to Mr. Hale's house in the first place?"

I recapped the whole story for him—starting with my eavesdropping on Hale, Mike, and Principal Spencer yesterday, and ending with a calmer report of everything I'd just seen.

"Did you see which direction they went?"

"No!" I shouted into the phone. "I was in the closet."

"Calm down. I need you to breathe."

I was breathing. If I weren't breathing, I'd be dead.

"Did your friends see where they went?"

I pulled the phone away from my mouth. "Did you see which way they went?"

Lauren shook her head. "In the other direction. Through Hale's backyard."

"Through Hale's backyard," I repeated into the receiver. "But that's all they saw."

"Okay good. Do *not* follow them. Do you hear me?"

Did the man think I had a death wish? "We're not. We didn't even see where they went." Although if we *had* seen where they went, I probably would have suggested we follow.

"Go home. All of you. Do nothing. Do you hear me?"

"Yes, sir."

"Let's not make a bad situation worse."

CHAPTER THIRTEEN

I'd called Reyes twice over the weekend, but I didn't manage to get him on the line. By Monday morning, I was contemplating showing up at the Practitioners Bureau to demand an audience with him. What was happening with Mike and—more importantly—Richard Hale? Was he alive?

As Lauren stopped her car in the tech-side parking lot of the school, my phone rang.

"It's Reyes," I told her as we hopped out of the vehicle.

I leaned against the passenger-side door and took the call. "What's going on? Did you find them?"

He took too long to answer, and I squirmed. "Yes . . . and no."

"What does that mean?"

"If you let me speak, I'll tell you." He paused, and I bit my lip to keep from jumping in with more words. "We have a decent idea of who this Michael person might be.

There's a Mike who used to work with Hale in research at the Bureau, and I've confirmed he was at your school early last week. I wasn't able to get in touch with him on Friday, but I spoke to him personally on Saturday."

"But that would be too late—"

"Maddy, let me speak. I'm going against my better judgment by updating you at all, but maybe it will convince you to lay off this."

I said nothing and went back to chewing my lip.

"This Mike says he was at home all afternoon and through the evening. He lives with his wife, and she confirmed it."

"He was there. I didn't see his face on Friday, but I recognized his voice."

"A voice you'd heard on exactly one other occasion?"

"Yes."

"Isn't it possible you made a mistake?"

"No . . . I don't think so. And they have the same name."

"A very common name."

"What about Hale? Did you find him?"

"I left him several messages."

All my hopes took a nosedive into the pit of my stomach. "Then he's dead."

"One way or the other, he'll turn up. In the meantime, there is nothing you can do. Do you understand that? Tell me you understand."

"Yes, sir."

"Good. I'm going to go now. But I'll—"

"You'll update me if you hear anything else?"

He let out a long-suffering sigh. "That's what I was about to say. Be good and . . . for the love of God, stay out of trouble." He disconnected.

I zipped my phone into the front pocket of my backpack and joined Lauren on the school's front steps. She raised her brows in question.

"He knows nothing," I said. "Our Michael supposedly has an alibi, and Hale has disappeared."

"Damn."

"Exactly what I was thinking."

My phone rang again, and I fumbled in my rush to get my bag's zipper open. It was on its third ring by the time I connected the call, without even checking the caller ID. Maybe Reyes again?

"Hello?" I motioned for Lauren to start walking with me into the school building.

"Maddy, it's Bryan."

In the excitement of last Friday—between Principal Spencer's seizure and practically being held at knifepoint —I'd forgotten about Bryan's watch. "I'm on it. I haven't forgotten," I said before he could even ask.

"Today is the deadline, remember. It's been a week."

"No problem. I'm all over it." I disconnected the call before he could say anything else.

I would have loved to tell Bryan exactly where he could shove that watch, but unfortunately, the cheater had paid me good money. First, I needed to swipe the keys to the AV room. Ms. Louise kept them in her desk in the reception area of the principal's office.

"We have some time before class," I told Lauren. "Want to do me a favor?"

She laughed for five whole seconds, and I waited for her to finish. "Oh, you're serious. Okay. What do you need, and will it get any of us killed?"

"I'm a hundred percent sure everyone involved will come out alive." Then I remembered that last time I'd planned to grab those keys, I'd walked in on the principal's seizure. "Okay ninety-nine point nine percent sure."

"Hurry up and tell me before I change my mind."

"I'm going to distract Ms. Louise, and you'll grab her keys from the top drawer of her desk."

Lauren's mouth dropped open.

"Or you could distract her, and I'll grab the keys?" I asked.

"I distract. You grab."

I gave her my best smile. "You're my favorite."

"I damn well better be."

In the school office, Ms. Louise sat at the desk, clacking away on her keyboard. The door to Mr. Spencer's interior office stood closed, and I couldn't help staring at it as I approached the receptionist.

She stared up at me. "Miss Cooper?" Her brows rose toward her neat white hair, tied back into a bun. She followed the direction of my gaze and added, "He's still in the hospital."

"Oh." No time to wallow in my misery. I had a job to do. I nudged Lauren's foot with mine.

"I think I want to change out of my Art History class," she said, "and pick a different elective."

I stifled a groan. Worst distraction ever. I needed to get Ms. Louise *away* from her desk, not working at it.

Ms. Louise typed on her keyboard, then looked up at Lauren, expression transformed from sympathetic to crisp and businesslike. "Your available periods for electives are first and fifth—or fourth if you're willing to switch your lunch period. You can pick anything in those slots. What's it gonna be?" Her French-tipped fingernails tapped against the desk as she awaited a response. "Hmm?"

Lauren gave her an apologetic head shake. "What's available?"

"Just a minute." She clicked a few times with her computer's mouse. The printer to her left jumped to life and spit out a sheet of paper. She slid the page toward Lauren.

Lauren pretended to scan it, but her gaze kept straying to me. This wasn't getting us anywhere.

I spun and strode toward Mr. Spencer's door. "I think I left an earring in here last week."

"Please don't go in there." Ms. Louise shot up from her desk and hurried to stop me. "I'm sorry, but I'm under strict instructions."

Her back now faced her desk, and I shot a pointed glance at Lauren. It was now or never. Lauren shook her head, eyes wide.

"But it's my favorite earring," I said.

"It's out of the question."

"It was a gift from Cora. You understand." I was a horrible human being for going there, but the end justified the means. I widened my eyes at Lauren, and her shoulders slumped in surrender.

Ms. Louise's face crumpled, and she did that sympathetic head tilt I'd seen a hundred times over the last couple months. "I'm sorry. One of the parents expressed concern about contagions, and the administration asked that we keep everyone out of there until they confirm it's safe. But I'm sure it's nothing to worry about."

Lauren reached over the top of Ms. Louise's desk, pulled out the drawer, and extracted a ring full of keys. She pushed the drawer back in place and stuffed the keys into her backpack. She finished with a flourish that involved two middle fingers in my direction.

"I understand," I said. "I'll get it when the office is open again."

Ms. Louise returned to her desk and faced Lauren, who wore an expression of utter innocence.

"I've decided not to change my classes after all," Lauren said. "Really sorry for the trouble."

"No problem, dear. Final schedule changes are due on Wednesday, so you have only two more days to change your mind."

Lauren nodded and hurried from the room. "Have I told you today how much I hate you?" she muttered once we were outside earshot of the office.

"Not today, no." I grinned. "Want to come with me to the AV room?"

"Sorry. I've done my sidekick duty for the day. You're on your own."

She passed me the keys, and I zipped them into my backpack. I headed for the theater in the school's annex.

Almost no one occupied the space inside. The sets for the most recent community play had already been taken down, and it was too early in the school year for a Pritchett performance. On the other side of the rows of seats, a janitor swept the floor. He ignored me as I took the back steps to the AV room.

At the top of the stairs, I dropped my backpack and pulled the keys from it. They jingled while I flipped through each one until I found the one labeled *AV*.

The blood spot on the map had stopped at the far edge of the room, opposite the entrance. A closet stood in the middle of that wall. I opened it and, inside, found a box on the floor labeled *Lost & Found*. I tossed stuff from the box onto the floor—sweatshirts, notebooks, a phone—until I uncovered the platinum watch at the bottom of it. I stuffed everything else back inside and closed the door.

I breathed a relieved sigh. If someone had moved it between Friday and now, I would have been screwed.

I hated paying the price of a finding spell even once. No way did I want to pay it twice. I'd triple-checked my backpack before I left for school this morning to make sure I still had all my homework. The anticipation about what I would lose was driving me nuts.

Made of shiny platinum, the watch had a solid weight to it. I turned it over. On the back, an engraving included Bryan's full name and a symbol that looked like an abstract tree overlaid with a spiral. This thing must have cost a fortune.

I tucked the watch in my backpack and called Bryan. "I got it," I told him.

"Awesome. When can I get it back?"

"We have a few more minutes before class. Meet on the tech-side front steps?"

"Make it the west entrance. Fewer people around."

I bit back a snappy response. Of course he didn't want us meeting in front of the school, where the girlfriend he cheated on might see us. "Why don't I give the watch to Sheryl, and she can pass it along?" I had officially failed at holding my tongue.

Bryan didn't respond.

"Yeah. West entrance," I muttered.

"On my way."

Bryan was already sitting on the stairs on the side of the school when I arrived. He stood, slapped a few bills in my palm, and held out his hand.

I made a show of counting the money before handing over the watch.

"It's all there," he said. "So are you going to tell me how you found it? Did you . . ." He mimed slashing a knife across his forearm.

"That would be illegal." I kept my face blank and my voice flat.

"Come on. Tell me."

He'd paid me to find something, not to satisfy his curiosity. Now, as far as I was concerned, he could shove that watch into a dark orifice of his body. Instead of answering him, I pocketed the money and left. I had more important things to worry about than Bryan.

CHAPTER FOURTEEN

I convinced both Lauren and Marshall to study at my old house after school on Monday. I'd known Lauren for two years, and the lack of modern appliances at my place still weirded her out as much as the constant noise and whirring at her place did me. But she agreed to hang out there because she knew I missed it.

We stopped at a pizza place on the way, and Marshall bought us a large pepperoni to share. I had an ulterior motive for wanting to go home, and I'd handle that first—while pizza distracted my friends.

The car made it all the way to my driveway, which wasn't all that unusual since I lived close to the edge of the water line. Inside the house, I hit the switches, and the gas lamps on the walls lit up with a soft clicking sound.

"Plates are in the kitchen," I said. "You guys dig in. I'm going to be a minute."

When they turned their backs, I hefted my backpack

more squarely onto my shoulder and hurried into the master bedroom. It still looked like a disaster, with clothing and belongings strewn everywhere. As much as I hated to go into that bathroom, it was my best chance of summoning Cora. She'd crossed over in there, so that was where her spirit would be most connected to the living world.

I dropped my bag by the bed and removed my knife and a sheet of notebook paper. Inside, the cowardly part of me screamed, begged not to go any farther, but the rest of me had made up its mind. I stepped over the threshold into the bathroom.

When I blinked, behind my eyelids, Cora's lifeless body sprawled in the bathtub. She'd gotten most of her blood in the tub itself, but blood also striped the white tile of the far wall and spotted the floor beside her.

Dark red splattered all over the room's white canvas, painted by some twisted artist.

The Bureau had washed the place clean, but they couldn't scrub my mind. I swallowed hard and tried to push the image away.

With the knife blade, I opened a new cut on my upper arm. I rubbed my finger into it and wrote one word on the paper in my own blood: *Cora*.

With my gaze glued on the word, I pictured Cora the way she'd been before my father died. Always wearing a serene smile. She'd never had that internal fire my mother had. Cora was softer—scatterbrained and sweet. She never tried to be my mom, but she cared in her own way.

After the accident that killed my dad, I'd rarely seen that smile anymore, so at first, I had trouble picturing it. But when I did, my chest ached. I was ready.

Summonings were the most powerful spells I did, and I braced for the impact.

Millions of warm pinpoints slammed into me, bringing with them the sharp aroma of burnt flower petals. At first, I could feel the magic particles individually, like hot needles across my skin. They blended together, a familiar pressure pushing against me on all sides, enfolding me in spring on fire.

The pressure released me, and I was twisting and turning while shoved into a swift current. My head spun. My body rushed faster and faster like a ragdoll tossed about in the laundry—even though I was standing still.

Suddenly, my body slowed and dropped into the Deep. Floated. Instead of shoving me along, the pressure caressed every millimeter of my skin. I sank into darkness. But unlike the darkness of my room in the middle of the night—the kind that reminded me of horror movies and nightmares—this soothed me.

Cold crawled inside me and settled in my bones, burrowing deep. My teeth clacked together, but I didn't care. The transition left me breathless—like walking through violent chaos and then stepping into a room of utter silence. Still and numb and perfect.

I expected to feel Cora right away, but she wasn't there, waiting, as my mother usually was. Invisible, unidentifiable spirits floated around me. I shivered each time one rushed through me or brushed against me. Waited.

Waited.

Where was she?

Maybe I'd done it wrong. Maybe I didn't yet have the skill to summon anyone other than a blood relative. I would count down from three, and then I'd disconnect if she didn't show up.

"Cora," I whispered when my count was up. "Please. Please, please, please. I need to know what happened."

I waited a few more beats and was about to break the connection—but decided to make good of this little trip. I felt my mom nearby, and since I was already connected to the Deep, I wouldn't need to write her name. I pictured my mother and reached out to her.

"Mom."

Her spirit bobbed nearby, as energetic and full of life as she'd been before she crossed to the other side. I opened my eyes, and the space in front of me shimmered into a translucent human shape. It became more defined until a ghostly version of my mom stood before me. As always in my summonings, she wore blue jeans and a pale-blue blouse. Although her hair had a kinkier texture than mine, the style was the same—pulled back into a single hairband with a curly poof spilling over the back.

My nose filled with the familiar springtime scent of her shampoo. She had no body anymore, so of course her smell was gone too. Yet it always followed when I visited her here. Maybe I imagined it, but it added to the experience. The feeling that she was here, that we were together.

My legs trembled, reminding me my time was limited.

"I miss you," I told her.

I miss you too. When her lips moved, her voice echoed in my head. No body meant no vocal cords.

"Sorry it's been so long since we talked. Things have been crazy. Cora died—they're saying it's suicide."

I know. Her translucent brow knitted. *How are you?*

"I don't know. I was sure she was murdered, but maybe . . . Maybe that's just easier than believing she chose to leave me. My friends think I'm crazy."

Cora thought about death differently than most people. The dead are never really gone. She knew that. She might not have thought of it as leaving.

"But she retired from summoning. Why now?"

Maybe it had nothing to do with summoning. Maybe she was depressed.

"I guess."

You're living with Sara now? She phrased it like a question in my mind, but she knew the answer. She watched over me, even when I didn't call her.

"Yeah, for the last two months."

Adjusting okay?

I shrugged.

That's not an answer, Maddy.

I chuckled—my dead mother was scolding me. "I don't know her, but it's fine. It's only until graduation, and then I'm off to college."

Give your aunt a chance. She loves you.

"She . . . looks a lot like Dad."

My mother nodded, and the sympathy in her eyes told me she understood.

I couldn't summon him. I'd tried probably twenty times, but he never showed up. I should have been happy for him, happy that he'd found true peace from which not even a relative's blood magic could pull him back. But I'd never see that face again—not angry or happy or sad—not at all, and Aunt Sara's made a poor substitute.

What's wrong?

"I don't want to live with her."

Why not?

"Like I said, I don't know her."

You'll get to know her.

I didn't want to have this conversation, and I couldn't afford to. I gripped the side of the sink and braced myself against it to keep from falling over when my legs shuddered beneath me. As a novice, I could summon a spirit for three or four minutes tops. Some professionals could connect for fifteen whole minutes, but not me.

"I have to go, Mom."

Give your aunt a chance. I love you.

"I love you too."

A force slammed against my chest, and I was thrown back from the Deep and into the living world. The hole of loss in my chest widened again. Summoning my mother dulled the pain of having lost her, but it was fleeting.

I slid down to the floor to catch my breath. My hands

trembled, and I pressed them against my thighs to stop them. My stomach twisted, and I knew my lunch was about to make a second appearance. I reached the toilet bowl just in time.

Blood magic came with a price, and the price of calling the dead was the touch of death. A short stay made me sick. A long stay . . . People didn't survive those.

When I'd heaved everything in my stomach, I leaned against the wall and tried to gather my strength. Lauren and Marshall would worry if I didn't go back out there. I splashed cold water on my face, straightened up, and smiled into the mirror. Better to look like I hadn't just been summoning, especially with Marshall around.

I concentrated on each step back to my friends, careful to keep myself upright, even though I wanted nothing more than sleep. Marshall and Lauren were sitting at the kitchen table, and they had already disappeared half the pizza. My stomach growled when the smell of pepperoni and marinara hit me in the face.

Before I could dig in, the doorbell rang.

Lauren screeched—she hadn't quite gotten over her unsettled feeling about the house. Even Marshall jumped a little. After their initial reactions, the three of us exchanged glances. No one had lived here for two months. Who would come calling?

I went to check the door, and Marshall jumped to his feet to follow. When had he gotten so protective? I peeked through the peephole and found Aunt Sara standing outside, an unsure expression on her face, with Cassie and Ryan nearly hidden behind her.

"It's my aunt," I called over my shoulder before flinging the door open.

My eyes narrowed at the plastic food container in their hands. "What's up, guys?"

"We made a picnic," Ryan announced, still only partly visible behind his mother.

"Okay." I glanced at Aunt Sara and waited for the punch line.

She shifted to the side to give me a better view of the multiple food containers piled in my cousins' arms. Ryan wore a grin almost too big for his little face, while Cassie tried for cool indifference. She failed though—her lips twitched upward.

"You made a picnic," I confirmed.

My aunt stood still and waited for more of a reaction.

My growling stomach broke the silence. I stepped aside to allow her and my cousins inside. We already had pizza, but what could a little extra food hurt? Plus, I was touched they'd bothered.

In the kitchen, Lauren grabbed the pizza box and moved it from the table to the counter. Cassie and Marshall set the plastic containers on the table and began flipping off the lids.

"Are you okay with this?" Aunt Sara asked, her voice too quiet for my cousins to overhear.

I hugged her, tentatively at first but then tighter. My mom wanted me to give her a chance, and I had to admit this was thoughtful—bringing dinner to the place she knew I felt most comfortable. "It's perfect."

Once she made it past the foyer, my aunt gaped at the old home office. Lauren had started stacking the array of books and papers strewn everywhere, but it still looked like a Category Five hurricane had hit it. "What happened?"

"Bureau search." I waved my hand as if I didn't care, but mostly I was trying not to think about it.

"Cassie, Ryan." Aunt Sara set her food containers down on the table and grabbed theirs. "Why don't you guys straighten up?"

Cassie opened her mouth to protest, but Aunt Sara's glare stopped her. Ryan headed for the office while Cassie went to explore the rest of the house. Maybe having my aunt here wasn't so bad.

I couldn't help smiling as I grabbed a stack of plates and some silverware. Marshall and Lauren helped my cousins while Aunt Sara and I arranged the food. Then, all of us sat down to eat cold pot roast and pepperoni pizza, with sides of pasta salad and veggies, and it all tasted delicious.

"How's the school year so far?" Aunt Sara asked me. "Any favorite classes?"

"Art History's cool, I guess." I spoke around a mouthful of food, and bits of it sprayed from my lips. "I've never been into history classes, but I love learning about the art."

Ryan giggled, then flushed bright red when Lauren glanced at him.

"Don't talk with your mouth full," Cassie said. She copied the same singsong tone her mother always used, and I nearly spit out the rest of my food laughing.

Aunt Sara glared at her, but the look held more humor than annoyance.

"It makes her want to travel though," Lauren said. "She's been talking about seeing some of the pieces in person."

I nodded my agreement.

"Well . . . if you ever manage to save for half of the trip, I'll find a way to foot the bill for the other half, somehow."

My fork froze halfway to my mouth. Had she really just said that? Of course, I couldn't imagine earning half the cost of a trip to Europe—or even to DC to see the National Gallery of Art.

"And I could even come along with you, if you like." She added this part more quietly. "You two could join us if you could come up with your funds, of course." She gestured toward Lauren and Marshall.

Marshall nodded without looking up from his phone, where he was texting something, his fingers flying across the screen like an air raid. "Sure." He finally looked up and gave my aunt a tired smile. "If my folks let me."

Lauren grinned around a mouth full of pot roast, holding one hand up to let us know she wanted to speak. She rushed to finish chewing. "My parents will definitely be okay with it." She looked at Marshall, who was still on his phone. "They probably won't even notice I'm gone."

"I'm sure that's not true, honey." My aunt reached across the table and squeezed Lauren's hand.

Lauren returned the squeeze and then pushed her chair back from the table. "Let's make this plan official." She grabbed her backpack from where it leaned against the wall next to the table. From it, she extracted her planner and dropped back into her seat.

"So when would this trip happen?" she asked, flipping to one of the last pages.

My aunt leaned forward in her seat. "As soon as possible. But first, Maddy has to start saving."

Lauren glanced up from her book. "When will that be?"

"I don't know," I said. "A year, maybe. I'll get a job next summer."

"I'll put it down for next summer before school starts. August." She wrote something on the page and then snapped the planner shut. "Think of it as a target for your savings plan."

"Can I come too?" Ryan asked, his eyes big and staring at Lauren.

My aunt patted him on the arm. "No, this will just be me and Maddy and her friends. But I'll take you somewhere special soon."

His shoulders slumped, but Cassie dropped another slice of pizza on his plate, and he perked up again.

"I love your calendar," my aunt said, a big smile on her face. "It makes the plan seem more real. This trip is going to be epic."

I didn't know whether I could come up with the money, but for a second, I wanted to hug my aunt anyway. To throw myself at her and squeeze and thank her for trying so hard. In that moment, I didn't care that she looked like my dad, or that she could never replace the family I'd lost.

But then I remembered that her presence with me was temporary—that was how it always worked. It would be better not to get attached.

I shoved my chair back from the table, and the loud scraping called five gazes to me. "I'm going to get some air." I started for the front door but then changed my mind. I spun and exited through the sliding-glass door in the family room.

Aunt Sara's footsteps whispered across the carpet after me. I left the door open so she could slip through, and she pulled it shut behind us. But I didn't turn to look at her.

Instead, I went straight for the bench swing where Cora and I used to sit. Beside it, a vintage gas lamp hung on a wrought-iron post. The sun had started to set, so I reached up to turn the light switch. A small flame flickered to life and cast my shadow onto the bench as I dropped into it. I started it swinging, all the while keeping my gaze on the spot beside me. My shadow shifted back and forth with each swing and creak of the old bench swing.

Right there, a week after my dad died, Cora had carved a heart with the numbers *1+1* inside it. I'd been sitting where I was now, crying my eyes out, worried about where I'd go now that I had no parents. Cora ran inside to grab a knife, and as she carved the heart and the numbers, she told me that neither of us had to be lonely. Two individuals who had no one else could make their own family: *1+1.*

The etching had faded a bit as the bench aged, but the numbers still stared up at me. I brushed my fingers over it and wished to the universe that the last two months had been a dream.

I wasn't asking for much—not asking for my mother and father. Just Cora. Just two months rewound. I'd earned that much. Right? I clenched my jaw and refused to cry.

Aunt Sara dropped down onto the bench, blocking the heart from view. The old swing jolted and stopped under her weight. "What's going on?"

I stared up at the darkening sky. "Nothing."

"The same *nothing* that's been going on for the past couple months, I assume?"

I shrugged.

"This isn't easy for anyone. But the rest of us"—she gestured through the glass to the four people seated at the table around containers of food—"are doing all we can to make it work. We need your help."

I stared her in the face. "Why?"

She blinked, baffled by my question. "So we can be a family."

I laughed.

Aunt Sara laid a hand on my shoulder, but I shook it

off. "Fine." She stood and brushed the dust off the back of her jeans before walking to the sliding door. She turned back to me. "You know where to find me. I'll be here as long as it takes—but I think it will be better for all of us if that's soon." When she slid the door open, a burst of laughter sounded from inside. Aunt Sara stepped into the house and closed it behind her, taking the laughter with her.

I envied their joy. My chest ached to feel that kind of freedom in happiness again, but I didn't know how to crawl my way there through everything in my head. Cora's death always floated at the surface of my thoughts, questioning my loyalty every time I felt a twinge of joy. I needed to know the truth of it.

It was the only way to move forward.

CHAPTER FIFTEEN

By the time classes ended on Tuesday, I itched to go back to my old home again. Having dinner there had made me more homesick than usual for my old life. To smell faint whiffs of my father's aftershave at odd moments. To hear the sound of Cora's voice as she walked through the door. To catch vague snatches of memory of my mother standing in this corner or that.

"Do you mind if we stop by my old place again on the way home?" I asked Lauren when I joined her in the parking lot that afternoon. "I know we were just there yesterday but . . . Not for long, just to hang out for a minute."

She squeezed my hand and then released it, her expression spilling over with sympathy I pretended not to see. "I have to start writing a paper. I can take you to your aunt's if you want, but no pit stops today. Can your aunt take you to your old place?"

I cringed at the thought of asking Aunt Sara to bring me home. Dinner the night before had been fine—good even. But still, I couldn't have my aunt invading my old life. That space was sacred, and as much as she tried, she would never replace my mom, my dad, or even Cora. "No."

"What about him?" Lauren nodded over my shoulder.

I turned to see Marshall waving on the way to his car —a fancy car, as I'd suspected. A shining black sedan with chrome accents that had all the angles and curves that reeked of luxury.

"Call me later," I told Lauren. "Hey, Marshall." I hurried across the parking lot toward him.

He stopped with his hand on the car door. His bright smile was contagious, and I found myself grinning when I caught up to him.

"Lauren has to study. Any chance you want to take me to my aunt's, maybe with a detour along the way?"

"Sure. I can squeeze you into my busy schedule."

"I can call my aunt if you—"

"No." He held up his hands. "It's no problem."

"Good. I really didn't want to call her."

"What's the detour?"

"Can we . . ." I almost asked him to bring me by my old home, but I changed my mind halfway through the sentence. "Can we stop at my stepmother's grave first?"

"No problem. My folks will survive if I'm a half hour late." He laughed. "Maybe."

"I really appreciate it."

We hopped into the car, and he set the navigator to go to the cemetery. The school stood right on the water line, and the cemetery lay inside it but near the opposite side. We circled the outside of the water line to get there and then crossed a bridge closer to the cemetery.

Two minutes inside the magic community, Marshall's car sputtered, slowed, and then shut off completely. All the dash lights blinked out.

Marshall turned the key to the off position, waited a second, and then tried to turn on the engine again. The car remained dark and silent.

"So we walk," I said, without moving from my seat.

"I guess so." He opened his door and stepped out.

I sat still and tried to work up the nerve to get out. I'd been to this graveyard a hundred times to visit my parents—but never to visit Cora. It felt different. Cora's death felt unsettled, and I didn't know whether I'd yet earned the right to pay respect to her resting place. But what was the big deal? It was just a gravestone, marking the place where they'd buried a body. Cora didn't occupy that body anymore. Just a stone marker of a flesh-and-bone marker.

"Maddy?" Marshall had come around to my side of the car. He opened the door and gestured for me to get out, his expression soft in sympathy. "We don't have to do this."

Without answering, I got out of the car and closed the passenger door behind me.

We abandoned the vehicle in the middle of the road and, ten minutes later, walked into the parking lot of a small church. The building had been standing for a century, since before blood magic became public. Its original occupants had abandoned it in their race to the other side of the water line, but people with magic blood had kept it running, maintained, and in its vintage state. The redbrick walls and white steeple looked fresh and clean, perhaps newly pressure washed.

My mother hadn't believed in God—not completely anyway—she had her doubts, but she'd always respected my father's faith. I straddled someplace in between. I *hoped* God was up there. But I knew an afterlife awaited me on the other side regardless.

My dad had wanted to be buried in the graveyard behind the old church where his parents had been buried before the water line existed. Despite not being a church-goer, my mom agreed.

The graveyard behind the church was well-kept, with flowers marking both sides of the walkway that led down a small hill toward it. An older man, pushing an old-style mechanical mower, waved at us as we made our way down. Although I wasn't a member of this church, I appreciated the care taken here. It made the place slightly less heartbreaking. Only slightly.

I'd expected to have to search for Cora's grave. After all, I'd been to it exactly once before, for the funeral, and that had been months ago. But my legs brought me straight to the grave. A rose-colored gravestone marked the spot. I sidestepped a couple feet to one side so I wouldn't be standing on top of her—just in case. Not that it mattered.

I opened my mouth to speak and found my tongue too thick for words. I swallowed and then managed, "My parents are over there." I pointed to a spot twenty yards away. "She wanted to be near them, even though they're buried together."

"That's kind of sad," Marshall said, his voice soft and heavy.

"Is it?"

"She's all alone here, just to be near your dad."

"*She's* not here. It's just a body."

"So why come?"

I dropped to my knees and laid my hand on the rough stone of the grave, still cold despite the warmth of the morning. "I'm not totally sure. I feel like I owe her an explanation." I considered telling him I'd tried to summon her, but in the end, I decided to skip the lecture that would answer that confession. "I wanted to feel close to her again—I think."

"Do you?"

I closed my eyes briefly and tried to imagine Cora's hand resting on my shoulder, the same way my hand lay on her gravestone. "I'm not sure I deserve to."

Marshall dropped to the ground beside me and sat cross-legged, the same as he had the day Cora died. He leaned forward and rested his chin on his fist. "Why?"

"When she died, I told the emergency operator that she'd killed herself. Then when your mom and Agent

Reyes showed up, I kept to that story. I didn't stand up for her until it was too late."

"Maddy—"

"Don't." I pushed myself to my feet and brushed the dirt from my knees. "I'm going to fix this," I whispered to her grave, to her flesh and blood and bone, to her empty shell where she wasn't anymore. I didn't know if she could hear me. But my options were limited. The summoning hadn't worked, and I couldn't live with the silence anymore.

My eyes stung, so I rubbed them until they stopped.

Marshall stuck close behind me as I returned to his car, my back straight, head high.

He didn't speak until we'd climbed back into the sedan. "You don't have to be strong all the time."

I choked on my own short laughter. I hadn't been strong when my mother died or when my dad did. I hadn't been strong after Cora bled to death in the room next to mine. I hadn't been strong when the Bureau stood in my living room and I told them that my stepmother killed herself. If I were strong, I might have been able to stop some of it. But none of that was my reality. "No chance of that."

"You didn't let me finish before. I was going to say that I'll help you. We have a deal to find the truth, and I'm with you until we do."

"I thought you would be out after what happened with Hale."

"I'm not out until I say I'm out—and I won't say I'm out until it's over."

"I'm not your sister. Maybe you feel like, if you're watching over me, you can save me. Like you didn't do with her. But I'm not her. I don't need saving."

"Okay."

I expected him to say more, so I let the silence settle between us until it got too heavy to hold. "Just okay?"

"I'm in. Does it matter why?"

"I guess not."

"So what's the plan? You have one?"

"It's kind of a long shot. We know the first name of the guy who kidnapped Rick Hale—Michael—and he has to be involved with Cora's death. The Bureau's website is useless, but his practitioner's license has to be a public record. If we go to the Bureau's local headquarters, won't they have to give us his information?"

"It's worth a shot. Hold on." He reached into his pocket and grabbed his phone, typed something into it, and then slipped it back into his pocket.

"Texting your parents?"

"I told them I'm studying with you in the library." He started the car. "Let's go."

Soon, we pulled up to the brand-new, two-man security station that led to the Bureau's building. Faded parking spots marked the space underneath the station, where the new security encroached on what used to be part of the parking lot. A tall, wrought-iron gate blocked a freshly paved driveway that was surrounded by faded parking lines on all sides. A sharp spike tipped each baluster of the gate. More metal spikes poked upward from the cement beneath it, threatening the tires of any vehicle that managed to get through.

Two security guards, a man and a woman, peered down from the small security station. "Names," the man said.

"Marshall Tanner and Madison Cooper," Marshall said. "We don't have an appointment or anything."

"That's fine. What's the reason for your visit?"

"We're here for Bureau information that's public record."

The guard nodded toward his female colleague.

She lifted a clipboard and flipped a few pages into it, where she wrote something—our names, I guessed. She handed the clipboard to the man, and he stepped out of the station to Marshall's window.

"Identification."

Marshall dug his ID out of his wallet and handed it over.

The guard held it up to Marshall's face and shifted his gaze back and forth, comparing his real-life features to the ones smiling up from the card. After returning the ID, he thrust the clipboard and a pen at Marshall and pointed to a line with his name. "Sign there."

Marshall did, and the guard came around the car to my side, where we repeated the same thing.

The gate in front of us whirred to life and slid to one side. The spikes in the ground retracted, allowing us access to the Bureau's headquarters. Indistinct from its surroundings, the three-story office building that housed the Practitioners Bureau could have held any other organization. The building had two parking lots, a back one for employees and a front one for visitors. Back when this had been the Practitioners Aid, the front lot had been larger, but it had been sized down to make room for enhanced security. We parked in the small front lot.

My guess was that whoever chose this building for the Aid had gone out of their way to make sure it blended in with the remainder of the city. A private organization designed as a resource for practitioners, the Aid had been concerned with being non-threatening to both magical and non-magical societies. After having been integrated into the government and rebranded, the Practitioners *Bureau* could not care less how threatening it appeared.

Marshall got out of the car first, while I stayed inside, staring up at the building. I started when someone tapped on my window and glanced up to find him standing there. I hadn't even seen him come around to my side of the car. He opened the door and held it for me as I stepped out.

"You ready for this?" Marshall asked.

I leaned close to him and whispered, "Do you think I should leave my bone knife in the car?"

"I don't know. Do you think it would be safer in *my* car, in *my* control?"

"Good point. I'll take it inside. It's not like they're going to search us."

I grabbed my backpack, and Marshall and I walked to the building.

"I'm dead if my mom catches me here," he said at the front doors.

"Why didn't you just tell her the truth?"

"You mean that we're investigating your stepmother's death, which most likely involves killer blood magic?" He pressed his lips together, and a short snort of laughter came through his nose. "You think I should have told her that?"

"Fair point."

Inside the doors, we stepped over the threshold and onto a white-tiled floor. Bare tan walls greeted us on both sides, with faded rectangles where portraits of old practitioners, including founders of the Aid, used to hang. A white-painted steel barrier separated the waiting area from everything beyond the front desk. The barrier—a new addition to the place since my last visit—stopped a couple feet shy of the ceiling. On each side of the desk, a door was set into the barrier, with a security card scanner next to it.

From this side, we couldn't see anything beyond the white wall. A reception area stood on the right, with three white desks separated from the lobby by an acrylic window. Customer service people occupied two of the desks, and one of those two had a customer. I stepped up to the other desk, where a man in his thirties pounded at his keyboard.

"I'm trying to get information from your public records," I said.

"Mm-hmm." The man didn't glance up at me. "Specifically?"

"There's a man named Mike—or Michael—who is—or was—licensed to practice. He might also have a license for a six-inch blade. Could you search for someone like that?"

The man paused typing and peered up at me. He pushed his plastic-rimmed glasses farther up his nose and leaned forward, as if noticing me for the first time. "Why would you need that information?"

"I . . ." I hadn't been prepared for that question.

Marshall stepped forward and stood hip-to-hip with me. "She's not required to tell you that. The information we want is public."

"Indeed it is," the man said. "One moment." His computer screen faced away from me, so I couldn't see what it displayed. The man moved his mouse, clicked the mouse button, moved the mouse again, clicked—several times—until he nodded. "I think this is what you need. Hold on. It's printing."

A printer behind him jerked to life and spit out a few pages. The man leaned back in his chair, and his smile grew wider as the printer spat more pages. Page after page after page.

"Is there anything else I can help you with while we wait for your document to print?"

The printer chunked out more pages.

"No," I said. "Are there other documents printing ahead of mine?"

"Nope. That's all you."

A few minutes later, the printer finally stopped spitting out pages. The man pushed back his chair, and it rolled away from the desk far enough for him to stand. He lifted the stack of pages from the printer tray and tapped each edge of the stack against his desk to straighten them. Then he snapped a large binder clip on the top.

"The last year's worth of national licensing records will be enough. Yes?"

"Can't you just search for the criteria I gave you?"

"Unfortunately for you, I don't have search capabilities like that at my disposal. *Public* record does not mean *convenient* record." He pushed the pages toward me across his desk so that they sat in the window's opening. "Are you going to take this, or shall I recycle it?"

Marshall reached across me and grabbed the stack of papers. "Thanks?" The word came out more as a question than a statement.

"You're quite welcome. And I'm sorry for the inconvenience." The wide grin on his face said otherwise.

Marshall handed the stack to me and hurried back to the car, with occasional glances over his shoulder—to make sure his mom was nowhere in sight. But for me, our walk back felt as heavy as the pages in my hands. I held them in my lap as he started the car, in silence, and pulled through the exit gate and out of the parking lot.

The first page showed about thirty records, each with

someone's name, address, type of license applied for, date of application, and status of the license. The record at the top listed a Belinda Harwood, who'd applied for a standard practitioner's license yesterday, and her application was pending. The second record also had an application dated yesterday, as did all the records until I reached halfway down the page. For kicks, I flipped to the last page and checked the page number—192.

Every page had numerous diagonal lines spanning it—protection from digitizing the document. That meant we couldn't scan it and search it digitally.

"Total waste of time." I leaned my head back against my seat's headrest.

"Come on," Marshall said. "The information you want is there. You just have to find it."

"You think I should read thousands of records to look for someone named Michael—a popular name, by the way—who applied for a six-inch blade? There's not even a guarantee that he's in there. This is only a year's worth of records. His application could be older. Or maybe he illegally bought that knife I saw him with, and he never applied at all." I shook the stack of papers at him and then tossed it onto the backseat. It hit the leather-clad cushion, bounced, and flipped onto the floor.

The car went silent except for the soft hum of the motor and faint rhythm coming from the speakers.

"Sorry," Marshall said after a while. His mouth opened and then closed again without any more words.

"For what? That I'm now out of options for proving

my stepmother didn't commit suicide?" I blew out a long stream of breath. *"I'm* sorry. This isn't your fault. You've been perfect—except for stealing my knife."

He gave me a weak smile. "I wish I could have done more."

CHAPTER SIXTEEN

"I want to try one more thing," I told Lauren on our drive home from school on Friday. It had been three days since my disastrous trip to the Bureau, and since then, I'd been at a loss for new information about Cora. That was what I needed—information.

"What's that?" she asked.

"A knowledge spell."

She took her eyes off the road long enough to treat me with an expression of extreme skepticism. "Is that actually a thing?"

"Sure, why not? If I'm willing to lose something I know, there's no reason I can't gain knowledge with a spell in return. I'd have to focus it on a specific piece of knowledge though."

"What are the chances this will get someone killed?"

I mimed counting on my fingers and thinking deeply. "Nearly zero. *And* I'll be your best friend for forever."

"Don't threaten me."

"All you have to do is drive me to my house. It's private there."

She took the next exit off the highway and rerouted toward my old house, across the water line. The car made it all the way to my driveway.

When we pulled up, Lauren turned off the car and faced me. "Maybe I'm dense because all of this is new to me, but this doesn't sound like anything you've tried before. How is this spell going to work?"

"I'm still figuring that out." The truth was that I'd never heard of a knowledge spell. But why not?

"Tell me." She gestured toward herself, beckoning for more information. "We'll work it out together."

I breathed in deeply while I sorted through my thoughts, deciding which to reveal and which to hide away. "Magic exists everywhere. But it can be used only in moments. We focus our minds and bodies, pull the energy into us, and channel it into use. I need to use that moment to get information."

She nodded slowly. "But crossing into the Deep or finding an object—those take only a second. How do you use a short moment to see information when you don't know exactly what you want to see?"

I would need a focus—a specific piece of knowledge, something the universe could locate instantaneously. But knowledge wasn't a watch—I couldn't just *find* it, because I didn't know precisely what I wanted to find. That was the whole point. If I knew what I needed precisely, then I wouldn't need this spell.

"I'll focus it," I said. "I'll ask for a specific piece of information located in Mike's head. It's no different from a finding." I opened the door and stepped out of the car before she could figure out I was bluffing. "It'll work or it won't."

"I guess." Instead of opening her own door, Lauren reclined her seat and donned her sunglasses. "I'll be here if you need me."

Inside the house, I headed for my bedroom and sat at the small desk where I used to do homework.

This was *nothing* like a finding. This wouldn't work. It couldn't.

But I'd hit a brick wall, and I needed a bulldozer to knock it down. I didn't have the liberty to think about *wouldn't*s and *couldn't*s. It *had* to work.

I needed information—about Cora's death, and Michael, and Richard Hale. I could narrow it down a bit. I could direct the spell at Michael, to transfer any knowledge he had about my stepmother into my own head. The spell would need a more complex intention than any I'd worked with before.

I grabbed two sheets of paper from a notebook. After digging my knife out of my backpack, I lifted my arm and drew blood from the soft flesh underneath. In my blood, I wrote four words on the page: *Mike knows Cora's death.*

It was a crude intention, and I cringed while I wrote it —not only because of the sting of the open wound on my arm, but also because I knew someone with more skill could come up with a better intention. For the first time, all my self-taught skills seemed wanting. But skilled or not, I was giving this a shot.

What was the worst that could happen?

By the time I finished writing, my stomach was flip-flopping inside me. Writing four words had taken a lot more blood than the intentions I'd done in the past. I wasn't concerned about blood loss—it wasn't *that* much. But spreading this much of it around was not for the squeamish.

I kept my eyes open, staring at the words on the page, turning them over and over in my head. Nothing happened at first, and I pushed more energy into the intention. I willed Mike's knowledge to come to me through the blood, through my magic.

Magical energy concentrated around me like fiery needles pricking against my skin. Images flooded over me—Mike and Rick Hale visiting Mr. Spencer's office to discuss Cora. Hale standing in his living room, his face filled with terror. A symbol covering a concrete floor—a large spiral, a five-pointed star. The images came faster and faster until they all weaved together, none making any sense.

They repeated, this time overlaying a scene with which I was all too familiar. I saw it every time I closed my eyes: Cora in the bathtub. Spilled from the jagged cuts along her wrists, blood covered the lower parts of her body and nightgown.

The stinging scent of blood drew tears to my eyes. I gasped for fresh air, but my nostrils clogged with the sickeningly sweet stench of smoke and flowers.

Despite the horror surrounding her, Cora wore a mask of serenity. She might have drifted off to sleep while she waited for the life to flow from her. In the tub beside her hands, sticky with red liquid, lay a knife with a long white blade. Her straight reddish-brown hair fell to one side. And on her back, beneath the right shoulder, she had a small circular rash.

Blood on the tile floor, on the wall, in the tub, all over her nightgown. And Cora a picture of peace within that disaster of red on white.

The picture of Cora faded, leaving behind only the symbol on the concrete floor. The symbol kept repeating —a spiral and a five-pointed star. A spiral and a five-pointed star and a concrete floor. A wet, red spiral and a five-pointed star.

It burned my eyes, until I had no choice except to squeeze my lids shut. Sweet-smelling smoke suffocated my nose and mouth and lungs. I gulped for air, but there was none. Pain blossomed outward from behind my eyes until it filled my entire head. My head throbbed. Tears streamed down my face. I tried to scream, but I had no air to shape into sound.

I curled on the floor, my mouth hanging open. Stop. Stop. Stop. Why wouldn't it stop?

Far away, I heard the front door open and a high-pitched scream that wasn't my own—I didn't think it was my own anyway. All I knew was the star—the five-pointed star—and I was drowning in it.

Something pressed against my shoulder. A hand? Someone whispered my name from far away, and then more sounds that I couldn't distinguish. I tried to crawl toward the surface of the deep, viscous liquid surrounding me, but my arms hurt. My body hurt. My head hurt.

And then it all stopped.

CHAPTER SEVENTEEN

I woke lying in my bed, my purple comforter tucked in all around me. For the briefest moment, I convinced myself that all of it had been a dream.

Cora never killed herself. I hadn't moved across the water line. It was morning in summer, and I could slip out of bed to find Cora fixing breakfast, freshly home from her latest trip. When I breathed in, I smelled the pancakes and bacon. Later, we'd go shopping, and she'd tell me about her trip.

Everything was perfect.

"Maddy."

That man's voice was not part of my fantasy. I squeezed my eyes shut and willed it away.

"Maddy, how are you feeling?"

I groaned and opened my eyes.

Agent Reyes stood over me, with Lauren just beyond him. She leaned toward me on her tiptoes. Compared to her, Agent Reyes looked less relieved to see me awake. He had his arms crossed over his chest, and his expression told me I was not going to like what was on his mind.

That was fitting. After all, I had the sinking feeling I'd thoroughly screwed something up.

"Are you with us? How are you feeling?" Reyes asked again.

I licked my lips to bring some moisture back to my mouth—which felt like a desert had formed in there while I slept. "Like a truck ran over my skull—and then backed up to make sure the job was done right."

Lauren stepped in front of him and handed me a large glass of water. I sat up and gulped it down without stopping for a breath.

"What were you doing?" Reyes asked.

I licked my lips again. "If I say I was doing a spell, will you arrest me? Hypothetically."

He glared at me, and I wanted to burrow under the covers. "*Hypothetically*, what kind of spell would you have been doing?"

"To access someone else's knowledge about Cora's death."

"Someone else? Who—Michael Lynch?"

Lynch—that was his last name. If I didn't feel like I'd been flattened—twice—I might have smiled. I tried to nod, but a dull throb vibrated through my skull, and I cringed with the effort. "Yes."

Reyes's face remained unreadable.

"What?" I asked him. "What's that look?" With effort—

because my limbs felt like lead—I raised a finger and pointed at his face. "You're making a face."

"This is why we require licenses to practice," he said. "We make sure the people who practice actually understand the tools of the trade."

I didn't appreciate his attitude. "What am I missing?"

"Two things." He held up a finger. "First, you never ever perform a spell without knowing exactly what your goal is—which basically means all knowledge spells are out unless you can make your question really narrow, which of course requires a complex intention from a *skilled* and *licensed* practitioner."

I tried my best not to take offense at the emphasis he put on the word *skilled*. Not much I could do about the *licensed* part.

"Second." Reyes held up another finger. "For argument's sake, if you're right that Mike is involved with your stepmother's death, and if it's an ongoing spell, *and* if it involves other people like Rick Hale—these things point to some serious magic. So—"

He was taking too long to get to the point, so I cut him off. "That's why I need to find out what's going on."

Reyes held up a hand to stop me. "No, that's why the *Bureau* needs to figure out what's going on. No bloodmagic practitioner worth his salt performs a big-time illegal spell without a protection element thrown in for good measure."

"Huh?"

Reyes threw up his hands. "You don't know nothing about nothing, do you?"

I gritted my teeth.

"This is exactly why you need to leave law enforcement to professionals. You could have died." He leaned in close enough that I could smell the spicy scent of his aftershave—and the onions on his breath. His gaze met my eyes with no amount of humor. "Your spell couldn't complete. And because your intention wasn't fulfilled, your magic kept trying to fulfill it—over and over—until I pulled you out of it with my own magic."

That explained the dark circles under his eyes and the tired slouch of his shoulders.

This wasn't entirely my fault. I'd called him last Friday to ask for help, and all he'd done was blow holes in my theories. Had I really seen the guy from the principal's office? Was it the same Mike? Was he really involved with Cora?

"When I called you, you didn't believe me."

"I believed you," Reyes said. "I *believe* you. But I need evidence."

"That's why I was trying to—"

He held up his hand. "The one good thing that's come from this is that it's now a hundred percent clear that the Michael you heard at Hale's is into some serious shit. Unfortunately, we can't confirm his identity because you didn't see his face."

"I saw his face at school."

"And you can't prove the man you saw at school is the same man from Mr. Hale's house."

"What about a voice lineup? Isn't that something the cops do?"

"Yes." He hesitated. "But they're not considered reliable. And without probable cause, we can't force him to come down to the Bureau to do a lineup anyway."

I opened my mouth to ask him what our next move was, but Lauren beat me to it.

She stepped between me and Reyes so we couldn't ignore her. "Is Maddy okay now? She hasn't caused herself any long-term damage? Not that she doesn't deserve it." She glared at me.

"She should be fine. She'll just need to take it easy. No more spells for a while—until she's eighteen and licensed."

For now—until I felt strong enough—I'd just have to figure out another way to get to the bottom of this.

By the time the sun set, my head felt less like it had been run over by a truck and more like the culprit had been only a small coupe. I moved knowledge spells onto my brand-new list of things never to try again.

"Ready to head back to your aunt's now?" Lauren asked from where she lounged on the big chair across from me in the living room of my old home.

"Give me another hour. It's so noisy there with that TV." The couch I lay on right now cradled my sore head and tired body, and I had no desire to face the world again. Not yet.

"And your aunt," Lauren said. "Much easier to avoid her here."

"Am I that transparent?"

"You're a window—without glass."

"I'm okay with that." I snuggled deeper into the couch and covered my face with one arm to block out everything.

"Don't you have to be there for dinner?"

"Yeah." I grabbed my phone from the coffee table and texted my aunt to let her know I couldn't make it. Ten seconds later, my phone rang and my aunt's name flashed across the caller ID on the screen.

"Hey," I answered.

"I want to chat with you about something." The weight of Aunt Sara's tone could have dragged down the *Titanic*.

"Can't it wait until later?" I didn't have the energy for another of her you're-a-part-of-this-family-now heart-to-heart chats.

"It can. But you'll want to hear this sooner."

She'd officially piqued my interest. "Okay. Go ahead."

The call line went silent for several seconds. "This would be better in person."

"Now you *have* to tell me. I'll just be thinking about it until I see you."

Lauren caught my eye across the room and mouthed the word, *What?*

I waved her away. She picked up a pillow and tossed it

at me. It landed in the middle of the floor, feet away from me. I stuck out my tongue at Lauren and gave her a thumbs-down.

"After our talk last Thursday, when I drove you to school," Aunt Sara said, "I called the Bureau about Cora's note."

"Reyes still can't turn it over. That's what he said last time I asked." Still, my soul ached at the thought of never reading Cora's last words.

"I know, and that didn't seem right. The note was for you."

"I know that. But it's not like my life is going to start being fair sixteen years in."

"Things will get better, Maddy. I promise you."

I'd heard that before, so I didn't waste my words on a response.

"I talked to six different people at the Bureau over the past week," my aunt continued, "until I reached someone in the public relations department. I convinced the guy you'd go to the press about finding Cora's body, and they'd look bad because all their psych exams do absolutely crap to stop the suicide problem. Excuse my language."

"Okay." I didn't know what else to say because I didn't want to guess where this conversation was going.

"They emailed me a copy. I printed it out for you to read when you get home."

I held my breath, scared the words would prove Cora had killed herself—or that she hadn't. Scared they would prove she had been murdered—or that she hadn't. Scared of knowing the truth and moving on and facing the present—whatever that was. "What does it say?" I wanted to reach out and wrangle those words back into my mouth. But knowing would be better than not knowing. Wouldn't it?

"Wouldn't you rather read it when you get home? When you have a moment to really take it all in?"

"Now. I've got to know now. Please."

"Are you sure you can—"

"I can handle it." When she didn't answer right away, I added, "I promise. I won't freak out."

Paper rustled on her end of the line, and I clamped my jaws together to keep from shouting at her to hurry up— or slow down—or rip the note into a thousand pieces and delete all traces of the email.

"*Dear Maddy,*" she read. "*I'm sorry for doing this to you. I love you like my own blood. I hope you know that. You have to know that. Remember that always.*"

I cut her off. "Then she couldn't have killed herself."

"She loved you, Maddy. But it's not that simple. You want me to keep reading?"

"Yeah, go ahead. Sorry."

"*I got involved in something. Maybe I shouldn't have, but I was trying to help, trying to do a good thing for good reasons. But I made a mistake. And things that are done can't be undone. No one knows that better than you, and I'm sorry about that. I'm so sorry. Please forgive me. Love always, Cora.*"

By the time my aunt had finished reading, tears

streamed down my face. I didn't notice them until one rolled down my lip, and the salty taste invaded my mouth.

"You okay?" Lauren asked. She slid off her chair and hurried over to me.

I nodded and wiped away more tears.

"Maddy?" Aunt Sara said, her voice soft. "What are you feeling?"

I didn't know how to answer that. Was there an emotion that covered both furious and heartbroken? Because that was the word I needed. "Thank you for reading it," I whispered.

"Are you okay?"

I pulled in a long breath that whistled through the empty space where my heart should have been.

My heart—it had been broken too many times. My mom's death caused the first crack. A clean split down the middle that interrupted the flow of blood to the rest of me. Everything went cold.

But my dad was there with extra-strength glue. He held the halves together, blowing on the adhesive while it dried. But it never did. And when he died, my heart wasn't strong enough to stay whole on its own. It shattered.

Cora swept up the dirty shards—the ones she could find—and shoved them together with tape and glue and safety pins. Not fully back together, not mended. But strapped and pinned, with gaping holes and sticky bits of adhesive on the outside.

And now this.

There were only so many times a thing could break

before it stopped being fixable—before its tiny pieces dissolved to dust that could not be pasted back together.

"Are you okay, Maddy?" my aunt asked again after I'd let the silence suffocate us for too long.

"This means she killed herself. No one murdered her. After everything. She chose to go."

But that didn't make sense. What did Mike Lynch and Rick Hale have to do with a suicide? Had I made up the mystery surrounding her death? Was it just a coincidence that Hale had gotten himself into trouble, and it really had nothing to do with Cora? Maybe the Michael at Hale's wasn't even Michael Lynch from Principal Spencer's office.

How could I have been so wrong?

"Maybe you should . . . Never mind," Aunt Sara said.

"What?" My instinct was to disregard everything my aunt had to say. She couldn't understand how I felt. She hadn't lost two parents, only to be abandoned by a third. But I'd been wrong about everything else. Why not try something new?

"Maybe you should accept this, and then forgive her."

"No."

"Not *now*, or not ever?"

I didn't answer right away. Did I plan to spend my whole life angry? Did I want to mar all the good memories I had of my stepmother because she chose this? "Not now."

"That sounds fair."

I didn't want to be on this phone call anymore. Somehow, it felt even worse that Aunt Sara knew about the suicide. I'd been a fool. A complete fool. An utter fool. Queen of the fools. "Aunt Sara, I'm really sorry, but I have to go. Would you email a copy of the note to me please?"

"Sure. I'm sending it now. Let's talk more later."

"Thanks." I disconnected the call and let the phone fall from my hand onto the floor. "She read me Cora's suicide note," I told Lauren.

"Oh, honey. I'm sorry."

"Yeah. She's going to email it."

My phone beeped at the email's arrival. I couldn't bring myself to open it, but Lauren swiped up the phone and opened the email.

I threw an arm over my face, covering my eyes. "Any chance it's a fake, planted by her murderer?" I laughed at my own words, even though I yearned for them to be true. How delusional was I?

Wordlessly, Lauren passed me the phone with the email still open. The words matched exactly what my aunt had read, but I had to zoom in on the lower left-hand corner. Cora had drawn a small heart surrounding the numbers *1+1*.

No one could fake that.

CHAPTER EIGHTEEN

"So what now?" Lauren asked. "You mean have we officially proved that Cora wasn't murdered?"

Lauren stared down at her hands, and I could tell she took no joy in being right.

"Yeah," I continued. "We're done." With a groan, I swung my legs to the side of the couch and stood. I extended my arms and stretched, working the kinks out of my muscles.

"We can stay a bit longer if you need to. My mom's not expecting me home until eight—and she probably won't notice if I'm late anyway."

"Lucky."

"Am I?" She still stared at her hands instead of at me. "I guess it's better than having her calling and texting all the time, but I wouldn't mind just a *little* attention. She's studying for some kind of certification to help her qualify for better nursing jobs post-divorce. It takes up all her free time." She pushed out of her chair and pressed her palm against my forehead. "You're not feverish."

"And you're fussing over me," I said, slapping her hand away.

"It's my right as your best friend." She plucked a long hair off my sweater and let it drop to the floor. "Since when do you shed straight hair?"

"I borrowed the sweater from Cassie—one of the few perks of living at my aunt's." Its wide collar and short sleeves made it perfect for wearing off one shoulder. "Let's get out of here." This pain didn't hold a candle to the pain of summoning. I felt tired—but not like my guts were being twisted inside out. I never wanted to repeat the experience of being stuck in that spell, feeling like I'd lost control of my mind and actions, but the aftermath I could handle. "Just give me a minute to grab some more of my things from my closet."

"Sure. I'll be on my phone. Shout if you need help." She flopped back into the big armchair.

I dragged myself to my bedroom closet and flipped through my shirts until I found a few T-shirts, a cool blouse, and a pair of jeans I might still want. I cringed at the sight of a bright-blue dress with a ruffle hem and collar. What had I been thinking? Maybe the one good thing about moving from here could be that I finally culled my wardrobe of clothes I no longer wore. I grabbed the items I wanted, hangers and all, and tossed them into a pile on my bedroom floor.

The sheet of paper I'd written my intention on still sat on the desk, next to a clean page and . . . no knife. Where the hell was my knife?

I yanked the desk chair to one side and crouched to peek on the floor. Not there either.

"Lauren?" I shouted, panic rising inside my chest. I ran into the family room. "Please tell me you—"

"Yeah, I have your knife," she called back, gaze still glued to her phone. She lay on the couch now, the back of her head facing me. "I wouldn't be able to live with you if I let the Bureau have it."

"Agent Reyes didn't try to take it?"

"He asked about it, and I played dumb."

"He bought that?"

"Doubtful. But his options were limited. You can't just go around searching teenage girls because you feel like it."

From behind her head, I reached over her and squeezed her head and shoulders in a tight hug. "Did I ever tell you you're my favorite?"

"Only every time I bail you out." She shrugged me off. "Go on and get your things. I have to get home soon."

Back in my bedroom, I passed my desk on my way to my closet. I grabbed the paper with my bloody intention written on it and started to crumple it into a ball. But I stopped mid-crumple as I realized more than my words covered the page. Over the intention I'd written in my blood, now dry, were three arrows extending outward from a point at their center. I set the page back on my desk and pulled the corners apart to smooth the page as much as I could without smearing the blood.

Reyes must have written the arrows in his blood to get me out of the spell.

Before I realized what I was doing, my phone was to my ear and ringing Agent Reyes. This was a terrible idea. He'd just insisted I stop practicing blood magic, and I was calling to ask him about whatever advanced spell he'd just performed.

A woman answered before I could disconnect. "Tanner."

I hesitated, too surprised to respond.

"Hello? Reyes's phone. Agent Tanner speaking." Marshall's mother. With her perfect posture and grim expression, she came off a little scary. According to Marshall, she was new to the Bureau, which meant she'd never been part of the kinder, softer Practitioners Aid—and there was nothing kind and soft about her.

"Can I talk to Agent Reyes, please?"

"He's driving the car right now, but I'm his partner. What can I do for you?"

"This is Madison Cooper. I met the two of you when my stepmother—Cora Cooper—died a couple months ago. Marshall introduced us again at your house."

"Cooper . . . Suicide, right?"

I gritted my teeth at the word *suicide*. No point in arguing about it. I'd seen the note. Of course, if the Bureau had given me that note months ago, I wouldn't have spent that time driving myself crazy trying to prove that Cora hadn't killed herself.

"What can I do for you?" Tanner continued.

"I . . ." I didn't know whether Agent Tanner would be anywhere near as sympathetic as Reyes was about my situation. Did she know that Marshall had taken my knife that day? Had Reyes told her? "I'd rather speak to Agent Reyes."

"Then hold on a second. We're pulling into a parking lot now." She must have moved the phone from her face because, after that, I heard only muffled voices, one male and one female.

While I waited for Reyes to get the phone back from his partner, I flipped through the clothes in my closet once more. I grabbed another pair of jeans from the back and spun the hanger in front of me. They had an ink stain on the left thigh. Right. That was why I hadn't worn them in forever.

"Maddy," Lauren called, "I think someone's at the door."

"Get it. It may be Aunt Sara." I should have known she wouldn't be able to leave the whole suicide-note thing alone until I got home.

Seconds later, Lauren's scream reached inside my gut and twisted. I dropped the pants at my feet. The clothing pile I'd been building entangled my foot as I scrambled to the door. I shook my leg loose and ran into the family room.

Lauren stood at the edge of the foyer, eyes wide.

Behind her stood a man, his cold, pale eyes just as odd as I remembered them. It took me too long to register the scene. I didn't want to see what I saw. Michael Lynch, once again holding that bone knife.

But this time, he pressed it against my best friend's throat.

CHAPTER NINETEEN

Slim and white, the blade shone under the overhead light. I knew the hand holding it. I knew that knife. I liked them both even less than the last time I'd seen them. And I knew the face too—I'd seen it in Principal Spencer's office.

Finally, I had the evidence I needed to prove the two Mikes were one and the same.

"Wait!" I held both hands in front of me, as if that could stop him from slitting Lauren's throat, from spilling her blood all over the carpet, from depriving me of all I had left in the world. "What do you want?" My voice shook so violently that I could barely understand my own words. "Whatever you want."

"I'm more interested in what *you* want." His lips barely moved when he spoke, as if none of it was worth the effort. My friend's life wasn't worth the effort.

I wanted to answer, but my mouth kept moving without words. Why couldn't I make words?

"Was it you?" He moved the knife from Lauren's neck and pointed it at me. "Or this one?" He returned the blade to her throat, and Lauren and I flinched in unison.

I shook my head—like an idiot. A *mute* idiot.

"Who cast the spell?" he asked, his voice as smooth and sharp as glass. The knife brushed Lauren's neck, but the skin remained intact.

Lauren yelped. She closed her eyes, and her lips moved without words. But the shape was clear enough. *Please, please, please*, her lips formed. Her eyes opened again, and this time she directed her silent words at me. *Please, please, please.*

The panic simmering in my stomach boiled over, and I could see nothing but the knife. The knife and the smooth brown skin beneath it. If Lauren had to suffer this, I wished anyone else in the world were here with her instead of me. Not because I wanted Lauren to suffer without me, but because I had proved I couldn't be trusted with life.

I was cursed. My presence here made this situation a hundred times worse. If anything, Lauren was more likely to die because I was here. That was how it worked with me.

"Who cast it?" Lynch shouted. He inhaled hard, sniffing the top of Lauren's head. "There's no magic here."

Lauren whimpered, and her lips stopped moving.

"I did." I raised my hands higher in front of me. "It was

me. But I was wrong. I thought you'd killed Cora. I thought—It doesn't matter. I don't care what you're doing. It has nothing to do with me. Or with her."

His brows rose a fraction of an inch. "Who was Cora to you?"

"She was my stepmother."

"Ah, I see. I'm sorry about that. She didn't have to die, if she'd left well enough alone. I'm not a murderer, you know. My specialty is life."

"Sorry about what?"

A tinny voice came from the phone, still in my hand, too quiet for me to make out the words.

Lynch's attention flicked to my hand and then back to my face. "Who's on the phone?"

Before I could think better of it, I said, "Agent Reyes of the Practitioners Bureau. He was here three minutes ago, and he can get back here in that same amount of time." It had been more like sixty minutes, but Lynch didn't need to know that.

Lauren's whole body vibrated, and I felt her panic as plainly as if the knife were pressed to my throat instead. But I'd already said the words, and I couldn't back off them. Without glancing at the phone's display, I moved my thumb to press the speaker button.

Reyes's voice blasted into the room. "Maddy, what's going on over there?"

The room went silent. No one spoke. No one breathed.

"Madison—" Reyes started again.

I cut him off. "So you're Michael Lynch?" I said to the

man with the knife at my best friend's neck. My voice had gained some of its strength back—or a good imitation of it.

"What?" Reyes said. "Is Lynch there with you?"

Lynch started to mouth something at me, but I turned my attention fully to the phone. If I couldn't see him, he couldn't threaten me. Right? And he wouldn't kill Lauren while I was on the phone with the Bureau. Right?

"Yes," I said, gaze pinned to the phone's display—which took every bit of my willpower. "He's here, and he has a knife on Lauren."

"I'm on my way. I'm going to keep this line open. Tell me everything that's happening for as long as it's safe."

"It's not safe," I said, "but I'm saying it anyway."

Out of the corner of my eye, I saw Lynch drop his hand from Lauren's neck and lunge at me. Instinctively, I shouted and dropped the phone. He hit me hard in the chest, and air exploded from my lungs as my back slammed into the floor.

"I can't move," Lauren shouted. "I'm frozen. Maddy!"

Lynch hovered over me, and for just an instant—a wonderful moment of calm—almost like visiting the Deep —I thought he'd kill me. I expected the cut of the knife. The searing pain of a bone blade, deeper than I'd ever cut myself. I expected to see my own blood spilling onto the carpet. I should have shoved him off right away, slapped at him, scratched his eyes out—*something*. But I did none of that. Instead, I imagined my dad, my mom, Cora, and me.

Together.

But I was scared to die, so not today.

I lashed out with my hand and struck the man across the face, nails first. My fingernails scraped flesh from his cheek, and he roared—in pain or anger, I didn't know. His eyes went wild, and for an instant, I thought he'd punch me.

But then he calmed, a smile stretching his face.

My entire body went rigid. I could see him, feel the pressure of his weight, but my mind felt disconnected from the rest of me. I tried to claw him again, but I couldn't move. My limbs wouldn't obey. My heart could do nothing *but* move, and it went on a rampage in my chest.

Despite that, somehow, I felt stronger than ever before. My breathing brought in more oxygen with no effort, and my chest felt full. My muscles felt coiled and ready. I could run a marathon right now—if only I could move.

Lynch bent his face closer to mine, slowly, his expression gleeful at the terror mounting in me. He stroked my left cheek with the back of his fingers, and then moved them away farther to the left. My head was tilted to the right, so I could no longer see his hands, and my terror rose to panic. I knew I could throw him off, but when I tried to shove him, nothing happened.

My body whimpered, but no sound came from my lips.

Lynch's hand brushed my left shoulder.

My heart had been crazy before, but now it seemed to stop beating, like it was going so fast that each beat blended into the next, and soon it would burst entirely from my chest.

Then Lynch was back on his feet. He shot toward the foyer, and the door slammed behind him as he left.

Lauren was at my side a second later. "Maddy? Maddy, are you okay? Say something!"

"I'm fine. He didn't hurt me." My limbs felt like mine again, and I shifted into a sitting position. "*Why* didn't he hurt me? And what the hell was that?"

"That was a horror movie in real life," Lauren whispered.

I nodded mutely.

For a long time—a full minute—the two of us sat in silence.

"Reyes," Lauren said.

"What?"

"Agent Reyes. Is he still on the phone?"

"We're fine," I said loudly, for Reyes's sake. "We're both okay."

No response.

"Reyes?" Maybe the magic had killed our connection? I scanned the room for my phone. "Where'd it go? We need to call him back—tell him what's going on."

She nodded and, with shaking hands, grabbed her backpack from the couch and searched inside until she withdrew her phone. "It's dead. The battery was low earlier. I should have charged it." Her voice went high-pitched, and she could no longer hide the fear with her usual rationality. "What if he comes back? We can't call for help."

"He's not coming back." I squeezed her shoulder. "But we still need to call Reyes, so he doesn't get away." For good measure though, I jogged to the front door and locked it before returning to the family room.

I'd fallen in front of the couch, so I lay on the floor and peeked under it. When I stood up, Lauren raised her brows at me, and I shook my head.

She knelt on the floor too, and the two of us looked under the overstuffed chair and the coffee table. Lauren even checked the hallway, although I couldn't imagine the phone flying that far. The search took less than a minute, and by the end of it, all I could think about was Lynch getting farther and farther away.

"It's the spell," I said after a couple more minutes of fruitless searching.

"The knowledge spell?"

"No. The finding. I found something, so . . ."

"Now you lost something."

I nodded.

Lynch was going to get away. Again.

I didn't know his connection to Cora or her death, but he'd attacked us. He'd attacked Lauren. That, I knew. And he might have killed Rick Hale. Someone had to stop him, regardless of whether he'd killed my stepmother.

I sucked in a deep breath and looked Lauren straight in the eye. "He is going to get away again."

"Oh, God. Don't." She buried her face in her hands. "You want to follow him. Don't you?"

"You stay here. I'm only going to follow for long enough to see where he's going. I'm not going to confront him." As a second thought, I added, "I'm not even going to get out of the car. So I can take off right away if he sees me."

"He's long gone by now anyway."

"No," I said. "Not if he had car trouble. And not if he got stuck at the water line."

I swiped Lauren's keys from the coffee table. Before she could object again, I hurried to the front door and flung it open.

Lauren stayed right behind me. "Haven't you caused enough trouble today?"

"We don't have time for this." I stopped in the open doorway and blocked her path. "I'm going, and I'm doing it alone."

"We both go, or neither of us. We're safer together."

I didn't move from the doorway. "Just me."

She tapped her wrist, where a watch would have been if she wore one. "We're fresh out of time. Besides, we're not getting out of the car. Right? Nothing to worry about." Despite her confident words, her fisted hands at her sides told me she felt as terrified as I did.

With a quick nod, I shifted to the side to let her through the door, and then locked it behind her.

"I'm driving my own car," she said, thrusting her hand at me.

I dropped the keys into her palm, and we both climbed into her convertible.

Before we left the driveway, Lauren pressed a button, and the convertible top whirred closed. To her credit, she drove at a good clip toward the water line. We passed a stalled luxury coupe with a small dent on its rear, but no one sat inside. The whole time, I leaned forward in my seat, squinting ahead in hopes I'd spot the guy we were chasing, and praying the car would keep moving.

We turned a corner, and the crossing point came into view. I slumped in my seat—there was no vehicle waiting there.

Lauren pulled into the nearest driveway and threw the car into park. I slammed my fists against the dashboard and let out a string of curse words that none of my parents would have let me get away with. Not even Cora.

Lauren chewed her lower lip.

"What?" I asked her. "What are you thinking?"

She glanced briefly at the ceiling, as if contemplating, then sighed. "If I were smarter, I'd turn around and head back to the house—because this is a terrible idea. But I guess I'm stupid." She pointed in front of us. "The water is up."

I glanced back at the bridge and saw that, yes, red liquid covered the bridge and lapped over the side of the land. "So we missed him."

"*Or* he got here and had to hide somewhere to wait it out, because waiting by the bridge would be too obvious after he'd just attacked two teenage girls."

I sat up straighter. "So we wait here until the water falls, and then see what happens."

She gave me a grim nod.

For the next few minutes, I bounced my foot against the floor in front of me while the water took its sweet time dropping. I'd never considered myself impatient before, but now I itched to get moving. Eventually, the water dropped low enough to drive across the bridge.

No vehicle showed up.

"Give it a little longer," Lauren said, five minutes after the water had reached a crossable level. Her words came out clipped, but when I checked her profile, her expression was calm and determined.

As if on command, a dark-blue sedan pulled up to the bridge and drove across. Lauren backed the car from the driveway where we'd waited and then followed at a safe distance. I leaned forward, trying to see the person driving in front of us. But the combination of the tinted rear window and the fact that he faced forward made it impossible.

The sedan headed toward the city. Eventually, the driver exited the highway and continued east. Soon, I recognized the neighborhood.

"We're going to East Square," I said.

Lauren said nothing.

The driver stopped the car across the street from Practitioner Paraphernalia, the same shop where I'd bought my bone knife. Street parking was sparse, so he parallel parked in front of a driveway. As he jumped out, someone shouted at him to move, but he waved a dismissive hand and didn't look behind him.

His back faced us the whole time.

Lauren kept the car moving forward.

"What are you doing? We need to see his face."

"But we don't need him to see ours, and he will if we sit here."

I didn't argue as she moved the car farther up the block. She found a lucky parking space and pulled into it to wait. I unbuckled my seatbelt and twisted in my seat so I could keep my eye on the shop door.

Five minutes later, the man emerged from the shop with a parcel tucked under one arm. He slid back into the vehicle.

"I'm too far to see his face," I said. "We have to keep following."

Lauren glared at me, and I squirmed under the pressure of it. But when the car drove past us, she obediently left her parking space and followed at a distance.

The sedan returned to the highway and took the exact route we'd taken to get to East Square, but in reverse. We took a highway exit north of the one that would have taken us back to my house, and then drove until we reached the tall, sparkling wall that marked the water line. This particular bridge, Bridge Three, stood on almost the opposite side of the water line from the one I used to go home. I usually took Bridge Seven.

The water remained low, so the dark sedan passed over the bridge without waiting.

Lauren slowed her car until the sedan turned a corner up ahead, inside the water line. Then she shot forward, bumping over the bridge, and followed. The world brightened as we passed into the shining, white-blue air.

"You're good at this," I said.

"I'm an overachiever." She smiled for the first time since we'd started this chase. "Always have been." Her face went solemn again.

We followed the sedan to one of the city's older neighborhoods, one that had existed long before the water line. It stood less than a half mile from the church where Cora and my parents were buried. We passed one-story homes with brick facades, many with roofs scattered with broken shingles. The car in front of us slowed and then jerked to a stop. Its brake lights went out and stayed dark.

A few seconds later, the driver's door opened and a man got out. He reached back into the vehicle to grab the package, slammed the car door, and continued on foot.

"Did you see his face?" I kept my voice at a loud whisper. There was no way the man could hear me at this distance, but something about following someone like this sent my nerves on high alert.

"No." Lauren shushed me.

When he reached the end of the street, Lauren started her convertible moving again. But it jerked to a stop, and all the interior lights blacked out.

"Any chance you want to give up and go home?" she whispered. "You said we'd stay in the car."

Without a word, I opened my door and stepped out. I

closed the door softly behind me, holding onto the handle until the last second and pushing the door into place. Lauren did the same, and then we ran on tiptoes to where the man had disappeared around the corner.

We followed for what must have been close to half an hour. The whole time, my heart played double dutch at top speed, skipping so quickly my lungs couldn't keep up. I focused on keeping my breathing steady and my feet silent.

Finally, the man turned up the front walk of a single-story house with faded blue siding. Lauren and I froze, still fifty yards away.

"That's it," she said, her voice barely audible. "End of the line. We can tell Reyes where he went."

"We haven't seen his face since catching up with him at the bridge. We don't even know this is Lynch."

Lauren mumbled something under her breath as I took off at a tiptoed run. Her soft, quick footsteps followed behind me. We tried our best to look casual and like we belonged there as we hurried to the house and pressed close against it. I tried to peek through the windows but found the blinds tightly closed all across the front.

Lauren and I circled around to the back. I checked the windows as we went, while Lauren lagged behind me with her arms crossed over her chest.

Blinds covered all of them. I'd just about given up when I spotted a small window level with the ground. This one had no blinds, but black paint had been used on the inside of the glass to shield the interior from nosy onlookers. The paint only piqued my curiosity. Someone wanted privacy.

But unfortunately for whoever that was, he hadn't gone far enough. The paint had chipped in one corner of the glass. Silently, I pointed at the spot for Lauren's benefit, then lay on the ground to line my eye up with the gap.

No one occupied the room, but that made it no less fascinating. In many ways, the place looked like an average basement, with a cement floor and unfinished walls of foam and wood. Stairs led up to the first floor, but a closed door blocked my view up there.

That was where any resemblance to *normal* stopped. A red symbol covered most of the floor. I recognized it right away—only this time, I could examine it without the searing pain that had accompanied my knowledge spell.

A five-pointed star, with an arrow pointing outward along an edge of each point. A candle sat on the floor just outside each point, and those faint flames were the only sources of light in the entire room. A spiral shared a center with the star.

The star. The spiral. The arrows hadn't jumped out at me during the knowledge spell, but I couldn't deny how familiar they were. This was the symbol I'd seen.

I'd asked for whatever knowledge Lynch had about Cora, and I'd seen this. On a cement floor, just like the one in the basement here. And then Lynch had shown up and he knew who Cora was. He'd said he was sorry for her death.

But Cora had committed suicide. She'd even written me a letter to say goodbye.

So what was the connection between Michael Lynch and my stepmother's suicide?

I traced the symbol in the air and tried to commit it to memory.

The star and the spiral shared an overlapping center on the floor, and on that center point stood a small table. Someone was performing a spell down here—only I had no idea what kind.

"What do you see?" Lauren hissed.

"It's set up for a spell—a big one."

I squinted and tried to memorize everything I saw. Symbol. Table. A door at the top of a short flight of stairs. Unfinished walls and a concrete floor. The floor had darker splotches, like it had been discolored. My stomach dipped, as if *it* figured out what I was looking at before I did—blood. Blood had covered the floor near the symbol's center. So much that the stain remained, even after someone had cleaned up the liquid.

"A big spell," I said again, my voice probably too low for Lauren to hear.

Bright light sliced across the room as the door opened. By instinct, I jerked away from the window.

"What?" Lauren asked.

"I think someone just came into the room."

"He can't see you." She jabbed a finger toward the tiny little crack in the paint, and of course she was right. Even if he stared right at me, he wouldn't see me through an opening this small.

I returned my face to the crack.

The man's back faced me. He had a full head of dark hair. I couldn't tell how tall he was from this angle, looking down at him, but I could tell he wasn't huge. Maybe average height or shorter. Too nondescript to be sure this was Lynch. And after the unconfirmed accusations I'd already made—not to mention the letter that suggested Cora had killed herself—I needed to be sure this time.

Lauren tugged my sleeve. "Let's go. We've seen enough."

"Turn around. Turn around," I muttered.

The man stood between me and the table in the center of the giant symbol on the floor. He was holding something in his hands, and he stripped brown wrapping paper away from it. The wrapping fell to the floor. The man raised his arms, and it looked like he might be placing something on the table.

He shifted to one side, bringing the table into my full view. A white bowl now sat on top of it. I assumed it was bone china—sometimes used to contain blood during spells. He must have bought it from the shop in East Square.

I could see his face in partial profile now—not enough of a view to be sure.

"It could be him," I told Lauren. "He bought a bowl from the shop and added it to his spell arrangement."

The man drew a white knife from inside his jacket and dragged the blade across his forearm. He dragged it slowly, his face expressionless as far as I could tell. Whenever I performed blood magic, I did the cutting part as quickly as possible. I got it over with. This man didn't even flinch.

He raised his arm over the table, and blood dripped down his wrist and into the bowl. Arm still raised, he circled the table until his face came into view.

A narrow face with a sharp chin and cold, wide-set eyes. He stepped back toward the doorway so he could scan the entire area. I had a perfect view now—it was *him*.

CHAPTER TWENTY

After the trek back to the car, we drove straight to Lauren's from the odd house with the creepy symbol. She ran inside to plug in her phone.

"What's Agent Reyes's number?" she asked when I joined her in the kitchen.

"No idea. It was in my phone."

She groaned. "I'll call the main line." On her phone, she ran a quick web search for the Bureau and found their number. "What's his partner's name again—Marshall's last name? Tanner?"

"I don't trust her. She was never part of the Aid."

"Trust her not to arrest you, you mean? Because she's not sympathetic to practitioners."

I shrugged in place of an answer.

Lauren drummed her fingers against the oversized kitchen island as she waited for someone on the other end to answer. "Yes, hello. I have some information on a case being handled by Agents Reyes and Tanner." She turned to me and added, "They're transferring me." Into the phone, she said, "Hi. This is Lauren Evans. I have information—"

I snatched the phone from her. "Hi. It's Madison Cooper. I have evidence related to my stepmom's death." That wasn't entirely true, of course. I had proof that Michael Lynch and his creepy intention were somehow connected to Cora. But how else might they be connected if not through her death?

Lauren shot me a withering glare. I ignored it.

"Where the hell have you been?" a female voice said from the other end of the phone call. Her voice sounded farther away as she called to someone, "She's fine. She's on the phone now." Back to me, Agent Tanner added, "We've been looking for you for over an hour—ever since your call got disconnected."

"You have?"

"Of course we have." Although her voice stayed calm and even, I didn't miss the annoyance in her clipped tone. "You insist you want to talk to him. Then you put him on speaker and get all weird, mentioning a man you already accused of kidnapping someone. There was a shout—he said—and then the call disconnected. What did you expect him to do?"

"Yeah." I saw her point. "Sorry about that."

"Hold on. Here he is."

"Maddy, where the hell have you been?" Reyes asked when he came on the line.

I launched into an explanation of everything that had

happened today after he left me. I was grateful not to have to relay it to Agent Tanner. Judging from Marshall's feelings about blood-magic practice—or at least about summoning—I doubted I'd get sympathy from Tanner if she knew about my illegal magic. When I finally stopped talking, the line went quiet. "Agent Reyes?"

"We'll pick him up right now."

"Great." I slumped into one of the kitchen chairs.

For the first time, it hit me how exhausting today had been. I'd failed massively at a spell, gotten stuck in it, learned my stepmother's death was a suicide after all, watched a man press a knife to my best friend's throat, and then followed him to his house, where he was planning some kind of spell that could not be the least bit good.

"Can you let me know when you get him?" I asked.

"Of course. Sketch me a copy of that intention as best you can, and email it to me. It may come in handy if we can interpret it."

"*If* you can interpret it?"

"Unfortunately, yes. Intentions are an intensely personal language. Only amateurs use words on a page."

I suspected he meant that as a dig at me, given that he must have seen my intention for the knowledge spell. But I kept my mouth shut and let him continue.

"More advanced practitioners learn to encapsulate their intentions in symbols, which can be different for each person. With experience, each person develops a language that works for him and succinctly describes his goals."

"So there's no way you'll be able to interpret it?"

"Not necessarily. We're all familiar with the same spoken language—English—and the same symbols—things like letters, signs, shapes. So our personal intention languages tend to be related. Just send me what you saw, and we'll see what we can do."

"What about the freezing thing he did? What was that?"

"It's Lynch's area of study. Interpersonal control, he calls it. It started as a theory that no one else bought. He thought he could physically control someone, without paying a cost himself, if he offered some of his physical strength to the target in return. Temporarily. But of course, that strength is useless to someone who can't move. Initially, his targets volunteered for him to experiment with them, but the volunteer pool dried up when his theory proved correct. He got rather good at it too, to the point where he could focus on specific body parts. Freeze some and not others."

"Isn't it illegal?"

"To perform on someone who doesn't volunteer? Yes, highly illegal. Don't worry. We can arrest him this time."

We said our goodbyes, and just as I disconnected, the sound of keys jingled in the foyer. I hadn't even heard the door.

"Mom?" Lauren called, her eyes widening at me.

"Who else would it be?" Marla Evans joined us in the

kitchen, a large stack of books and pamphlets under one arm. Her attention flicked to the phone in my hand, then to my face, and then Lauren's. After a pause, she added, "Why don't you take your backpack upstairs?" She pointed at the bag Lauren had tossed in the middle of the kitchen floor. "So Maddy doesn't think we're slobs."

"Yeah, Mom. We're barbarians. No one's vacuumed this floor in like twenty-four hours. The rats are having a field day."

Her mother glared until Lauren swept up the bag and, with an apologetic glance, disappeared into the next room to head upstairs.

Mrs. Evans set her books down on the kitchen island and folded me in a tight hug. Then she stepped back and looked me square in the eye. As always, it struck me how much she looked like Lauren, despite the difference in skin tones. Mrs. Evans was biracial and light skinned, while Lauren had inherited her father's darker tone. Still, she could have passed for an older sister, with neither a wrinkle nor a gray hair in sight. Today, her long locs were braided down her back. Mrs. Evans gave me a smile that contrasted the concern in her dark eyes.

"How are you? You know you can always call me if you need to talk."

"I'm fine. Really."

She bent her knees a couple inches to bring her face level with mine. "I know when you're lying." She pressed her lips to my forehead. "But when you're ready, I'm here." This time, when she pulled me close, I hugged her back, taking in the soapy scent of her hair and the smell of ammonia or some other cleaning supplies that covered the rest of her.

"Thanks, Mrs. Evans," I whispered. My voice came out heavier than expected.

"All right then. As much as I like seeing your lovely face, I'm going to ask Lauren to drive you straight home today. I need the peace and quiet, and I'm sure your aunt will want to see you."

"I need to get back anyway. I lost my phone, and she worries."

"Good. You deserve someone to worry after you. And I imagine you'll have more of that than you can handle tonight."

Ten minutes later, Lauren and I were back in her car on the way to my aunt's house.

"We need to talk," she said. I could tell from Lauren's tone that this talk was definitely not going to include praise for how great a friend I was.

"Okay."

She inhaled a deep breath and let it out. "I feel like you're taking advantage of our friendship."

I said nothing because agreeing with her would make me look bad and disagreeing would be a big fat lie.

"You know that when I said we'd find out what

happened to Cora, I meant it. And I honor my commitments."

"I know you do—"

"Let me finish." She held up a hand and waited until I looked properly cowed. "You are taking this too far. Loyalty goes both ways. As your friend, I stick by you when you do stupid stuff—really stupid stuff. But as *my* friend, you shouldn't keep asking me to do things that could kill me."

"I totally agree. Friendship rule number one: do not get your bestie killed."

"Could you stop making jokes for five seconds?"

"Would counting to five right now count as a joke?"

"Maddy!" She cracked a smile, but it lasted only an instant before melting away.

"Look," I said. "I get it. Today got out of hand, but I didn't know the guy would show up. How could I?"

"That's the point. We're involved in something way over our heads. We don't know what's going to happen because we're amateurs facing off against professionals."

"So what do you want to do? We're not done yet."

"Aren't we? You read the suicide note."

"And then Lynch attacked us. Why would he do that if Cora killed herself? It doesn't add up."

"Then we need ground rules. For starters, think about how your actions affect me. I know you don't care about yourself, but I need you to care about me. I really need that right now."

"Because of your parents?"

She waved a dismissive hand before returning it to the steering wheel. "They have their own lives, and that's fine. I'll deal with it. But you and me are different. When everything else goes down the toilet, we have each other." She turned her convertible into my aunt's driveway. "Deal?"

"Always." I leaned over and hugged her tightly around the shoulders. "I'll do better. I promise."

"Great. Call me later."

I hopped out of her car and headed to the front door. When I opened it, my aunt was standing not ten feet on the other side. She spun on me as I stepped into the house, a vein popping out on her forehead—never a good sign. Her face looked so red I thought it might burst into flames.

"What were you thinking?" she asked.

I made a show of closing the door behind me, slowly and softly, as I stalled.

Did she know about what had happened today? And if so, *how much* did she know? Had Reyes ratted me out? He'd been pissed about my disappearing act. When Reyes had called her, had it been a vague talk-to-your-niece call or more of a your-niece-is-a-delinquent call? I hoped for the first one and intended to keep my mouth shut until I knew. Better not to dig this hole any deeper than it needed to be.

"I *said*—what were you thinking?"

"I don't know." Vague—that was the way to go.

Beyond Aunt Sara, I had a view of half the kitchen table. At it, Cassie and Ryan sat eating their dinners—

except Ryan stared at us wide-eyed, a fork halfway to his mouth. Cassie wasn't even pretending to eat. She'd twisted around in her seat and had her arms propped on the back of her chair for a better view of the spectacle.

"Lauren's mother overheard part of your call to the Bureau at her house," my aunt said.

This was what Mrs. Evans had meant about having someone worry about me tonight. She'd known Aunt Sara would flip out when she tattled.

"You followed a strange practitioner across town to spy on him *after* he attacked you? Have you lost your mind?"

"Technically, he attacked Lauren."

Her eyes got so big I could see more of the whites than the irises.

I took a giant step backward and slammed into the front door. No escape. "There's nothing to worry about. Agents are on their way to pick him up right now. He's probably already in custody."

Aunt Sara pressed her lips together and shut her eyes for a few seconds. When she opened them again, some of the fire had gone out. "Does this have to do with Cora?"

"How could it?"

"Don't lie to me, Maddy. Marla said she heard you mention Cora on the phone."

"I honestly don't know what it has to do with her. The guy who attacked Lauren said he knew her—that's all. The note she left made it pretty clear she killed herself, so I don't see how this could have anything to do with her. But

. . . it feels like there's a connection. Too many coincidences."

"Cora's note was supposed to bring you peace, not send you on a mission to hunt down dangerous criminals." Aunt Sara sucked in an audible breath. "You are grounded, Maddy."

My mouth fell open, and I jerked my head up to meet her eyes. In my entire life, I'd never been grounded. It was the one good thing about not having parents.

"After school, you will come straight home. If you need to study with friends, you will do it here. You . . . uh . . ." This grounding thing must have been new to my aunt too, because she didn't know the rules any better than I did.

"No TV," Cassie called from the kitchen.

"Right, no television," Aunt Sara repeated.

I didn't much care about television. I was used to not watching it inside the water line anyway.

"And no phone," Cassie added.

Aunt Sara turned to glare at her. "I don't see you eating. Put your dish in the sink and go upstairs to do your homework."

Cassie pouted but obediently swept up her dish, stepped out of my view toward the sink, then passed back across my line of sight on her way to her room.

"You too, Ryan. Go. Now."

He moved a lot faster than Cassie, and then my aunt and I were alone again. I envied their quick escapes.

"As I was saying," Aunt Sara continued. She folded her arms over her chest. "No phone either. Except when you're outside the house. We need to be able to reach each other if there's an emergency."

"In that case . . ." I hesitated under Aunt Sara's glower. "I'm going to need a new phone. I lost mine."

"Maddy." She closed her eyes again, and her lips moved in shapes that looked like counting—to calm herself, I guessed. "Can you get one of your friends to take you sometime this week?" she asked after looking at me.

"I'll ask Lauren."

"Give them my information at the store and have them put it on my account. But I want you straight home after that. Call me from Lauren's phone when you leave campus, and call me again from your new one when you're on the way home."

Aunt Sara spun away from me and headed for the kitchen. The conversation had officially ended.

"How long am I grounded for?" I called after her.

She didn't turn around. "Until I get tired of seeing you everywhere I look." She waved in the direction of the stairs. "Go to your room."

The house phone rang when I was only a few steps up the staircase. Aunt Sara hurried to the kitchen, where the cordless phone sat in its cradle on the counter. Before she could answer, she looked up and noticed me still standing on the stairs.

I pointed at the phone. "That could be Lauren. She's supposed to call me when she hears from the Bureau."

Without a word, she held out the phone. I ran toward

her and snatched it from her hand before she could change her mind.

"Hello?" I answered.

"They picked him up for questioning," Lauren said, "but they can't hold him long. He wasn't home at first, but his wife gave him an alibi again—said he was home all afternoon. The creepy house is empty. No intention on the floor, no blood, no nothing. And when they finally caught up to Lynch, he didn't have a scratch on him."

"What do you mean?"

"I mean it was like you never scratched up his face. Reyes said he's *pristine*."

"That doesn't make any sense."

"You think he pulled off some kind of spell to heal himself?"

"No," I said. "It's not possible. Practitioners keep trying to develop spells like that, but it never works. Magic can't mend the human body. The only thing permanent is mortality. Impermanence."

"What's going on?" Aunt Sara said in a loud whisper.

I held up a finger to stall her.

"That's probably why they can't arrest him," Lauren said. "It's our word against his now, and the evidence is on his side. No scratch makes it look like we're lying."

"Why would we lie about something like that?"

"I don't know." Lauren paused and then added, "You haven't exactly been rational since Cora died—from Reyes's perspective, I mean. You've been performing illegal magic."

I didn't miss the hint of accusation in her tone, or the way she'd added *from Reyes's perspective* as an afterthought. "And from your perspective?"

"I don't know." She paused for so long that I thought the call might have disconnected. "You'll do anything to prove your stepmother was murdered. We almost died today because you botched a spell."

"I thought you were over that."

"Forgiven but not forgotten. Anyway, I'm not sure Reyes believes us."

I cursed, and Aunt Sara lunged for the phone. Instinctively, I hit the call-end button and dropped the device. It clattered to the vinyl floor, and my aunt glared at me.

"So they didn't arrest the man, I take it?" Her voice came out tight, barely controlled.

"No." I scooted back toward the stairway. "There wasn't any evidence. Well, there was—but it was all on his side."

"Why is that, Maddy?" My aunt's voice had gone too smooth.

"You think I'm lying?"

"Are you?"

I could have been offended—*should* have been. But if I claimed that Lynch had attacked Lauren and then covered it up with impossible magic, and if Aunt Sara believed me, she would never let me off the leash she'd just put me on. She'd be so worried about my safety that I'd be grounded forever.

On the other hand, if I lied, maybe I could convince

her I was turning over a new leaf. She might step aside and let me do whatever I needed to do to prove Lynch's involvement in . . . whatever was going on.

I bit my lower lip. "Maybe I should see that grief counselor."

"I think that's a good idea." She pulled me into a tight hug, pressing my face into her neck. "And you know I'm always here for you. We'll deal with this together."

I put up a dam to block the wave of guilt threatening to crash down on me.

For a moment, I'd thought Cora's death was suicide, because why else would her note exist? But it somehow connected to Michael Lynch, or else he wouldn't have shown up today. He wouldn't have attacked us.

At this point, I didn't know whether Cora's death was a murder, suicide, or something else entirely. But I was still invested, more than ever, whether I liked it or not. No need to drag my aunt into it too.

CHAPTER TWENTY-ONE

As soon as I woke on Saturday, I dug up Reyes's business card and dialed his number from the house phone. Everyone else in the house was still asleep, so now was the best time to make a call—before Aunt Sara decided my being grounded meant I couldn't use the house phone either.

"Pick up. Pick up. Pick up," I mumbled into the phone as it rang. When it hit the fourth ring—just as I was about to hang up and redial—he answered.

"I was just about to call you," he said as soon as the call connected.

"Then why didn't you?" I realized I'd snapped at him, and took a deep breath to calm my nerves. "What happened with Lynch? You didn't arrest him?"

He took a long pause, and my insides twisted in nervous anticipation. If he had good news, he wouldn't be searching so hard for the right words. If he had good news, he would have spat it out already.

"I'm sure you've spoken to your friend Lauren already, and little has changed. We've been questioning him on and off for most of the night, but he sticks to his story."

"We need to get him to tell us how he's involved in Cora's death. I know—I know there was a suicide note, but he wouldn't have come after me and Lauren if it was that simple. He—"

"Madison, let me finish."

I snapped my mouth shut.

"We have to let him go. Your story doesn't check out."

"My *story*?"

"Are you sure you scratched his face?"

"I didn't imagine that."

A pause and then, "No one thinks you imagined it."

"You think I'm *lying*? You're taking his word over mine?"

"It's more than his word. He has no scratches on his face. No old ones, no new ones, nothing. His face is pristine. Hardly so much as a wrinkle."

"Can't you just hold him until he confesses?"

"We can't hold him without charging him, and we can't charge him without reliable evidence. I'm sorry." He disconnected before I could respond.

I cursed so loudly that, for a moment, I was afraid I might have woken the whole house. I pressed my lips together and listened. The place remained quiet except for the sound of my own breathing and the constant buzz of too many electronics.

I headed to my room and was about to crawl back into bed when a better idea hit me. Reyes might not be able to get a confession out of Lynch, but maybe I could. He had come after me in my own home. That meant he considered me a threat.

Without showering, I grabbed the nearest items of clothing I could find on the floor—a purple short-sleeved shirt and a pair of jeans artfully ripped in the thigh—and pulled them on. I brushed my hair to pull it back into a band, tossed the brush on my bedroom floor, and headed for Aunt Sara's room. I threw the door open without knocking.

She lay asleep in bed, turned to one side. I shook her shoulder until her eyes popped open.

"I need to go to the Bureau's headquarters."

She stared up at me, eyelids blinking rapidly. "Maddy?"

"I need to go to the Bureau's headquarters," I repeated, pushing more urgency into my tone. "Can I borrow your car?"

Aunt Sara sat up straight, throwing the covers off herself. "Is something wrong?"

"Of course something is wrong." My voice went shrill. I hated that, but I couldn't help it. "Something is always wrong. My parents are dead. Cora is dead. I need to . . ." I'd already let Aunt Sara believe that no one had attacked Lauren and me, so I didn't want to tell her the truth now. I spotted the keys on her dresser and stalked toward them. I fisted them in one hand. "I need to borrow your car. I want to talk to Agent Reyes about the suicide."

Aunt Sara's face went solemn when she nodded. "I can go with you if you want. You don't have to do everything alone."

"It's better if I'm alone," I said as I hurried from the room.

I sped for most of the trip to the Bureau, my gaze flitting across the sides of the highway for police. The last thing I needed was to get pulled over and have to wait while a cop took his sweet time ticketing me.

At the security gate, I searched my imagination for a reasonable excuse for being here, a reason they should let me past the guard station. "Madison Cooper," I said when asked. I handed over my identification.

The guard lifted his clipboard and scanned the top page on it. As he flipped to the second page, he said, "The reason for your visit?"

I licked my lips to stall.

"Ah, here we go." He tapped a line on the page. "To see Agent Reyes?"

"Y-yes. Does it say that?"

The guard turned the list toward me and pointed at one row. "Madison Cooper for Agent Reyes. Sign here."

I signed next to my name, too baffled to argue.

He handed back my ID, and the gate in front of me split in the middle and slid open on both sides. Before he could change his mind, I raced through the gate and parked in an empty space.

I jumped out of the car and started running for the door. When someone else in the lot gave me a curious stare, I slowed to a fast walk. Inside, I shifted from foot to foot as I waited behind a blonde woman for the only receptionist on duty. The woman walked stiffly to the reception window.

"Has Michael Lynch been released yet?" she asked.

I stopped bouncing on the balls of my feet and inched closer to the woman's back.

The receptionist, a man in maybe his early twenties, clicked the keys of his keyboard, pressed his mouse button a few times, and then looked up at the woman. "Mr. Lynch is being released as we speak." He gestured toward the waiting area behind us. "You can have a seat if you like."

"I was with my husband all yesterday afternoon," the woman told the receptionist, her head bobbing up and down.

"I don't know anything about his case, ma'am." The reception guy gestured again to the waiting area.

The woman turned and settled into the nearest chair. She crossed one leg in slim-cut tan pants over the other, her back stiff and straight. Her blouse's short sleeves displayed arms that showed no signs of scars. She probably didn't practice—at least not much. That meant she wasn't involved with whatever Lynch was up to, but she was covering for him anyway.

"Next." The receptionist waved me forward, but I ignored him.

I dropped into a seat beside the woman and grabbed a

magazine from the low, circular table in front of us. The woman's stare remained locked on the white security door leading deeper into the building. Her head didn't move an inch.

Eventually, I stopped pretending to read and slapped the magazine back on the table.

The woman's eyelids fluttered, and her attention shifted to me.

"Are you Mrs. Lynch?"

Her head tilted. "Do you know my husband?"

Before I could answer, the white security door slammed open, and Agent Reyes stomped toward me. I flinched as his boots clomped against the tile floor.

He stopped almost right in front of me, angled just enough to block the blonde woman from my view. "Why didn't you let reception know you were here?"

I shrugged.

He grabbed me around the bicep and yanked me to my feet. "This is not appropriate, Madison. You cannot speak to people involved in my investigation."

"Even if her husband attacked me?"

"I was with my husband all yesterday afternoon," Mrs. Lynch said.

When I craned my neck to see her around Reyes, she was nodding. Her eyes looked glassy, distant.

I let Reyes lead me to another group of chairs and out of the woman's earshot. "What's wrong with her?"

"Nothing we can prove." He released me right over a chair, and I dropped into it.

"You put my name on the list with security?"

"That was not an invitation to come here and screw with my investigation." He breathed in deeply, his chest rising and then falling. "You are more predictable than you think. And I'd rather have you here, where I can keep an eye on you, than standing out by the curb when Michael Lynch walks out of here." He jabbed a finger in the wife's direction. "I did not expect her to be here when you arrived."

"How can you release him?"

"We've been through this. The evidence is in his favor." He glanced behind himself at the security door, which stood closed again. "Let's go to my office."

"You mean where I won't be able to watch him leave?"

His non-answer was answer enough.

I crossed my arms over my chest.

Reyes sat across from me and leaned forward until I could no longer see the security door.

How had I not noticed how large this man was before? It was getting inconvenient.

"You never sent me a sketch of the intention you saw when you followed him from your house."

Was Reyes trying to distract me? "I couldn't. I don't have a phone right now."

"No problem." He withdrew a small notebook and pen from his jacket pocket and set both on the table in front me. He stared at me until I flipped the notebook open and started drawing.

"This is it." I shoved it back toward him.

He lifted the notebook and rotated it to view the sketch sideways and upside down, then sideways again.

"Do you know what it means?" I asked.

"Offhand? No. But I hope we can figure that out." He slid the notebook and pen back into his jacket pocket. "What do you hope to accomplish here, Maddy?" He gestured toward the security door, where Lynch could exit at any moment.

"I need to see his face."

"His face is perfect."

"Maybe it's a glamour or something," I said. "There's got to be a spell that makes you look prettier, covers your scars and acne and all that."

"We checked him for that. Trust me on this."

I gritted my teeth, stood, and shifted into the chair to my left. From there, I could once again see the security door—where Lynch would exit when they released him. Out of the corner of my eye, I saw Reyes lean back in his chair.

The clock on the wall over the door moved too slowly. And each time the door opened, my heart galloped in anticipation. Ten interminable minutes later, Lynch stood in the doorway, escorted by a guard wearing all black. The guard ushered him through the door and pulled it shut behind him.

Mrs. Lynch jumped to her feet and waited, like a good little wife, for her husband to join her. He held out an elbow, and she settled her hand in the crook of it, allowing him to lead her toward the front doors.

Reyes kept his eyes on me the entire time. I squirmed under his stare like a bug pinned in place.

"I was with you all yesterday afternoon," the woman said to her husband as they passed Reyes and me.

Lynch patted her hand at his elbow. "Yes, you were, darling." By the time he reached the glass front doors, a smile filled his face, all white teeth and glee.

My feet twitched.

"Don't," Reyes said.

"If he attacks me in front of the Bureau, you'll have to hold him. Right?"

"He's not that stupid."

I twisted in my chair to watch as Lynch opened a car door for his wife and then let himself in. No one stopped them as they exited through the gate.

CHAPTER TWENTY-TWO

By Monday, I'd had enough of this whole being-grounded thing. I'd gone two straight days following every rule thrown at me, and it was a wonder I didn't have bruises from all the rules being chucked in my direction. It was time for a little rebellion.

In my last class of the morning, I packed my textbook and notebook in my backpack a couple minutes before the bell rang. When it finally sounded, I shot out of my chair and hurried to my locker. Lauren had the one right next to mine, so she'd meet me there.

I beat her by less than thirty seconds, and she waved as she hurried toward me. "Did your weekend suck as much as mine?" she asked.

Aunt Sara had dropped me off at school this morning, and since I was still phone-less, that meant I hadn't spoken to Lauren since our disastrous Friday.

"Twice as much." I gave her a quick hug.

She hugged me back, but it took her a second longer than usual.

"You okay?" I asked.

"I'm still kind of shaken up about Friday. But I'll be all right."

"Can you text Marshall and ask him to meet us here?"

She cast me a questioning look but sent the message anyway. "What's going on?"

"Wait until he meets us. I'd rather get one combined mega-lecture rather than two separate ones."

"I'm not going to like this. Am I?"

"Have I told you today how much I love you?"

She didn't smile.

A few minutes later, Marshall sauntered toward us down the hall, his blond hair an artful mess. "What's up?"

"I finally got a copy of Cora's suicide note," I told him. Since I'd been phone-less all weekend, I hadn't had a chance to update him.

"Really? What did it say?"

I risked a quick glance at him and was pleased to find he was not doing the sympathetic head tilt I'd seen so often in the past few months—and in my entire life. He just stood there, expression open, attentive—as if I weren't the pathetic orphan kid whose parents couldn't manage to keep themselves breathing.

I quoted it word for word, then added, "And at the bottom, it had a heart with the numbers one plus one in the middle. It's something Cora came up with right after my dad died. It's a sappy story, but basically it meant she loved me."

"So . . ."

"If you're waiting for me to admit Cora killed herself, to admit defeat, I'm not doing it. I did it for one minute." I pointed one finger in the air. "But then Michael Lynch showed up and threatened us, held a knife to Lauren's throat."

Marshall glanced over, mouth agape, to confirm this with Lauren.

She nodded gravely. "Maddy was already on the phone with the Bureau though, and that scared him off. But first, he lunged at Maddy, and she scratched up his face. We followed his car back to this house that had an intention painted on the floor in the basement. But—"

"And blood on top of it," I said.

"It *might* have been blood. But the Bureau caught up with him later, and he had no scratches. And his wife alibied him again."

"It doesn't add up," I finished.

"Okay." Marshall took a long breath. "A promise is a promise, and I said I'd see this through. So what do we know?"

I didn't know much.

But I knew Michael Lynch was involved in my step-mother's death. Maybe she'd known she was going to die, and that was why she wrote me her final letter. She'd known he was coming for her. Then he slit her wrists and arranged her body to look like a suicide only thirty feet away from my bed.

I shuddered at the thought of his being in our home in the middle of the night.

I also knew that I needed proof. And so far, I'd come up with none of that. Instead, I looked like a desperate child making up lies to console herself. Somehow, Lynch had used magic to get rid of the evidence. He'd healed himself.

"There's this old Sherlock Holmes saying," I said. "'Once you eliminate the impossible, whatever remains, no matter how improbable, must be the truth.' We didn't *imagine* Michael Lynch with a knife to Lauren's throat, and we didn't *imagine* the scratches on his face. So we're left with the improbable—that Lynch healed himself."

"That's more than improbable," Marshall said.

"Just because it's never been done, that doesn't mean it *can't* be."

"That would make him unmatched in blood magic, Maddy. No one else can do that."

"Which is exactly why we have to make sure this guy gets caught. Evil and powerful—not a good combination. And I have an idea."

"That's never a good sign," Lauren said.

"It's not bad. Really. But if that's the kind of magic we're up against, it's time I took my education more seri-ously." I pointed at Marshall. "We need your mother's library."

Twenty minutes into our lunch hour, Marshall unlocked his front door and led us inside. For the second time, I tried not to ogle the majestic—but entirely impractical—pair of spiral staircases. Really, why did they need two?

"I can't believe I'm doing this," Marshall said for the third time since I first told him my plan.

"You made a deal to see this through," I said.

He muttered something under his breath. Lauren laughed and then shushed him. It was probably for the best that I didn't hear it.

"My mom's office is this way." Marshall pointed to the right.

I knew the way already, but I let Marshall lead so he could feel like he had some bit of control over the situation. Like last time, the French doors to Agent Tanner's office stood open. Unlike last time, though, she was not in there.

He stopped directly in front of the doors, blocking our path. "Seriously, guys. Whatever you move, you need to put it back exactly where you found it. My mom caught me in here playing hide-and-seek once when I was younger, and I was grounded for weeks. And back then, I didn't even try to read the books."

"We got it." I bounced on the balls of my feet.

"And, Maddy, I'm showing you these books so you can possibly discover what kind of magic Lynch is using. This is not a how-to seminar. Do you understand?"

"Yes!"

In just a few seconds, Marshall was going to lead us into the first actual blood-magic library I'd ever seen. Over his shoulder, I could see the two bookshelves and the worn paperbacks on their shelves. There'd be books on magic I'd never heard of. I might burst with the excitement expanding inside me.

Marshall stepped aside, and I hurried past him. I moved so quickly that I banged my hip against his mom's desk. I flinched but didn't slow down. This was worth the bruise.

Before Marshall could say another word, I was scanning the titles: *Blood Magic: A History*, *Magic Art and Theory*, *Dangers of Summoning*, *The Power of Blood*, and so many more. These weren't professional printings like most books I'd seen in my life. Faded paperbacks without cover art or bar codes. Pamphlets printed on plain letter-sized paper and bound with staples. I grabbed a pocket-sized one titled *The Art of Intentions*, slid into a cross-legged position on the floor, and flipped it open.

Lauren scanned both full bookshelves before selecting a book and sitting beside me. The tension between us had slipped away, and she seemed back to her usual cheerful self. Marshall sat at the desk and propped his feet on its surface.

"You're not going to help?" I asked him.

"I am helping. Whose house do you think this is?"

"We have ten minutes before we have to turn around and head back to school. We can use all the eyes we can get." I stood, grabbed a pamphlet called *Blood and the Body*, and set it in front of him on the desk. "Thank you," I said, my voice syrupy, before settling back on the floor in front of the bookcases.

Over the next ten minutes, as we flipped through book after book, we learned that most of the spells written in them relied on *other* spells or on techniques whose names were given but without details on how to perform them.

"It's like the authors went out of their way to make these things as cryptic as possible," I said, resisting the urge to throw the book in my hands across the room. The thing was so old and tattered that it would probably disintegrate on hitting the wall. Instead, I slipped it back into its previous place on the shelf and selected another.

"They probably did," Lauren said. "Just in case an untrained teenager got it into her head to try some magic she didn't understand."

"I'm going to pretend I didn't hear that."

She tore her attention away from her book to grin at me. "I could say it again."

"This is cool," Lauren said a couple minutes later. She read from a brown book in her hands. "It talks about differences between the blood of people in magic families versus non-magic ones. Apparently, it's harder to perform certain spells on people with magic in their blood. They think the same gene that causes blood magic also protects against it."

"Interesting," I said, "but not helpful." I returned my

attention to the spiral-bound book open on the floor in front of me.

"Can't you just appreciate learning for learning's sake?"

"I said it was interesting. Maybe we can focus now?"

She closed the book and slid it back onto the shelf, regret on her face. "What a waste. I wish I could read all of these."

In our fifteen minutes there, I leafed through almost thirty different books. Between Lauren and me, we covered almost every one in the small library, and even Marshall flipped through a few. But by the time he insisted we leave, we hadn't found a single helpful thing.

"There's nothing here about successful healing spells," I said. "Not even a vague reference. This one"—I tapped the spine of a book titled *The Failures of Magic*—"refers to some failed attempts at healing, but that's it."

Marshall set his latest book on the shelf, aligned its spine with the ones adjacent, and waved for Lauren and me to follow him to the door.

As I pushed to my feet, a short black book caught my eye. *Theories of Life, Death, and Living.* It was a thin one, but it called to me. The title was like the theme of my life. I slid the book from the shelf, tucked it into my backpack, and followed Marshall and Lauren from the house.

Marshall broke the speed limit all the way back to school, and we arrived on campus with only three minutes to spare before our lunch period ended. The three of us got out of the car in silence and hurried down the school hallway. Lauren took the lead at a half-jog, with every few steps alternating between running and walking. The halls were almost empty, and only a few stragglers were making their way into classrooms.

"Could you have made a mistake?" Marshall asked as he and I approached Lauren's and my lockers again.

"About what?" Lauren said. She was already grabbing the books for our next class, Physics.

"No way," I said. "We saw what we saw. He was injured, and then he wasn't."

Lauren slammed her locker just as the bell for class rang. She cursed and then slapped a hand over her mouth when the word rang out through the now-quiet hallway. "If this affects my class ranking, I'm hurting both of you. I am this close to making valedictorian next year." She pinched her thumb and forefinger less than an inch apart.

"You don't get graded down for being late. Detention, maybe, but that's it."

"I can live with detention."

"Even if that's true," Marshall said loudly enough to draw our attention back to him. "Even if he somehow healed himself, what makes you so sure Lynch is involved with your stepmother? What if that part's a coincidence? Maybe Rick Hale dragged him along to Principal Spencer's office that day, and Lynch had never heard of Cora before then. Maybe the only reason you're on Lynch's radar is that you told the Bureau he kidnapped Hale, and he found out."

"No." I shook my head. "That doesn't explain why I saw that same intention when I did the . . ." I let my voice trail off when I realized I'd started to tell him about the knowledge spell. Up until this point, I'd been strategic about telling him everything except that, and now I'd gone and screwed that up. I turned toward my locker and started spinning the combination, my gaze now firmly planted on the locker door. "That would be too much of a coincidence."

Marshall grabbed my locker door as I popped it open. "That's not what you were going to say."

Lauren identified an invisible stain on her shoe and bent down to rub at it.

"Traitor," I whispered to her under my breath.

"What don't I know?"

I opened my mouth to tell him about the knowledge spell, but I couldn't bring myself to do it. This would not go well. He didn't seem to have an objection to magic in general—mostly just to summoning. But he'd flip about my using magic I didn't understand, especially given the result.

"Maddy?"

I sighed and spit it out. "I did a spell to find out what Lynch knew about Cora's death. The spell showed me the same intention we saw in that basement."

Marshall's jaw tightened. "What else?"

How the hell did he know there was more?

In reply to my unasked question, he added, "Knowledge spells are hard-core. I don't for a second believe you pulled that off."

"Hey!" I said, but his glare shut me up.

"What else?"

"I got stuck in the spell. Lauren called Agent Reyes to drag me out of it."

His chest rose and fell, and his barely contained anger vibrated through him, right down to the hand he fisted around the strap of his backpack. "The whole point of my agreeing to help you with this was to keep you from doing dangerous shit." His voice was low and quiet, like the beginnings of an earthquake. "Instead, you do an advanced spell and almost kill yourself."

"It's fine." I reached out to lay a hand on his shoulder. "I'm—"

He jerked away. "Yeah, right now you are. You're alive, thanks to Agent Reyes. And by the way, if he'd brought my mother along, you'd be in jail right now. You risked both your life *and* your freedom. I know you don't care about the *life* part. You think yours is over because everyone you love already went to the other side. But guess what?" He paused for long enough that I wondered whether he really expected me to answer.

I opened my mouth to reply, but before I did, he was talking again.

"Your life isn't over. Your family isn't all gone. For God's sake, you're living with your aunt and cousins, and every time they try to show you they love you, you run away like a coward." His voice grew louder with each word. "You think you're so tough and brave because you're searching for your stepmother's killer. But you're not. Brave would be moving on with your life. Brave would be listening to people when we tell you we care about you, and not running around like you have a goddamned death wish."

He slammed my locker so suddenly that I barely yanked my hand out of the way to avoid getting my fingers broken. He hefted his backpack onto his shoulder and stormed down the hall.

For a moment, Lauren and I stood there in silence, and I rested my forehead against my closed locker door.

"Quick. Say something to cheer me up," I said to Lauren with a forced laugh.

"He's not wrong." She turned and followed Marshall down the hall. "I'll see you in class."

CHAPTER TWENTY-THREE

"You are late, Madison." Ms. Parker, my Physics teacher, was standing by the door when I walked in. She handed me a sheet of paper and pointed to the remaining empty desk in the room. "Five-minute pop quiz. But only two and a half minutes for you." She gestured toward the analog clock on the wall, which read two and half minutes after the hour.

Lauren was already seated, hunched over the quiz in her usual desk in the front row. The only desk remaining was behind her. As I passed, I tried to catch her eye with a silent apology, but she stayed lock-focused on the quiz.

Bryan was in the seat next to mine. He looked up at me with boredom etched into every millimeter of his expression. I pretended not to notice him as I dropped into my seat.

All the quiz questions were about the speed of different round objects set in motion down hills at various angles. An illustration of a ball on a hill accompanied each one. I remembered the formulas the teacher had given us for solving these, but it took me a full minute to figure out how to plug the values for the first question into them. The next two questions went easier.

Three questions down, and two to go. The second hand of the clock by the door ticked too quickly, and the twenty seconds left would not be enough to wrangle the final two questions into submission.

I drew a square on the hill illustration for the fourth question, blocking the ball's route downhill. I did the same for the fifth question. From each square, I drew an arrow to the bottom of the page, where I wrote: *Oh no, a cement block! These balls are stuck.*

"Time is up," Ms. Parker said from the back of the classroom.

The sounds of furious scribbling stopped, replaced by pencils being slammed onto desktops. In front of me, Lauren kept writing, still hunched over her desk and emanating more tension than a tightrope.

"Lauren Evans. Stop writing now, or you will earn a zero for this assignment."

Lauren froze and then slowly placed her pencil on top of her paper, as if any quick movements would cause Ms. Parker to misunderstand and follow through with her threat. The teacher snatched up Lauren's quiz and weaved through the aisles to collect all the others. She slowed as she approached my desk and spotted mine.

"You could have gotten some points on those last two

if you hadn't wasted your time drawing on them." She made a *tsk*ing sound with her tongue and teeth as she slid the page off my desk. "Or if you'd been on time. Priorities, Madison. Reexamine them."

Ms. Parker returned to the front of the classroom and set the stack of quizzes on the edge of her desk. "Let's start by going over the correct answers."

I spent the rest of class staring at the back of Lauren's head, but she never once turned around in the entire remaining fifty-five minutes of class. I put my notebook and pencil in my backpack a minute before class would end. When the bell rang, Lauren stuffed her things in her bag and shot from her desk. Still, I beat her to the door.

"Not cool, Maddy," she said as she brushed past me and continued down the hall.

I let her go. She needed time to cool down, but we'd be good later. We always were.

Since Aunt Sara had to work until five o'clock, Lauren was supposed to drive me home. That was the plan, anyway. But after this afternoon, I thought she might take off without me. I wouldn't blame her either.

Before my last class of the day, I made sure to pack my backpack with everything I'd need for homework. So after the final bell, I went straight out to the parking lot. I was leaning against Lauren's red convertible when she got there.

"Are you still mad?"

The convertible top was closed, so she pressed a button on the handle to unlock the car door and climbed in. She paused for only a second before unlocking the passenger door from the inside. I slid in next to her.

"You can run me all around town looking for a man who may or may not have killed your stepmother. There are only two rules, and you've broken both of them. One: do not put my life in danger. And two: do not put my academic status at risk again."

"I thought you forgave me about that other thing."

"Forgiven. Not forgotten." She hadn't started the car yet.

"I'm really sorry about the quiz. How could I know?"

She slumped back into her seat and stared at the ceiling. "I'm more mad at myself than at you. You couldn't have known there would be a quiz. But I should have considered it as a possibility. I shouldn't have left campus with you at lunch. Or I should have insisted we get out of there sooner. It's—"

"You couldn't have known either. Give yourself a break. You don't need to be perfect all the time."

"But if I am, my parents will have to notice." Her voice trembled like soft thunder, and her reddening eyes called for rain to go with that storm. "If I make valedictorian, Dad will have to fly back for graduation. Mom will throw me a party or something. Right?"

I reached over and hugged her. "I love you whether

you are valedictorian or not. You're my very favorite person."

"Really?"

"No contest."

She laughed and wiped a tear from her lower eyelid before it could fall loose. "In that case, I guess I can drive you home." She started the car, and the engine purred to life. "But I have new rules. No field trips in the middle of the school day. And you have no more than an hour and a half of my time after school each day. Any more than that, and you're cutting into my homework."

"Deal."

We hugged again, and then she pulled out of the parking space. The ride to my aunt's place was mostly silent, but not that awkward silence we had during Physics class. More like the silence of two people who didn't need to speak. We waved goodbye in the driveway of my aunt's place, and I ran into the house.

I'd gone three hours with this book in my backpack, and the anticipation overwhelmed me. I didn't even make it to my bedroom before I opened it. I grabbed it from my backpack, tossed the bag on the floor, and slumped onto the couch in the family room.

I'd barely cracked it open when Cassie appeared on the stairway. Although Ryan would stay at school until his mother picked him up, Cassie was old enough that Aunt Sara trusted her to be at home alone.

"Maddy, can you help me with graphing?" she said, stomping her way down the steps toward me.

"Graphing?" I asked her, my gaze already back on the pages of the book.

"I have to graph these functions for math class. Can you just see if I did the first one right?" She thrust a sheet of graph paper in front of me, over my book. Then she scratched the back of her neck.

I shook the paper off and let it flutter to the floor. "Can't you ask Aunt Sara when she gets home?"

"Yeah, but if I finish early, I can go to a movie with Jen and her mom." She lifted the page from the floor and again set it on top of my book.

Since checking it looked like the only way I'd get to my reading, I glanced at the paper and compared the curve on the page with the equations below it. "Isn't this ninth-grade work?"

"Yeah. I'm advanced." She stood straighter and tapped the page in front of me. "This one has an *asymptote*." From the way she emphasized each syllable, I figured she'd learned it today. She pointed at how the curve came closer and closer to the horizontal line on the page but never reached it. "It gets infinitely close to the axis but never actually reaches it."

"Seems like an awful waste of time to me. If I were that curve, at some point I'd just decide I was close enough. I mean, what's the real difference between 0 and 0.000001?"

She rolled her eyes. "Is it right or not?"

"Looks good to me." I rubbed my hand on top of her head, mussing her shiny black hair. "Good job."

"Quit it." She shrugged away from me and scratched the back of her neck again.

"Why do you keep scratching?" I looked down at the hand I'd just rubbed in her hair. "Do you have lice? If you give me lice, I'm going to hurt you."

"It's just a rash." She rotated to give me a view of the circular red patch under the right side of her hairline. "I've had it since Saturday, and now I feel kind of tired too. I must be allergic to my new perfume."

"Call your mom and ask her to bring something home to put on it." I nudged my foot against her leg. "And get away from me in case it's contagious."

"It's an allergy. It's not contagious!"

"So you say."

She took the steps back upstairs two at a time and left me alone with my book.

Holding my breath, I flipped to the back of it and almost shouted when I found an index. This would have been easier with a digital copy, on which I could just run a search, but this was almost as good. I found the word *healing* in the index and flipped to the first page number beside it.

"Practically speaking," the book read, *"spells to extend life are impossible. These include spells for youth, healing, resurrection, and the like. The price of these cannot be paid by the usual methods. For instance, to achieve youth, what does one give up in return? The obvious answer is: To extend one's life, another's life must be shortened. As one might imagine, this hypothesis has led to spells involving animal or human sacrifice. But the*

result has been the same in most cases—a dead animal or human and no resulting positive."

My excitement burst, shattered into tiny, useless pieces. I'd allowed myself to believe this book could be the answer. But just like the rest of my life, there were no answers. Just one disappointment making way for another.

I kept reading anyway. After all, it wasn't every day that I got to read a book it was illegal for me to have.

"The problem with this hypothesis is that it assumes one life can replace another in the same way that one lost item can replace another in a basic finding spell. But this is not the case. Life is a unique entity, a combination of genetics and memory and soul that cannot be replicated by some arbitrary other life. By my calculations, a life-extension spell would take either the sacrifice of both of one's own biological parents or an infinite combination of other lives."

I grabbed a pen from my bag and underlined the words *both of one's own biological parents*. So it *was* possible —but it would take a monster to do it.

CHAPTER TWENTY-FOUR

By Tuesday night, I'd had as much time with Aunt Sara and my cousins as I could handle. We'd eaten every meal together this past weekend, and now the four of us sat around the coffee table with a board game spread out between us. I couldn't wait to be ungrounded.

"Maddy." Ryan nudged me with his fingertip. "Your turn."

I leaned back in my chair. "Sorry, squirt. I think I'm done with the game for now. Can we pick it up later?"

Aunt Sara glared at me across the table, but I was saved from a family-time lecture by her phone ringing. She held up a finger to indicate none of us should move, and then stepped into the kitchen to take the call.

Ryan picked up a few of the game pieces we weren't using and began stacking them into a tower in front of him, while Cassie let out a long sigh that could be meant for nothing except drawing attention to herself.

"What?" I asked her.

"I'm a little tired."

"You didn't sleep well last night?"

"Not really."

Aunt Sara's voice reached us from the kitchen, high-pitched and frantic. "Is she okay?"

Cassie, Ryan, and I all turned our heads toward the doorway, even though Aunt Sara was out of view.

"When will you be there?" she asked. Then she lowered her voice to say something else in hushed words I couldn't make out. A few minutes later she returned to the room. In the span of only the few minutes she'd been out of view, she'd loosened her ponytail, and now the light-brown strands fell all over her head. Her face was redder too, and tension stiffened her shoulders.

I jumped to my feet and went over to her. "What's up? Everything okay?"

"Their aunt Kate—their dad's sister—fell off a ladder while trying to clean the gutters. She broke a couple bones. I'm going to take care of her for a few days."

"She's not going to . . . die?" Ryan shot a glance at me—like I was the authority on dying.

"No. No, of course not." Aunt Sara hurried over to Ryan and wrapped him in a tight hug. "She just needs someone to take care of her for a few days until your father can get home to her."

She turned to me and added, "Jack and his sister both live in their hometown up north. He moved back there after the divorce. But he's on a business trip and can't get to her until the weekend." She clenched her jaw, and I had a feeling she wanted to say more but couldn't do it in front of her kids.

"When are you leaving?" I asked.

"As soon as I can get packed." Her face softened. "Kate's a good friend. If Jack's not going to care for her, I will."

"We get to stay here by ourselves?" Cassie asked, suddenly wide awake and grinning like she'd just been offered a million bucks.

Aunt Sara thought about it for a few seconds and then pointed at me. "You're officially ungrounded. Please keep the house from falling apart while I'm away. You're used to staying by yourself, so I know I can trust you with this." She turned toward Cassie. "Don't give Maddy a hard time."

"What about me?" Ryan asked.

"I bet George's mom would be happy to look after you for a few days. Won't it be nice to stay with your friend for a while?"

He gave a hesitant nod. "I can't stay with Maddy?"

"Not this time. Sorry."

"It's cool," I said. "I can watch him."

Aunt Sara shot me a glare that told me, in no uncertain terms, to shut my mouth. I couldn't blame her. I hadn't exactly been the picture of responsibility since I'd been here. I wouldn't have trusted me with a six-year-old either.

"Sorry, squirt. We'll hang out when your mom gets back."

"Can we go to the skate park?" He stared at me with big brown eyes that made me want to melt.

"I promise." I kissed him on the forehead. "This weekend."

Less than an hour later, Aunt Sara had packed a bag for her trip and helped Ryan pack a smaller one for himself. She dropped her car keys into my hand. "Get a new phone tomorrow—even if you have to skip a class to do it. I need us to be able to reach each other." She shooed Ryan toward the door. "The taxi will stop at George's on the way to the airport."

Pouting, Ryan wheeled his small roller bag to the door.

"I'm so sorry to do this to you guys," Aunt Sara continued, "but it's only going to be a few days."

Cassie and I stood solemnly in the doorway as the cabbie stuffed their bags in his trunk and then drove my aunt and cousin away. As soon as the car rounded the corner, Cassie cracked a huge smile.

"Can I have a party?" she asked.

"Are you trying to get me grounded forever?"

"Then can I invite a few friends over?"

"Maybe tomorrow night. Tonight, I'm inviting Lauren."

"But can't we—"

"Nope."

She glared at me. Her eyelids drooped, and she tilted on her feet for a second before righting herself.

"Maybe you should forget about partying and rest tonight."

Cassie tried to bat my hands away as I gripped her arm and led her to the couch. She leaned against me, heavier than I expected. Luckily, the front door opened right into the large living room, so the trip was short. As soon as she sat, her shoulders slumped.

She gave in and stretched out across the cushions. "Just for a little while. But I'm inviting friends over as soon as I feel better."

"Sure you are. We'll talk about it when you wake up."

I called Lauren from Cassie's phone, and by the time she arrived, my cousin hadn't moved from where I'd left her on the couch. Her brown skin had gone sallow. I hadn't been worried before. But now, between her damp forehead and the random exhaustion, I didn't know what to do.

Lauren placed a hand on Cassie's forehead. "Your temperature feels normal. What hurts?"

Cassie's right shoulder moved, which might have been intended as a shrug. "Nothing. I'm just sleepy."

I chewed my lower lip. "Should we go to the emergency room? Or call your mom?"

"And tell them what?" Cassie asked. "That I'm tired after not sleeping well last night. No thanks. I want to just lie here. Besides, Mom's probably on a plane right now. You can't reach her."

"What if I call *my* mom?" Lauren said.

"She's a nurse," I added.

Cassie gave a terse nod.

Lauren stepped out of the room, phone in hand, and returned a few minutes later. "She's on her way."

Mrs. Evans arrived surprisingly quickly and spent the next hour fussing over Cassie. Lauren and I gave them some space and hung out in my room until Mrs. Evans called us back downstairs. By that time, Cassie lay on the couch, mouth hanging open, loud snores emanating from her.

"I gave her some chamomile tea," Mrs. Evans said. "She's fine. Maybe stressed about something, but she doesn't appear to be physically ill."

"We don't need to take her to the emergency room?" I asked.

"No. She just needs sleep. I guarantee that if you take her to the hospital, they're not going to do anything more than I've already done for her. Without any symptoms, she'll sit in the waiting room all night, and then they'll send her home saying she's fine. Your aunt doesn't need the medical bills for a pointless trip."

"Got it. Thanks for coming by."

Mrs. Evans squeezed my shoulder. "She'll be fine. Try not to worry so much." She turned and headed toward the front door.

I didn't like seeing Cassie so uncomfortable. Somewhere along the way, I'd managed to care about her. I intended to take my babysitting duties seriously.

Lauren hurried after her mother. "I won't be out late. So you can make dinner, if you want."

"Stay as late as you like." Mrs. Evans kissed her on the

forehead, one hand on the doorknob. "I hadn't planned to cook anyway. I need to study. You understand?"

Lauren nodded. "I—"

"Gotta go, honey. I'll see you tonight." Mrs. Evans kissed her again and turned to me. "Call me if there's any change. Okay?"

"I will," I said.

And I tried my best to push the worry out of my mind.

CHAPTER TWENTY-FIVE

"Feeling better?" I asked Cassie the next morning before school.

"Much." She gave me a wide grin. "Well rested and my rash isn't itchy."

"If you want, I can probably get Lauren's mom to write a note for you to stay home."

"Not a chance. I'm having lunch with Kyle today."

"You sure you don't need me to chaperone? I could drive to your school and hang out in the cafeteria with you guys. I'll even tell bad jokes."

She rolled her eyes. "You're worse than Mom."

The doorbell rang, and Cassie grabbed her backpack. "That's Jen's mom here to pick me up. I'll see you after school."

"Do you want some fruit or something?" I called after her.

"I'm not hungry. And you really *are* worse than Mom."

I waved her out the door and snatched my own bag off the floor to head out myself. On the way to school, I stopped at a wireless sales store and picked up a new mobile phone.

When I arrived on campus, I still had some time before class, so I dropped in at the principal's office. I hadn't heard anything about Principal Spencer in over a week. Since I'd been one of the people who found him when he fell ill, I thought I had good cause to demand an update. He'd always been kind to me, and I wanted to hear he was feeling better.

When I entered the reception area, Dean Harris stood at the threshold of Spencer's inner office, looking lost. She wore a black skirt suit, and even in short, sensible heels, she towered over me. She had to be at least five-foot-ten, but she slumped as if that might help her hide from anyone who might notice her. She wore her long brown hair braided and twisted into a bun on the back of her head.

Dean Harris let out a relieved huff when she spotted me.

"Did I interrupt something?" I asked her, trying to peek around her into the office. It looked empty from here.

"I'm just moving in. It looks like your principal will be out for a while." She didn't look thrilled with the job—not that I could blame her, given what had happened to the last person who'd occupied that office. "You're Madison Cooper, right?"

"Maddy, yeah. Do you have any news on Principal Spencer?"

"Not much besides the fact that he'll be out longer than originally expected."

"But how is he? I was here when he had his seizure. I've been worried."

Her eyes lit with recognition. "Oh, yes. The administration mentioned that one of the students waited with him for the ambulance. I'm sorry you had to go through that, especially with all you've been through lately." She tilted her head to one side—the sympathy tilt—and waited. I suspected that was my cue to tell her my whole life story. But the last thing I wanted right now was therapy. Between Aunt Sara and Marshall, I got enough of that already.

"Yeah, it sucked. Any news?"

"Mr. Spencer is . . . resting comfortably in the hospital."

Something about her tone did not reassure me. "What does that mean? Is he better? Is he coming back to school?"

"The administration has asked me not to give details on the principal's condition, so as not to worry any of you. But I think you're a special case since you were with him. I imagine you're already plenty worried."

I said nothing, hoping she'd fill my silence with more words.

"The doctors don't understand it. He'll be fine for a couple days, and the next day, the rash will be back, followed by the exhaustion and more seizures. And despite the food they keep shoving down his throat, he keeps losing weight."

"Rash?"

"Yes." She tapped the left side of her chest—maybe that's where the rash was on Principal Spencer. "It first showed up a couple weeks ago—a week before the seizure you saw. When he stopped by my office a few days after that, he was complaining about the exhaustion. And it keeps going like that: rash, exhaustion, seizures. It's the strangest thing."

"And he's not eating?" A knot of dread grew in my chest. Except for the seizures, this sounded a lot like what Cassie was experiencing.

"Sometimes, yes. Sometimes, no. But either way, he keeps losing weight."

I'd seen a news report a couple weeks ago—something about a man going from rich and perfect health to dirt broke and dead of malnutrition in a matter of weeks. Was that happening to my principal too? "Has he had any financial problems?" I asked.

Her eyes widened. "That's kind of a personal question, don't you think?"

I came up with a lie on the spot. "I was just thinking about taking up a collection from my classmates, if he needs help paying for his care. So what's the deal with his finances?"

"I honestly wouldn't know." She scolded me. "And if I did, I'm not sure it would be my place to share that with you, despite your concern for his welfare. I assume his medical insurance will cover whatever this is."

"Right." Well, that was a dead end.

Ms. Louise entered the room, a bag of takeout food in her hands. "Dean Harris." She raised the bag in greeting. "Come to claim your new office, I assume?"

The dean nodded.

"If you don't mind, I'll finish my breakfast and then show you around the space. That okay?"

"That'll be fine," the dean said.

"Miss Cooper," Ms. Louise added in my direction. "I've been seeing a lot of you lately." She said it with a smile, but the expression held no joy. She slid into her office chair and removed a foam container of food from the bag she'd been carrying.

I turned back to Dean Harris. "Thanks for the info. If you get a chance, will you please let Principal Spencer know I'm rooting for him?"

"I'll pass the message along." She patted me on the shoulder in a way that I thought she intended to be comforting but came across as awkward.

With a last glance at Ms. Louise, who ignored both of us in favor of her food, I left the office.

When I reached my locker, I leaned against it and extracted my phone from my backpack. Cassie's symptoms looked too much like Principal Spencer's. Before, I'd been concerned, but now the situation had taken a flying leap into a crisis zone.

The dean had said he lost a lot of weight.

I ran a quick web search for that recent death by malnutrition. I hadn't paid much attention to it before, but now it might have everything to do with me. It was a long shot. Just because Spencer was wasting away didn't mean Cassie would, but I had to know for sure.

According to the search results, a man named Garrett Walker had died from what looked like malnutrition. One day, he'd been rich and gorgeous, with two kids and both a wife and a mistress. And two months later, both women had left him, and his wife had taken the kids. He'd lost his job, and then died despite doctors' efforts to keep him well fed.

How does a rich man in a big city die like that?

I searched the web for more cases like that one and came up empty.

Walker. Walker. Outside of hearing the name on television, I'd seen it someplace else. I stared at my phone and willed the memory to come back to me.

Rick Hale's house. His corkboard. Luckily, I'd set my old phone to automatically back up all photos to the cloud.

On my new phone, I navigated to my cloud folder and accessed the photos that had been uploaded. I scrolled through them until I found the two I'd taken at Hale's house. I scanned them until I found Garrett Walker's name.

It was a print version of the same article I'd just read. But next to it, cut out and pinned to the corkboard, was an article about Jay O'Hara. Unlike Walker, this guy hadn't died of malnutrition. He'd been stabbed during a mugging. The article that described his death was a human-interest piece, in which the writer marveled at the guy's utter bad luck.

On its own, the mugging wouldn't have caught my eye, but Hale must have put it on his board for a reason, so I examined it more closely.

O'Hara had filed for bankruptcy a week prior to his death. The mugging culminated a run of bad luck that included discovering his wife's affair with his best friend and breaking his leg on an open manhole. Plus, he'd been seeing a doctor about unexplained weight loss preceded by an odd, recurring rash.

As far as I could tell, Walker and O'Hara had nothing in common outside of awful luck and weight loss.

I moved to the second photo. It showed an article about a man named Sam Schneider. He'd died about two and a half months ago. The date caught my eye—the day before Cora killed herself. Schneider's death appeared to be the oldest in the set. And Hale had said Schneider's half brother was murdered only a week before that.

I slid down to the floor of the hallway, my back against my locker, and opened a spiral-ring notebook to a blank page. On the page, I charted the paths of the illnesses for each of the three dead men and my principal.

Schneider had died first. I didn't know whether he had a rash, but according to the article, he complained of being tired the entire week before he died.

O'Hara, the second death, had the rash for the first

time two months before he died. The exhaustion didn't set in for another month after that, and the seizures came another month later. He lasted a day after the seizures.

The articles about Walker focused on his marriage and wealth rather than the precise path of his health, so unfortunately, I knew nothing about his timeline. Only that he died two weeks ago.

Mr. Spencer's rash first appeared two weeks ago, followed by exhaustion a few days later, and seizures a week after that. He seemed to be holding on for dear life harder than O'Hara, because the seizures hadn't killed him yet.

From the information I had, the illness—if that was what this was—had no clear timeline. Principal Spencer had been sick for only a week before his first seizure, while O'Hara had lasted two months. The only certainty was death. And that could happen any time after the seizures started.

I turned to a fresh page of the notebook and began compiling all my information into a single timeline rather than a separate one for each man. I started from the present and worked backward.

Principal Spencer had a seizure almost a week ago on a Thursday. I marked it on my timeline. He'd first seen the rash a week before that—which was only a day after Walker's death, who had been third of the three dead men.

The *third* death.

Rick Hale had used that phrase when he and Lynch

visited Principal Spencer. He'd said the third death proved Cora was onto something. Could he have meant Walker?

What if Michael Lynch had killed all three men? He'd somehow cursed them, and maybe he killed Sam Schneider's brother too. He caused Cora's death because she knew too much, and then when Hale clued in Principal Spencer, Lynch cursed him too. And then he kidnapped Hale for knowing too much.

It made sense. Except *why* would he kill all those people? What was he hiding?

And Cassie had the same illness as these men. Why involve her? She didn't fit the profile. All the others who'd suffered the curse were men and magic users.

I didn't know the answers, but I knew Cassie could have a seizure at any moment.

I needed to confirm one more thing. Maybe all these connections were in my head. After all, I'd only tied the articles together because Hale had placed them near one another. And he was a conspiracy theorist, not to be trusted. Maybe it was a coincidence that O'Hara had had a rash—I couldn't confirm that the other men did too. Maybe Principal Spencer's illness had nothing to do with theirs, and neither did Cassie's.

All those men had had money problems. I needed to find out whether Principal Spencer had financial issues too. That would tell me for sure that his case was the same.

I'd seen the principal's son, Walt, in the lunch area with Bryan on the first day of school, so I guessed that was where he spent all his lunches. I headed that way and skipped the food line, moving straight through the cafeteria to the outdoor eating space. I spotted Walt sitting with Bryan and Sheryl. Beyond them, the wall of shining magical energy glowed, marking the boundary between the tech and magic sides of school.

Sheryl gave me a bright smile and patted the seat beside her, urging me to sit.

She could have done so much better than Bryan.

Speaking of the devil—Bryan kept jerking his head back toward the school building, a sign that he wanted me to leave. He worried I'd spill his cheating exploits to Sheryl. I wanted to, but thanks to the money he'd paid me, I felt ethically obligated to keep my mouth shut.

I ignored Bryan and spoke to Sheryl. "Not today. Rain check?"

"You got it," she said. "What's up?"

"I actually came over here to talk to Walt."

Walt stopped eating and looked up at me. Outside of seeing each other around campus, I couldn't recall ever interacting with him.

Bryan stopped signaling for me to get lost, as he finally realized this little visit had nothing to do with him. In that instant, I decided that—when things calmed down—I would have to take steps to get Sheryl away from that asshole.

I motioned for Walt to follow me away from his friends. He hesitated but then got to his feet. I led him far enough away that I was confident Bryan and Sheryl couldn't hear us.

"What's up?" he asked when I stopped walking.

"You know I found your dad in his office when he was in the middle of that seizure, right?"

"Yeah, I heard something like that." His shoulders slumped, and I regretted forcing him to think about the fact that his dad was lying in a hospital bed. It was probably hard enough for him being here on campus.

"How's he doing?"

Walt shrugged. "Still alive. That's something, I guess."

"I was thinking of taking up a collection from the students to help pay for his medical care. What do you think?" I held my breath and hoped he'd think I was offering to be helpful—rather than nosy.

"No point. Insurance is covering it." His gaze drifted off to the side. "Good thing too."

Bingo. Principal Spencer was definitely having financial troubles.

"Okay, cool. But let me know if I can do anything to help out."

Walt's eyes narrowed at me. I couldn't blame him—it was a weird conversation to have with someone he barely knew, especially from a scholarship kid who had to be less financially capable than just about any other student here.

Before he could question my motives, I hurried away across the grass.

CHAPTER TWENTY-SIX

I was just about to call Aunt Sara to tell her everything I'd discovered—even though she wouldn't believe me —when I heard someone calling my name.

"Maddy." Marshall ran toward me across the grass, his phone gripped in one hand.

"What's going on? I thought we were fighting."

He thrust the phone at me. When I hesitated, he stretched his arm farther toward me and shook the phone. "It's Richard Hale."

I tore it from his hands.

"Maddy!" came a strained voice that I recognized as Hale's. "I got out. But I'm—" He broke off with a coughing fit that sounded like he was spitting up half a lung.

"Mr. Hale?"

"Yes, yes, I'm fine. No, I'm not fine, but there's nothing to be done about that. I—" His voice cut off abruptly.

"Mr. Hale?" I shouted into the phone. "Can you hear me?"

"Quieter," Marshall whispered. "If the connection's bad, shouting is not going to help it."

I waved him away and concentrated on the call.

"Water line," Hale said. "Bad connection . . . at bridge . . . meet."

"Meet you where?" I said, more quietly this time. "Which bridge?"

"Meet me . . . three."

"Three o'clock? No, Bridge Three! Meet you at Bridge Three?"

"Come now." The call disconnected.

I handed the phone back to Marshall. "I need to meet him right now."

"That's a bad idea. I knew I shouldn't have given you that call."

"Why did you? Aren't you supposed to be mad at me?"

"I'm not mad. I'm frustrated. I just want you to be safe. And it sounded like an emergency. You heard him."

I struggled to keep from smiling. "You want me to be safe, so you bring me a call from a conspiracy theorist who wants me to meet him at a water-line bridge."

He shook his head. "No."

"We need to go here." I pointed at the phone's screen.

He held up both hands. "We can't skip school to meet a creepy old guy."

"Says who? It's not far. We'll be back soon." Since

Pritchett Academy stood on the water line, we weren't far from any of the bridges.

"That's not the point."

"Are you with me?" I said. "Remember your promise."

"As far as I'm concerned, you broke that deal when you did your little knowledge spell." He crossed his arms over his chest. "And nowhere in my promise did I say skipping school was an option."

"You didn't say it wasn't either. And lucky for me, I don't need your wheels today. I yanked my aunt's keys from my backpack and twirled the key ring around my forefinger. "I'll drive myself." I turned and sauntered across the grass. "You're welcome to join me."

"This isn't fair, you know?" he said as he caught up with me a few seconds later.

"Life isn't fair."

In the parking lot, we slid into my aunt's car and took off for Bridge Three. Marshall pouted for most of the ride, staring out the window with arms crossed over his chest. But he was there, under protest or not, and that was enough.

When we arrived, I pulled the car to the side of the road and jumped out. I ran to the edge of the water line and scanned the area beyond it. The red liquid flowed round and round. It lapped just over the edges of the bridge. On the other side, in the bright-white light of magical energy, a small road led from the bridge and forked. In one direction, it led to the house with the intention on the basement floor.

"Mr. Hale!" I shouted. When no response came, I said to Marshall, "Maybe he meant three o'clock, and not the third bridge."

Marshall pointed across the bridge. "There."

Hale was now running toward us—if *running* was the right word for it. He'd jog a few steps, trip, wobble to one side, and then jog again. His face flamed red, and he breathed heavily.

I hurried across the bridge to meet him, and the faint fragrance of sweetness surrounded me as the world became brighter. My feet slapped against the water, splashing translucent red liquid all over my pant bottoms. Within a few seconds, I'd almost reached Hale. He looked so fragile that I held out my arms, ready to support him if he fell over.

I didn't reach him fast enough.

Hale collapsed at my feet in a fit of vibrations.

Marshall reached my side and dropped to the ground beside the man. "What's happening?"

Hale's body shook in a way that was all too familiar.

"He's seizing," I said.

CHAPTER TWENTY-SEVEN

The cops blocked off the non-magical side of the bridge with bright-yellow police tape—but not before ushering Marshall and me to that side of the water line. From here, it was harder to see the body.

Also between us and Hale's corpse stood two police cars, angled to stop anyone from walking or driving across without having to go through them. Two uniformed officers stood near the cars, arms crossed over their chests like a pair of sentries on duty, guarding the white wall of light beyond. One of the officers eyed us as we loitered nearby.

"We were with him when he died," I told one of them, although he hadn't asked.

The officer grunted but said nothing.

"We were with him when the seizure started," I continued.

He stared at me, wordless.

"Stop talking," Marshall whispered.

I jammed my elbow into Marshall's ribs. "Can you tell us whether he has a rash? A circular one. Maybe on the back of his neck or his chest?"

"We can't release any information about the body."

"You don't have to say anything. But maybe you could blink twice if he has a rash."

Before I knew what was happening, one of my arms was wrenched behind my back, and the other followed. I twisted my neck as Reyes slapped handcuffs around my wrists.

"What the hell?" I shouted.

"You can't do that." Marshall lunged at Agent Reyes but stopped when Reyes raised a hand.

"Think about what you're doing. Assaulting a law enforcement officer. Are you sure you want to make this decision?"

Marshall took a large step backward.

"What are you arresting me for? You can't do this."

Reyes scratched the thin layer of stubble on his chin. "How about obstruction of justice? You're at a crime scene after all. Truancy is also a good option."

"I'm not obstructing. I'm observing—on public property. That's not illegal."

"Then how about I arrest you for the underage practice of magic? Add to that practicing without a license. Are those illegal?"

I snapped my mouth shut.

"Madison, I've gone out of my way to be sympathetic

to you. I could have arrested you on at least two occasions already, and I didn't because I know you're having a hard time. But you need to let this go. At some point, I'll decide you're better off in jail rather than chasing a bad guy who may or may not have healed himself."

I twisted my neck around to look at him as squarely as I could. "Do you know what happened to Lynch's parents? Are they both dead?"

His brow creased.

I hesitated to say more for only a second. Reyes already had more ammunition than he needed to arrest me. What could a little more hurt? "I have this book called *The Theory of Life, Death, and Living*. It says healing spells can succeed when the practitioner sacrifices both his parents."

"Where did you get that—" Marshall started, but Reyes stopped him before he could go any further.

"Don't believe everything you read."

"I don't. I believe what I see. And I saw Lynch's scratched face. *I* scratched him! I came away with flesh under my fingernails. How else do you explain it besides that he must have found a way to heal himself."

"I looked into his relatives and friends the first time you sent me after him. His father died of cystic fibrosis when he was a kid. His mother is still alive."

"But that doesn't make any sense. It's literally the *only* way to do a successful healing spell."

"Even if that were true, which I doubt, it's not the case here. He didn't kill either of his parents."

"Are you sure it's his biological mother who's still alive?"

"You're in this too deep, and you can't seem to make your way out. So I'm going to help you the best way I know how." He tugged on my wrists, and I followed instinctively—the alternative being to let him wrench my arms out of their sockets.

Handcuffs hurt.

"My cousin is dying!" I shouted just before we reached the black sedan he'd aimed me toward.

Agent Reyes spun me around to face him. "What are you talking about?"

"I would have called you earlier, but I got distracted by . . ." I nodded toward the corpse across the bridge. "She has some kind of magical illness related to Michael Lynch." I told him all about the three dead men and my principal, and about Cassie's rash and exhaustion. "So I can't let this go," I finished. "Even if I could have before, I can't now."

After a short pause, Reyes spun me away from him again, and my shoulder sockets loosened as he unlocked the cuffs and released my arms.

I rubbed my right hand against my left wrist, where the metal had bitten hard. "Those things hurt."

"They're not intended to be pleasant."

"You have to arrest Lynch right now."

"Not *arrest*, Maddy. If—and that's a big *if*—what you say is true, and Cassie is the victim of Lynch's spell, then arresting him won't solve your problem. Spells don't just end because the perpetrator is behind bars." He stared me in the eyes, his gaze full of deep meaning.

"He has to die," I said.

Reyes nodded gravely.

Either Michael Lynch had to die, or my cousin might. And I still didn't know what any of this had to do with Cora.

CHAPTER TWENTY-EIGHT

"We should go, Cassie," I told my cousin on Thursday morning. "I'm going to be late if we don't leave in the next two minutes."

Aunt Sara was going to kill me if I got *two* detentions while she was away. Marshall and I had already gotten one this week—thanks to our field trip to meet Rick Hale in the middle of the day. The school would send Aunt Sara a letter informing her, which meant I could already expect one lecture when she got home.

More importantly, I had approximately zero time to figure out how to kill Michael Lynch, and I couldn't do that sitting around the house.

"I'm coming. Quit your whining." Cassie tossed me a bright smile and set her cereal bowl in the sink. Her backpack already sat in the entryway, and she hefted it onto her shoulder with a grunt.

She looked a little better than she had over the past

two days. She usually straightened her natural hair so it fell in a thick, glossy sheet down her back, but today she'd tied it into a neat bun. It looked nice, but Cassie was in love with her hair, so it said something that she'd pulled it back today. Her face had its color back—maybe a little too much color.

I pointed at her face. "Are you wearing makeup?"

"I didn't want to look like death walking, so yeah."

"Are you still feeling bad?"

"Better. Still tired, but I'm eating, so that's an improvement." She pulled down the back collar of her blouse. "And the rash is almost gone." The skin there was now smooth with only a touch of red to suggest there'd been a cluster of bumps there the day before.

"Wait." I stopped her from releasing her collar and stuck my face closer. Was it just my imagination, or did the reddened skin make a pattern? I blinked and then squinted, just in case I was seeing things. Was I going crazy? A spiral—and a triangle perhaps.

More importantly, was it an intention? And was it the same intention I'd seen twice before? When I squinted one eye, that triangle could pass for a five-pointed star.

What did Cassie have to do with Michael Lynch and his creepy intention? What did either of them have to do with Cora?

I had no idea. But things did not look good for my cousin.

"Why don't we stay home today?" I said.

"No way. I'm having lunch with Kyle again. I had to get

Melissa to ask Kyle to ask me to eat together. I'm not letting all that hard work go to waste."

I laughed. "Fine. But go to the nurse's office at school if you start feeling bad again." Even though I wanted to watch over her today, I didn't want to take this small joy away from her. It was the small joys that mattered, after all. The little moments we could never get back, even when the people who made them special went away.

"Aw, you love me." She gave me a sickeningly sweet smile.

"Only a little."

She swiped at my head in mock anger, but I ducked. She locked the front door behind us, and we hopped into Aunt Sara's car.

After I dropped Cassie at school, I turned the car toward Pritchett and pulled into the parking lot with only five minutes to spare before the first bell.

I stepped through the front doors of the school just in time to hear the crackle of the public announcement system. "First period is canceled. All students are to report to the large auditorium in five minutes for an assembly."

I stopped at my locker to stuff my backpack in there and then, because I still had a few minutes, took a detour by the principal's office on my way to the auditorium. I'd checked on Principal Spencer only yesterday, but now I had even more at stake.

If he lived, if he beat this thing, then Cassie had a chance to do the same.

Ms. Louise wasn't at her desk, so I stepped inside. The

interior door to the office stood closed. I rapped on it. When I heard no response, I knocked again, this time harder.

"Come in," came a quiet voice inside.

I opened the door to find Dean Harris sitting in Principal Spencer's chair, her shoulders slumped, head bent over the desk. Not a single paper lay atop the desk's surface. Apparently, Dean Harris had just been sitting there, doing nothing.

"Can I help you, Maddy?" Her words came out like a long sigh. "Shouldn't you be on your way to the assembly?"

"Is everything okay?"

She opened her mouth to say something and then shook her head. "You'll have all the information you need in a few minutes. Please go to the assembly."

I stood in the doorway for a few more seconds, but Dean Harris didn't look up at me again. I left the room and shut the door behind me, careful to close it softly so as not to disturb the dean any more than necessary.

The knot of dread that had been forming in my chest since this morning grew even larger.

Almost every other student beat me to the auditorium, and when I got there, the seats were packed with my schoolmates. I scanned their faces for Lauren but didn't see her among all the others scrambling for the remaining seats.

I spotted Marshall without even trying, probably because he was already staring at me. The powder-blue shirt he wore made his eyes look so shocking that I could see the deep blue of them across the distance between us. Or maybe I imagined that, but either way, he looked amazing.

And seriously irritated. As soon as our eyes met, his gaze shifted to a boy beside him, and he chattered away as if we hadn't just connected. I probably shouldn't have roped him into watching a man die. Or stolen his mom's book. Or hid the knowledge spell from him.

"That's cool," I muttered to myself. "It's not like we're friends or anything."

"Maddy Cooper!" Lauren's voice boomed across the auditorium. A couple of girls near me stopped talking and jerked their faces toward her.

Lauren stood in front of a seat on the aisle on the opposite side of the room. She grinned sheepishly when I caught her eye, and waved me over. She'd done me no favors with her seat selection. The shortest path from me to her would take me right past Marshall, who sat in a row directly behind an aisle parallel to the stage.

I headed to the back of the auditorium and then crossed over—the long way around.

"Coward," I said to myself under my breath. I slid into the seat beside Lauren.

Her gaze bored into the side of my face.

"What?" I said.

"Did you just walk around the entire room to avoid your boyfriend?"

"Only half of it. And he's not my boyfriend."

"Not with that attitude, he's not. Here I was, thinking you weren't afraid of anything, and it turns out you're terrified of a boy who's crushing on you. Kind of pathetic."

"This is not making me feel any better."

"A little tough love never hurt anyone. Talk to him. You two—"

Dean Harris stepped onto the auditorium's stage, and I shushed Lauren. I made no attempt to hide my pleasure that her lecture was reaching an early end.

"We're finishing this later," she hissed.

The dean spent a full minute adjusting her microphone. She was stalling. Whatever she had to say was not good news—and I suspected I knew what it was.

"Good morning, students. As most of you know by now, Principal Spencer had a seizure a week and a half ago. He spent days in the hospital, and yesterday afternoon, the doctors sent him home."

I scanned the crowd of students for Walt but didn't see him anywhere. I assumed that, if the assembly was about Mr. Spencer, Walt already knew what we were about to hear. His presence would have meant good news. His absence meant he'd been dismissed from school—bad news.

Dean Harris cleared her throat. "I'm sorry to tell you all that Principal Spencer died last night in his sleep."

The room went silent except for the sound of Harris's breath on the microphone.

My throat closed, and for a moment, I couldn't breathe. I hadn't known the principal well, but he'd been a kind man. Quirky, with his colorful bow ties. And always generous with his smiles.

He'd been fine yesterday. They sent him home. This made no sense.

I waved my hand in the air.

Dean Harris stared straight in front of her, not meeting any of our eyes.

I jumped up from my chair, hand still in the air. "Dean Harris," I called across the room.

Every face turned toward me.

"Um . . . I guess I could take a question. Maddy?"

"You said he was doing better. What happened?" I dropped back into my chair.

"He was. According to his family, he was in good spirits and even showing a little more energy. He hadn't had a seizure in a couple days. But this morning, he simply would not wake up. He'd lost a lot of weight, and his body gave out under the stress of his illness."

So that was how it worked. They could get better, but not for long. In the end, they all died.

CHAPTER TWENTY-NINE

I was standing in front of my locker, staring at my books, when a hand landed on my shoulder. Numb, I glanced over to find Marshall standing beside me.

"I've been calling your name halfway down the hall. You avoided me in assembly."

I shrugged. Not because I hadn't avoided him—I had—but because I didn't care about that right now. I didn't want to fight with Marshall. I wanted to save Cassie. That had to be my priority right now—especially since I had a suspicion that saving Cassie meant getting to the bottom of Cora's death.

"About what happened on Monday—"

"I'm sorry about that." I wasn't sure I was the one who should be apologizing. *He'd* blown up at *me*. But could I blame him? He hated summoning because his sister had gotten trapped in a spell, and then I'd gone and done the same thing. I hadn't been summoning, but if it wasn't for

Reyes, I would be just as dead. Did I expect a pat on the back for that?

He raised his brows. "Sorry about *what?*"

I wasn't entirely sure why I was apologizing. Certainly not for the knowledge spell. I *was* sorry for that—but because it had failed, not because I tried it. "For not being honest with you about what I was doing, about how far I was willing to go."

"But not for the spell?"

I shook my head.

He opened his mouth—probably to introduce me to a sequel of his previous tongue-lashing—but I managed to speak first.

"Would you just stop?"

His eyes went big, and I realized I'd shouted.

More quietly, I said, "I don't want to fight with you. I have other things on my mind."

"Believe it or not, I came over here to see how you're doing. This whole thing with the principal is hitting you pretty hard, I bet."

"Not for the reasons you think."

"Not because you saw his seizure?"

"No." I meant to say more, to explain everything about the series of deaths and Cassie's rash, but I couldn't bring myself to voice it. Cassie was going to die, just like Principal Spencer, just like those three men.

"Maddy?"

"Yeah. Sorry." I needed to call my aunt. She'd come straight home and demand that the doctors in the emergency room give Cassie a full physical. If nothing else, she would *be* here. If the worst happened, if I didn't call her, if she wasn't here and Cassie died, Aunt Sara would never forgive me. "I should call her," I said, more to the contents of my locker than to Marshall.

"Let's take a walk." His fingers touched my hand and pulled it away from my locker door. Still holding it, he closed the door and led me out to the parking lot. Without a word, I let him.

It was like when we first met. Something about Marshall calmed the fury and heartbreak inside me. He was the calm to my tornado. His hand felt warm around mine, and I threaded my fingers between his. He gripped my hand more tightly.

Before I realized it, we stood outside his car on the tech-side parking lot, with Marshall holding the back door open.

I looked up at him, confused. "Where are we going?"

"Nowhere. I thought you might want a moment without everyone in school staring at you." He closed me inside the car, then walked around to the other side and slid into the backseat with me. He laid an arm across my shoulder, and I leaned against him. My head fit neatly in the crook between his neck and shoulder.

"You mind if I call my aunt?"

"Go for it."

I fished my phone from my bag and dialed.

Aunt Sara picked up on the second ring. "Everything okay?"

"Fine. I mean . . ." I'd gotten so used to claiming everything was *fine* that the word now came out on its own. "Something's wrong with Cassie."

"What kind of something?" The pitch of her voice shot upward. "Is she hurt?"

"Not exactly, but—"

"Don't scare me like that."

"She had a rash the day you left, and she was tired, and she wouldn't eat at first. These three men had the same symptoms, and they all died. Two from malnutrition, and one was shot."

"What do they have to do with Cassie?"

"She has the rash."

"Cassie might get shot because she has a rash?" My aunt did a poor job keeping the skepticism from her voice.

"I think that's the bad-luck part of it, but it would probably be malnutrition."

"Maddy." Her voice had gone low and soothing. "None of that sounds like it has anything to do with your cousin."

"But the pattern is the same." I didn't know how to convince her, but it was not with the whiny tone my voice was making.

"I have to go. Kate has a doctor's appointment, and we're running late. Can we continue this later?"

"Principal Spencer died," I said in a last-ditch effort to keep her on the phone.

"Oh, honey, I'm sorry to hear that. I know you were fond of him."

"He had a rash too."

"Lots of people have rashes. He also had a seizure, so he had health problems completely unrelated to that rash."

"They're not unrelated. That's what I'm trying to tell you. The illness—whatever it is—it starts with the rash and gets worse. The seizures come later."

"I'll be right there," Aunt Sara shouted, her voice farther from the phone. To me, she added, "I have to go or we'll be late."

"This is important. Life or death."

A long sigh and then, "Maddy, I'm glad you've grown to care for your cousin, but believe me when I say that you are overreacting. You've been through a lot, and understandably, you are sensitive about the lives of the people around you."

"I'm not making this up!"

"Why don't you have Lauren's mom come over and take a look at her? Would that make you feel any better?"

"She did already."

"And?"

"She said Cassie was tired and stressed."

"See—"

"But she's not a blood-magic practitioner. She doesn't know the signs."

"I'm coming," my aunt shouted away from the phone. "I have to go. I'll call you guys tonight." She disconnected the call.

"You think Cassie's dying?" Marshall asked when I'd stuffed my phone into my backpack.

"I think there's a damn good chance of it."

I glanced out the window at the cliques of students clustered around the school's front steps, with the wall of magic in the distance. Since first period was canceled, and it wasn't yet time for second period, no one was in a hurry to go anywhere. That meant they'd have plenty of time to pay attention to me—the girl who'd found Principal Spencer when he was seizing.

Marshall pointed to the school building. "You want to go back inside?"

"I really don't." My foot kicked something, and I looked down to find a large stack of papers rubber-banded together. I swiped it up and dropped the pages on my lap. It was the list of license applications we'd gotten from the Bureau. "You still have this?"

"I haven't cleaned my car."

With halfhearted flips, I turned from one page to the next, and to the next, page after page.

"What are you looking for in there?"

"Nothing. It's useless now that we know Lynch's last name. That's why I wanted it—for his name and address. But the name hasn't helped us get the guy arrested anyway." I continued to flip the pages. It was either that or step outside the car and face more classmates, or look Marshall in the eye—neither of which sounded appealing.

Something on one of the pages caught my attention. I flipped back, slowly, not sure I wanted to see what I'd seen. Even with it staring me right in the face, I couldn't believe it. I touched the page, moving my finger across her name. As if feeling the letters would bring us back together.

Marshall leaned over and peeked at the page. "Cora was approved for a six-inch blade?"

I shook myself out of the trance and tapped the date on the same row. "Only two days before she died."

"You think it's a coincidence?"

"I don't think anything's a coincidence." I stared at the words on the page and wished the ink could talk to me, tell me the deeper meaning. "Why would she need one of those?" The only person I'd ever met who used one was Michael Lynch—and that definitely wasn't for innocent spells. Maybe I had it all wrong. Maybe Cora wasn't the victim I'd assumed. "Do you think they were working together?" I asked, my voice barely louder than a whisper.

"With Lynch?" He shook his head hard. "No way. You would have known if she'd been into that kind of thing."

"I should have known she was dead in the next room when I went to bed that night—but apparently, I don't know as much as I think."

"There are lots of reasons to get a long blade, Maddy. It doesn't mean she was doing anything wrong."

"Doesn't it?"

He stared at me for a moment. When I didn't say more, he added, "It's not just about being able to draw more blood. It's also about the use of more bone."

"Huh?"

"For someone who knows so much about blood magic, you really don't know anything."

I glared at him.

He laughed. "There's a reason blood magic requires a bone knife. Bone makes up the body, just like blood does. Just like a spell that uses more blood can potentially be more powerful, so is a spell that uses more bone. Cora didn't necessarily want to hurt someone with the knife. She—"

"She wanted to perform a powerful spell," I finished for him. "We have to find Michael Lynch."

"Why?" he asked. "And how?"

"You don't want to know." I jumped out of the car and hurried back to the school building.

I had no more time to sulk, no more time to feel sorry for myself. Cassie could die any time. Aunt Sara wouldn't help me. Even though Agent Reyes appeared to be on my side now, he *couldn't* help me, since he couldn't find the man who needed to die to save my cousin's life.

Lynch was tied to Cassie's illness, he'd known Cora, and both he and Cora were involved in heavy magic. There was no end to the connections. Michael Lynch was the key to everything.

Behind me, Marshall's car door opened and closed, but he was moving too slowly. I quickened my pace and left him behind. The bell for second period rang as I stepped through the front doors to find an empty hallway. All the other students and teachers had found their way to class. I hoped Lauren hadn't. I needed her for what I had planned.

When I arrived back at my locker, Lauren was standing there, leaning against her own, her fingers twisting together at her waist. She stood up straight as I approached.

"I need to get to class. But how are—"

"I'm fine," I said without letting her finish. "We're getting out of here." I grabbed her wrist and towed her down the hallway. "Do you have a map?"

"Lauren. Maddy." Our Pre-Calculus teacher, Mrs. Green, stood in the doorway of her nearby classroom, hand on the doorknob. "Shouldn't you two be in here?" She nodded toward her classroom. "The bell rang already."

I blanked on a good excuse not to join the class. Lauren stood as mutely as I did. She ducked her head, shrugged at me, and slipped into the classroom. Mrs. Green gave me an expectant look, and I followed.

Finding Lynch would have to wait until after school.

CHAPTER THIRTY

I couldn't pay attention to anything my teachers were saying for the rest of the day. The whole thing felt like a waste of time. For each hour that passed with me sitting in a classroom using math and science and history that had no impact on my life, Cassie's life slid away.

When the final school bell rang that afternoon, I bolted out of my seat and across the private water-line bridge back to the tech side of school. As soon as I crossed the bridge, I got a text from Cassie saying she had a ride home and I was off the hook. That made me even more confident about my plan to save her. Nothing was slowing me down.

I beat Lauren to our lockers by a few minutes. By then, I'd grabbed the books I needed for homework and was bouncing on the balls of my feet, impatient for her arrival.

"What's the plan?" Lauren asked, breathless from having run down the stairs. She made quick work of unzipping her backpack and swapping books between it and her locker.

"We're doing a finding."

Her brow furrowed for only an instant before flattening out. "We're *finding* Lynch."

"Exactly. Do you have a map of the city?"

"My phone does. But what makes you think the Bureau hasn't tried that already?"

"I'm sure they have. I'm also sure they're not keeping me in the loop. Agent Reyes has threatened to arrest me twice already if I don't stay out of things. He says he's keeping me updated, but I'm betting he's not. And I need to know everything. *I'm* the one who figured out that Lynch was cursing people. Our best bet for saving Cassie is to work on this with the Bureau—whether they like it or not." When she didn't disagree, I added, "Your phone won't work. I need a paper map."

"We can grab one from a gas station." She slammed her locker door and hefted her bag onto her shoulder.

I led her to the parking lot. Automatically, Lauren turned toward her convertible, but I put a hand on her forearm.

"Let's take my aunt's car," I said.

Her eyes narrowed. "That way I have no say in where we go?"

She knew me too well.

"Between the two of us," she said, "one of us has to be the practical one. And that damn sure isn't going to be you. So we can go look, but don't do anything stupid."

I batted my eyelashes at her. "You must be confusing me with someone else."

"Yeah, that must be it."

I didn't miss her sarcasm.

"No repeats of last Friday," she added. "You've met your stupid quota for the month already."

"I'm going to need a higher quota."

She glared at me. "I'm not kidding. Promise you won't go near Lynch. We can find him and follow him, if necessary, but we keep our distance."

"I promise." I turned toward my aunt's car, but Lauren stayed put. "Seriously? What else?"

She crossed her arms over her chest. "Make it a blood promise. That's the only way I'm going and definitely the only way I'm letting you drive."

"You don't trust me?"

"Do it."

"You realize blood promises don't actually do anything? They're not magic. Just something little kids do for pretend."

"Do it, or I get into my car and leave you on your own."

I'd never actually made a blood promise before, but I'd seen them made and broken by children. As far as I could tell, they had no binding effect—no magical one anyway. But since blood ran our lives, we took the spilling of it seriously.

I moved to the back of Lauren's car, letting the vehicle shield me from the view of anyone in front of the school. I dropped my backpack to the ground and fished around the bottom of it for my knife.

I already had too many cuts in various stages of healing under my left arm, and although that spot was discreet, all the rubbing against my torso when I walked was beginning to irritate them. So this time, I quickly swiped the blade across my forearm to open a shallow wound. Lauren cringed, even though she kept her gaze on my face.

Non-magic people were so squeamish.

"I promise not to go near Lynch until you release me from this bond." I started to put the knife away, but Lauren held up her hand to stop me.

"Make it more specific."

I cut myself a second time and rolled my eyes while I spoke. "I promise not to get within . . . twenty feet of Michael Lynch until you release me from this bond." I met her eyes. "Good enough?"

She nodded.

I folded my knife back up, still sticky with blood, and dropped it into my bag. "Let's go."

"You've got an hour and a half. Then I have to be home for homework."

Lauren let me lead her to my aunt's car, and the two of us climbed in, with me in the driver's seat. We stopped at the first gas station we saw, and I bought a map of the city.

Back in the car, I laid the map out across Lauren's lap, while she stared at me with a look that didn't display nearly as much trust as I deserved. I leaned into the backseat and fumbled inside my backpack until I managed to extract a sheet of notebook paper and my knife.

"Wait." Lauren grabbed my arm to stop me. "What if he's inside the water line? Then we won't find him if you do the spell from outside."

"If he's inside the water line, then the spell will fail." I shrugged. "And we can try again from inside. I would have to lose *two* things, but I'll risk it."

Lauren released my arm. She cringed and turned her face away until I finished wiping blood onto the blade from one of the new cuts on my forearm. I drew the single word, *Lynch*, on the page. Then I captured a drop of blood on the knife's tip and dropped it onto the map close to where I figured we must be now.

I pressed a bandage to the cut, which hadn't stopped bleeding yet. Messy. But I needed to start the spell while my blood on the map remained fresh. I closed my eyes for a few seconds to clear my mind of everything but this, and then opened them, focused on the intention I'd written. After a couple seconds, a few small pinpricks of heat touched my broken skin, skittered upward, and settled into my chest, warming me all over.

"It's moving," Lauren said, her tone low and flat. It held none of the excitement it had the first time she'd watched me find something.

I started the engine, and she pointed right as I pulled to the edge of the parking lot.

"Turn here," she said. "And make a left at the first light."

After I made the turns, she added, "Okay, stay on this for a while. We're headed east and so is the blood."

I stayed straight, my gaze twitching back and forth between the road and the page with the intention, still lying on the center console between Lauren and me.

"I . . . I think you need to turn right here," Lauren said, hesitant.

"You *think?*"

"Your blood on the map—it keeps disappearing. It shows up for a second, and then it's gone again."

I swiped up the page with Lynch's name and held it against the front of the steering wheel, trying to keep my eyes on both it and the road. This was harder than I'd thought—concentrating on my intention and not driving the car into a ditch.

"Which way now?"

Lauren bent closer to the map for a better view. "I . . . I don't know."

I gritted my teeth.

"It's gone, Maddy. I don't think it's coming back this time."

I cursed and pulled the car to the side of the road.

"What happened?" Lauren asked. "Last time, you were able to maintain the spell for as long as you wanted."

"I can't concentrate and drive at the same time."

"That's an easy fix." Lauren moved the map from her lap to mine and pushed her passenger door open. She came around to my side of the car and knocked on the window.

With a huff, I let her take the driver's seat and slid over to the space she'd abandoned. "Unfortunately, it's not that simple," I said. "Every time I perform this spell, I risk having to pay the price of it."

"But you didn't find anything last time."

"I don't make the rules." I picked up my knife from where I'd placed it in the cup holder between our seats.

She grabbed my hand. "Wait."

"I have to use fresh blood, Lauren. You can close your eyes if you want."

"It's not that. I mean, yeah, the cutting and the blood thing bother me. But since you're being charged for each spell, why don't we drive to where the blood disappeared on the map, and then you can do a new spell there?"

"Sure. I can't afford to lose too many more things. Where was it?"

Lauren pointed at a spot on the map. "Last time I saw it."

The dot had stopped in the middle of a section of small intersecting streets, some of which curved and dead-ended. "Looks like a neighborhood. Let's go here." I pointed to the nearest major road on the map. "I'll be ready with the spell as we get nearby."

Several minutes later, with less than a mile between us and the spot I'd chosen on the map, I lifted my knife again. Some of my blood still remained wet on the blade, but I didn't want to risk using old blood when fresher blood could be more effective. On the bright side, I didn't have to cut myself this time. I peeled the bandage off my arm, squeezed the cut I'd made a moment ago, and swiped up another drop of blood on the knife blade.

I smoothed the map across my lap and tapped the blade to our location.

For the first few seconds, the blood did nothing. Just a tiny streak on a map.

Maybe I needed to write the intention again. Maybe I needed a new cut to work with. Maybe I was just out of juice. After all, this was my first attempt at magic ever since the disastrous knowledge spell.

The blood shrank to a dot and jumped into motion.

"Yes!" I shouted. I pointed straight ahead. "Keep going. It's heading in this direction."

Unlike us, the dot didn't have to follow rules of the road. It angled across our street and headed northwest, while we continued west. I had to admit that it was much easier to maintain my concentration without having to drive.

I directed Lauren. She silently obeyed, both hands clutched around the wheel, her back stiff. A couple minutes later, the dot stopped moving and then faded into the map.

"Got him." I released my concentration and grinned.

A few minutes later, we stopped at a curb just outside a large park.

"Now, we report it to the Bureau," Lauren said. "When they get here, they can take over spying on him."

"The whole point is for *us* to spy on him. The Bureau doesn't tell us everything."

I climbed out of the car and scanned the green space for any sign of the man. Lauren followed, but I suspected that was only to keep me from wandering too far.

A tall line of trees extended away from me on my right, marking the edge of the park. On my left, a sidewalk and a low stone wall framed the park's edge. In front of me, one sidewalk trail snaked to the right and downward toward a lake with more trees beyond it, while another headed upward and to the left toward a picnic area.

"It was on this corner of the park," Lauren said. "He's nearby. Let the Bureau do the rest."

Before I could object, a faint wailing silenced us both. Lauren and I stared at each other, my nerves pulled taut. The sound got closer and blossomed into the full-on clamoring of a siren.

Three police cars zipped past us, whipping wind so hard that my hair lashed across my face. My eyes widened.

"No," Lauren said.

I ran back to the car and jumped into the driver's seat. "Get in or I leave you. You trust me to do this alone?"

A second later, Lauren was beside me, snapping her seatbelt in place. "I'm going to regret this."

I pulled out of the parking space and slammed my foot on the accelerator, heading in the direction the cops had gone. We didn't go far. The three cars jumped the curb and turned into the park entrance farther down the road. The entrance was meant for foot traffic, but if it was wide enough for them, it was wide enough for me too.

Lauren buried her face in her hands as I, too, jumped the curb.

The police cars stopped just beyond the lake. Two people got out and jogged toward the dark woods nearby. I stopped my aunt's car about fifty yards behind them, grabbed my mobile phone, and hopped out. They paid no attention to me.

When they disappeared into the shadow of the trees, Lauren and I hurried after them. It took my eyes a few seconds to adjust, and then my stomach turned. I grabbed Lauren's shirt and dragged her behind a large tree before the cops could see us. Both of us stuck our heads out to get a better look.

In a small clearing, maybe a hundred feet from us, two bodies lay across leaves and small branches that had fallen from the canopy of trees above. Two dark-haired women, with their limbs twisted oddly beneath them. Yellow police tape surrounded the small area, draped around nearby trees. The two detectives we'd followed spoke quietly with two uniformed officers just inside the police line. I couldn't make out their words.

Behind me, Lauren gasped. I turned to shush her, and then pulled her back into hiding.

"Stop looking," I said as she tried to peek around me again. "Do you really want to see that?"

"Do you think he killed them?" she whispered. The wind shifted, and it brought with it the stink of blood. Lauren gagged and covered her mouth.

"He must have. You think he got away already?"

Lauren leaned against our tree and arranged herself to face directly away from the crime scene. "Those cops have been here for a while," she whispered.

I caught up with her line of thinking. "So why would the finding take us here if he's long gone?"

"Maybe he was here when the spell started, but his protection spell notified him."

I shuddered. "We should have thought of that."

"Yeah, we're lucky he didn't counter again." She jerked her head toward the crime scene. "I imagine he was busy with other things."

"The spell ended almost ten minutes before we got here. Yeah, we followed the blood after that, but the actual finding happened right after I spilled it. For the cops to be as far along as they are, Lynch would have to be long gone —by more than ten minutes. So why'd my blood stop here on the map?"

She shrugged. "Your guess is as good as mine."

Another car pulled up to the lake, near where we'd left my aunt's car. In the distance, a man stepped out and hurried toward us. He strode toward the crime scene, and his swagger struck a familiar chord.

Lauren and I scooted around our tree to block his view of us as he passed. We slid back into our hiding place as he ducked under the police tape and stepped into the clearing.

"Agent Reyes is here?" I whispered.

"Of course," Lauren said. "It's his case. What's he doing?"

I peered around her just as he squatted beside one of the still, broken bodies on the ground. He lifted a small duffel bag from his shoulder and set it on the grass beside him. From it, he withdrew an object that flashed in a thin ray of sunlight.

"He took a plastic baggie out of his bag," I said.

From the plastic, Reyes pulled out a smaller object that I couldn't identify from this far away. He fiddled with the object and then jammed it into the corpse's bare leg.

I squealed.

"What's happening?" Lauren whispered. They couldn't hear us from this far away, but something about spying on a bunch of cops at a crime scene—even a public one— demanded silence.

"It looks like he's taking blood from one of the bodies."

Agent Reyes withdrew the syringe from the body and fiddled with it again—I couldn't be sure from this distance, but it looked like he put a cap back on the needle. He pulled a pen from his pocket and wrote some- thing on the syringe, then pulled out an empty plastic baggie to store it.

"He labeled it and saved it in another baggie."

Reyes stood, and I ducked behind the tree. I waited a few seconds and then peeked again. He was now kneeling, back to me, near the other body. From what I could tell at this angle, he repeated his actions of drawing blood, labeling the syringe, and sticking the syringe in the bag.

"He's taking blood samples from both," I said.

"Why?"

"How should I know?"

"We should get out of here before someone spots us."

My phone rang and vibrated. I jumped and fumbled to turn down the ringer. I didn't intend to answer it, but out of instinct, I checked the caller identification. It was Reyes. I turned the screen toward Lauren.

"You think he saw us?" she asked.

The phone stopped vibrating, and I breathed a sigh of relief—until it rang again.

"Answer it," she said.

I held my breath and connected the call. "Hello."

"Hello, Maddy," Reyes said, his voice booming from the phone. "Is that Lauren with you?"

"Um . . ."

"This is a crime scene. You think I don't have eyes at my own crime scene?"

I stepped out from behind our tree to find Agent Reyes standing just outside the police tape, staring right at us. One hand held his phone to his ear, while the other beckoned us toward him.

"He sees us," I whispered.

"I got that." Lauren sighed, grabbed my arm, and towed me to Reyes.

He took the phone down from his ear and crossed his arms over his chest. "How did you get here?"

"We drove." I flinched under the weight of his stare. "I'd rather not say more than that."

He rubbed his forehead and temple with one hand, frustration filling every movement. "I don't know what to do with you anymore." He spread his hands wide. "What do you expect me to do?"

Since he didn't appear to be dragging me toward his unmarked police car again, I took the opening. "We think Michael Lynch may still be here."

"He's not. And you shouldn't be either." He pointed back toward the lake. "Is that your car?"

Lauren started to head that way, but I wasn't yet convinced the Bureau had this right. "*Hypothetically*, if someone did a finding to locate a person—"

Lauren grabbed my arm to stop me from saying more. "How did you guys get here so quickly?" she asked Reyes. "Did you do a finding?"

I nudged her to let her know I approved of her tactic.

Reyes, however, was not fooled. "You can't find a person with a finding spell." His tone came out low, almost like a growl. "That's how you got here, I take it." He gestured toward the fresh cut on my forearm.

I shifted my body to move my arm behind me and out of his view. "Why can't you?"

"If you want to learn blood magic, grow up and take the Bureau's training course like everyone else. You know more than enough to do damage already."

"It's because people aren't interchangeable," Lauren said. "Right? That's the same reason there's no healing spell—supposedly. You can't find a person because it's impossible to pay the price for a spell like that. You'd have to lose the exact same person to pay for it or—or you'd have to lose yourself. Giving of yourself seems to always work with blood magic."

Agent Reyes scowled but said nothing.

"It makes perfect sense," Lauren continued. "With that one spell, we—whoever did the spell—would both find someone and lose him at the same time. So they'd end up finding a location where he used to be."

"Smart kid." Despite his annoyance, Reyes couldn't hide his admiration.

"But wouldn't they lose something else too? I mean, it's not enough. If they find an old location, that's still a win. The point of magic is to be equal—no better and no worse after any spell."

"Yes, you can find someone's previous location, but you'll lose something else in return. Very good. You should use those brains for something that won't get you killed." He gestured to the bodies behind him. "You're lucky you missed him."

"What about spells to harm people?" I said, thinking of Cassie. "By the same logic—simultaneously finding and losing someone—you'd need to hurt them and also *help* them. How does that work?"

Agent Reyes narrowed his eyes but, again, said nothing.

"I'm guessing the practitioner can pick and choose what parts of the victim's health to harm and which to help," Lauren said. "So they might, for instance, improve someone's blood pressure in return for a brain tumor." She did a little excited jump. "Which explains why I felt so strong when Lynch froze me. He gave me strength, but I couldn't use it since he was also freezing me."

"I felt that too," I said.

"Agent Tanner will be here any minute," Reyes said, his voice flat and firm. "Time to go."

"We're going." Lauren grabbed my shirtsleeve and tugged.

"My cousin has only two days," I said, feet planted in place.

Agent Reyes gritted his teeth. "We're going to save her. We're doing everything we can."

Only that wasn't good enough.

CHAPTER THIRTY-ONE

On Friday morning, I got to school early after dropping off Cassie and planted myself near Bryan's locker.

I'd burned all my bridges already. I couldn't *find* Lynch —because blood magic didn't allow it. And if I did, I couldn't prove any of my claims—because he'd figured out how to do the impossible—heal himself. I couldn't prove Cora's death was related to Lynch—because all signs suggested Cora had killed herself—and maybe she had. And I couldn't save Cassie—because I was useless in every way that mattered.

The one thing I had left was that intention. I saw it on the floor of the creepy basement, and I saw it during my failed knowledge spell. I'd seen a similar symbol on Bryan's watch. As much I hated to need anything from Bryan, the fact that he was a jerk was the least of my concerns right now.

While I waited, I tugged my long sleeves down to make sure they fully covered my arms. I hadn't been thinking when I put two cuts in my forearm the day before. The last thing I needed was to make someone suspicious—especially since I was asking about an intention. It took only a minute for Bryan to round the corner of the hallway, one of his hands intertwined with Sheryl's. She spotted me before he did and gave me a bright grin.

Bryan scowled.

"Hey. What's up?" Sheryl asked.

I jerked my head toward her boyfriend. "I need to talk to Bryan about a Physics assignment."

He folded his arms over his chest. "Lauren is in our class, so ask her. Isn't she in the running for valedictorian?"

"Let's go someplace quiet." I tipped my head toward the hallway beyond Sheryl, but he refused to move.

"It's about your watch," I said close to his ear in a voice I hoped was quiet enough that Sheryl wouldn't hear. As much as I wanted her to know that Bryan was a cheating jerk, I needed something from him right now. This was not the time to take a flying leap onto his bad side.

"His watch?" Sheryl glanced down at Bryan's wrist. "What about it?"

I needed to work on my inside voice.

"Nothing," Bryan said. "Why don't you head to class, babe? We're going to talk Physics."

She pursed her lips. "As exciting as that sounds, I'll catch up with you later." She kissed him on the cheek. "See you at lunch." To me she added, "See you in a few," since we had class together first period.

Bryan and I waited until Sheryl passed out of earshot.

"What the hell is wrong with you? I paid you over two hundred bucks to keep that secret."

"Technically, you paid me over two hundred to find your watch—not keep your secrets."

Bryan led me to the end of the hallway, where we could talk without other students passing us every two seconds. "Our business is done, and you weren't exactly a pleasure to work with. Why would I answer anything for you?"

"I did the job, didn't I? And so far, I've kept my mouth shut."

"So far?"

I let that question hang in the air without an answer. "What does the symbol on the back of your watch mean?"

"What?"

"The etching. It has something that looks like a spiral and a bunch of lines." I kept my voice soft and nonthreatening. I wanted Bryan to feel like he could talk to me without going on the defensive.

"It's some kind of blood-magic thing for good health." He shrugged. "Like I said before, Sheryl bought it for me."

"You never asked her what it meant?"

"Yeah, but I forgot. My family doesn't really do that stuff."

"But you have the blood for it."

"And my dad won't let anyone forget it, but it's more of a status symbol than something we actually use."

I held out my hand. "Could I see it?"

He sighed and then flicked the clasp to release the watch. He slid it off his wrist and passed it to me.

I flipped it over. I hadn't really examined the etching the last time I held it. More like, I noticed it and found it interesting, but that was all. This time, I compared the lines and arcs to what I'd seen in Lynch's basement. The symbol somehow managed to be both like and unlike it.

A vertical line split the whole thing down the center, with angled lines shooting from its top half. Four arrows extended outward from the four corners of the etching. The one part exactly the same as what I'd seen in Lynch's basement was the spiral that started at the center and swirled outward until it reached the arrow tips.

I tilted the back of watch toward Bryan. "What does this spiral mean?"

"No idea." He kept glancing toward the door. I couldn't tell whether he expected Sheryl to come back looking for him or he just had no interest in what I was asking him. Probably both.

He held out his hand for the watch. "I don't want to be late for class."

My shoulders slumped as I dropped it into his palm. This conversation hadn't been as productive as I'd hoped.

I stopped at my locker to grab the books I needed and then hurried to class. Sheryl was already waiting in the room, her phone sitting on the desk in front of her. She giggled at something on the screen, and then looked up as I came in.

"Hey again." She pointed at the desk next to her. "Sit with me today."

I slid into the desk.

Without glancing up from her phone, she said, "Tell me what's going on with you and Bryan."

Even though I'd planned to do just that, her statement took me off guard. "Excuse me?"

"You hate him. Always have."

"I have not."

"Oh please. Freshman year, when I was staring at him during Bio, you told me to do myself a favor and electrocute myself—it would be less trouble."

I didn't even remember that. "Sorry."

"No, you're not. You say what you mean. So why go out of your way to talk to him about *Physics*?" She made air quotes around that last word. "When you tell the truth too often, you become a terrible liar."

My cheeks warmed. "He lost that watch you got him, and I helped him find it."

She finally glanced up from the phone, her forehead crinkled in confusion. "Why did he ask *you* for help, and why did you help him?"

"It was kind of a coincidence. I noticed him looking for it and offered to help—for payment. I needed the money."

"And you used blood magic?"

I nodded. Sheryl was one of those people who noticed

everything but never said much—which was why I was amazed she'd never noticed that her boyfriend was no good. "I needed to ask him about the etching on the back of the watch. Trust me, if I had a Physics question, he would not be the first person I asked." I licked my lips and added, "Why do you stay with him?"

She flushed so bright red that it hid the smattering of freckles across her nose and cheeks. "I like him. Once a week, I tell myself I'm going to break up with him, and then he does something really sweet. And then I don't."

Neither of us said anything for a few beats, while I considered telling her that he'd cheated on her. Maybe then she'd stop coming up with excuses not to dump him.

I chose a different route. "What does that etching mean?"

She reached into her backpack, pulled out a notepad, and slapped it onto the desk. Then she flipped to the last page and sketched the symbol from memory. "It's a language of intentions my mom uses." She pointed at the line running up the center and the spikes coming out of its top in different directions. "This tree stands for good health." She pointed to the arrows extending outward from the outer edge of the drawing. "And these banish negative things."

"And the spiral?"

"It represents life. Literally, this intention banishes sickness and evil from life. The result is a long, healthy life —in theory, anyway. It would probably do nothing in practice, seeing as how in essence it's a healing spell. Plus, the watch has no blood in it. Just a token of well wishes, basically."

"You said this is your family's language?"

"On my mom's side. Why all the questions?"

"I've seen something similar, but I don't think it has anything to do with your family. So maybe I'm stretching."

"Maybe not," she said. "Intention languages can be really similar."

Reyes had said something like that too.

"What about this symbol?" I gestured for the notebook, and Sheryl handed it over. I flipped forward one page and sketched the symbol from the basement of the creepy house.

Sheryl gasped as I finished my drawing and angled the page toward her. She snatched the pencil back from me and scribbled dark lines all over what I'd drawn. When she'd almost completely obscured the figure, she leaned back in her seat and took a long breath. "Don't write that again."

Solemnly, I waited for her to explain.

As if on second thought, she ripped the page from her notebook, balled it up, and tossed it in the trash.

"I know it has something to do with life," I said, "because it has that spiral. Right?"

She took a deep breath and nodded. "It had the spiral, yes. Two spirals actually. And the arrows around one of them represent banishment."

"Banishing life?"

"Life at the expense of life. And the pentagram acts as a

general protection spell for the practitioner. There was also a symbol there for good health or good fortune. I'm just an amateur at this, so I can't be sure about what the connections between those mean, but given the clear meaning behind the spirals, I'd guess the overall intention is something about protection and good will for the practitioner, at the expense of someone else."

"Shit," I muttered.

"Shit is right."

"Where did you see that?"

I hesitated, unsure how much of this I should burden her with. "Some guy attacked me and Lauren last week. We followed him to a house and saw the intention there."

"If you're mixed up with someone who's performing magic with *that*"—she pointed at the trash can—"I suggest you get the hell out of it."

CHAPTER THIRTY-TWO

"Cora had an intention on her back," I told Lauren. We were walking toward the third-period art class we had once per week—on the magic side of the water line. I'd just finished summarizing everything Sheryl told me about the intention at Lynch's. "And Cassie had one on her neck."

We crossed the lunch patio and stepped onto the manicured grass, heading to the water line. Lauren took the lead while I hurried to catch up.

"They had circular rashes," she said. "That doesn't make them intentions. Lots of rashes have a defined shape like that—ringworm, for example."

"They didn't have ringworm."

"You know that's not what I'm saying. Look, I'll buy that Cassie's rash *maybe* is the same as Lynch's symbol. That fits. Lynch came after you thanks to your knowledge spell, and he accidentally cursed Cassie."

I shook my head. "It's bigger than that."

"Cora killed herself, Maddy. You read the note."

"She wouldn't do that."

"She might if she couldn't live with herself. How did she put it in the note? She got involved with something she shouldn't have, and things can't be undone?"

I repeated part of the note from memory—I'd read it so many times by now. "I was trying to help, trying to do a good thing for the right reasons. But I made a mistake—a huge mistake. And unfortunately, things that are done cannot be undone."

"See. It was regret."

"That doesn't explain the rash." I stopped walking as the truth of it hit me so hard in the chest that I struggled to breathe. "She knew she was dying."

"What?"

"Why else would she have killed herself?" My words came faster in my excitement, tumbling over one other, pushing and shoving to get out. "Cora saw the rash. She knew about Lynch's first kills—Sam and Timothy Schneider. They were brothers. He killed one of them." I mimed slitting my throat. "And then cursed the other—maybe when he started to figure it out. And then he . . . he cursed Cora when *she* started to figure it out too. And she couldn't stop him so . . ." I ran out of words. They'd all tumbled out, but in the process, they'd failed to come to an adequate end.

"So she killed herself?"

"Yes," I said with much less confidence.

"She killed herself because she was dying?"

I chewed my lower lip.

"Could you hurry up, please?" Lauren said. "You're making me nervous." She pointed down at the water-line bridge beneath my feet. I'd slowed to a stop while Lauren stood firmly on the magic side of the bridge.

"This thing is wide enough for a car. I'm not going to fall in."

"I know you're right, but it makes me nervous anyway. And I don't want to be late."

"We have twelve minutes left," I said. Pritchett gave us fifteen full minutes between classes, and Lauren and I had headed this way as soon as our previous class ended. Despite that, I picked my pace back up, and we continued to the small, one-story school building that sat on the magic side.

"So instead of spending her last days with you," Lauren continued, "showing you the best time of your life and showering you with love and happiness, she slit her wrists in the bathtub twenty feet away from your bed?"

"It was more like thirty feet."

"Maddy!"

"Okay. I admit there's a hole in my theory."

"A giant, gaping hole. It's the Grand Canyon of holes."

I didn't answer because I couldn't contradict her.

"I need to see the crime scene photos of Cora's death," I told Lauren just as she reached for the door of the small school building.

Her mouth dropped open, but no words came out.

Sheryl's words earlier that morning confused me more than they clarified anything. The more I thought about the intention Sheryl had ripped up, the more I was convinced that things didn't add up. The intention asked for life—at the expense of life. It was a blessing, not a curse. An ugly, twisted blessing based on the pain of others, but a blessing nonetheless. So why would Lynch put that intention on his victims?

"I'm ninety-five percent sure the rash was an intention—"

"Are we back on that?" Lauren asked.

"We never got off it." I spun and hurried back to the bridge. As I crossed over it, I extracted my phone from my backpack. I glanced back to see whether Lauren was following. And she was, slowly, dragging her feet across the ground as she walked.

Back on the tech side, I called Agent Reyes. For once, he answered on the first ring.

"I need photos of Cora's body," I said before he could speak.

A long silence met my request.

"Hello?" I said.

"I'm here," Reyes said, "but I'm baffled as to why you'd want something like that."

"There was a circular rash on her right shoulder. I think—I *know* it was an intention."

"I inspected that crime scene personally. There was indeed a rash, but no intention."

"Can't you just send me the photos? One would be

enough—with a view of her back." I couldn't be a hundred percent sure, but I was damn close. I needed more than Reyes's word to be convinced I was wrong.

"I'm sorry, Maddy. But I can't think of any scenario under which that would be a good idea." He disconnected the call.

With the dead phone still to my ear, I closed my eyes and tried to call up the same image I'd been pushing aside for months. Cora in the bathtub. So much blood. How did that much fit in one person's body?

I pulled my focus away from that and to Cora's back. The rash was there in my memory, perfectly circular. There was no way both Cora and Cassie had those by coincidence. I focused harder on the rash, trying to call up the details, but I didn't have them. Of course, when I'd found my stepmother's body, I hadn't inspected the red spot on her shoulder. I hadn't memorized its shape.

I'd thrown up my breakfast and then gotten the hell out of there.

"What did he say?" Lauren had caught up and now stood opposite me on the other side of the bridge, with white light sparkling all around her.

"He said no. He won't give me the photos." I started walking back toward the small, magic-side school building, and Lauren fell into stride with me.

She nodded, as if she'd expected that all along.

As soon as we entered the building, an idea hit me so hard that it almost knocked me over. "She slit her wrists!" I shouted.

Lauren shushed me when a nearby group of students looked our way.

I grabbed her wrist and towed her toward the girls' restroom. I let go of her when we entered the deserted restroom. Most students used the toilets on the tech side, which made sense since everything over there was higher end.

This building had been standing before Pritchett's founding but had been renovated to act as part of the school. Building new structures inside the water line often proved more trouble than it was worth. The construction machinery kept failing. Most of the renovation work here had to be done by hand, or done on the tech side and then transported across the bridge.

The result was a nice enough restroom but not luxurious like on the tech side. A narrow stone countertop was home to only two sinks. Thin wooden doors separated the two toilet stalls from the sink area. A traditionally styled armchair with a plush red cushion sat in one corner.

I jammed the chair under the door handle while Lauren eyed me as if I'd lost my mind—which maybe I had. I peeked inside each of the two stalls to make sure we were alone.

"She slit her wrists," I said again.

"We've established that. Wrist-slitting. Thirty feet from your bed. Got it."

"No, I mean that's the reason I first decided she couldn't have killed herself—one of the reasons anyway. A bloody death is not the way practitioners kill themselves.

They hang themselves. They take sleeping pills. They do *not* spill perfectly good blood all over the bathroom." My words were speeding up again. "You know when they *do* spill blood?"

Lauren shrugged, forehead crinkled. Then her mouth fell open, and she said what I was thinking. "When they're performing spells."

"She was trying to stop him—with a licensed long blade. That's why her blood was still in the tub. The stopper was down. She needed that blood to stay in there with her. Cora killed herself, but she did it for a reason." I paused to contemplate my next move. "I need to borrow your blood," I told Lauren.

She froze.

"To summon Cora," I continued. "The only person I've summoned is related to me. That can't be a coincidence."

"You've only *tried* to summon people related to you— and it doesn't work for your dad."

I waved a dismissive hand. "But it works for my mom. And logically, it makes sense that related blood would improve a connection to the dead."

"But my blood's not magic. That came from Cora's other side of the family."

"I'm not sure that'll matter, since it's *my* blood that needs to be magic to pull the whole thing off."

"If I do this, how are you ... going to ..."

"I'll have to cut you with my bone knife."

She frowned. "That's going to hurt."

"Think of it as part of the price of any spell. And if you

want, we can grab some ice from the cafeteria and numb you up a bit before I cut."

"We don't have time for that. And you never do that on yourself anyway."

"I'm used to it."

Her gaze searched my face. "You really need to do this?"

"I really do."

She checked the analog clock on the far wall, opposite the entrance. It read five minutes until class. She inhaled deeply and let out a long, audible sigh. "No ice then. Let's just get it over with before I change my mind."

It would be most effective to do the summoning back at my house—where she died. But Cassie's life was on the line, and we had no more time to waste.

I searched my bag for my bone knife and a clean sheet of paper and set both on the counter. "You ready?"

Lauren squeezed her eyes shut and raised her arm so I could access the fleshy part on its underside.

"It'll be over before you know it." I took a deep breath and pressed the blade into her skin.

She whimpered.

"I'm sorry. That's the worst of it. No more cutting." I squeezed the cut to get a good flow of blood going, which I swiped up with the side of the blade. On the blank paper, I wrote Cora's name in Lauren's blood. "That's it. All done."

I washed the blade with soap and water, then cut

myself on my upper shoulder and added my blood right over Lauren's. Lauren grabbed two bandages from my backpack, and I let her fuss over my cut while I got started.

I closed my eyes to focus and to shut out the soft pressure of Lauren's hands on my arm. When I opened them, I stared at the page in front of me with Cora's name spelled out. The name seemed to float above the page. Nothing existed but it and me and my desire to meet Cora, wherever she was.

The smell hit me first—like potpourri thrown into a fire. Then warm needlepoints pricked the skin at my shoulder. They spread outward until there were hundreds, millions, uncountable and spreading like fire across oil. Just before they became unbearable, the pinpoints blended together, leaving the familiar pressure on all sides. I broke through it with a gasp, and the transition left me breathless. I was floating in nothing, a perfect void without pain or worry or loss.

Everything I needed was right here.

"Cora," I whispered.

I felt her nearby, smelled her lavender scent. Her presence was quiet and calm, in contrast to my mother's, which somehow seemed so full of life even in death.

I opened my eyes.

The space in front of me brightened into a transparent gray figure. The facial structure became more defined. Surprise magnified Cora's large eyes and delicate features. Her lips moved, but her ghostly form flickered, and I couldn't hear her words in my head the way I did with my mom.

The connection was too weak. I could see her but not talk to her.

Cora held up a finger, asking me silently to wait. Her eyes closed, and an instant later, my head filled with an image of the Pritchett family crest. An ornamented shield surrounding a rose with its stem wrapped around a bone knife. I guessed Cora was trying to tell me she was surprised to be summoned.

"Hi." I gave her a guilty smile.

Another image of the crest. This time, she cocked her head to one side.

"Oh right. I took some blood from Lauren."

Cora shook her head, disappointed. While she was alive, I'd never told her I summoned my mom—or that I practiced magic at all. She would have disapproved, urged me to wait until I had a license and the proper training. Now, that disapproval played across her face.

I'd waited months to see her. Months missing her smile. Months missing the truth.

Tears slid down and settled at the edge of my lips.

My stomach lurched—a reminder that my time here was limited.

"Did you . . . did you kill yourself?"

She offered me a slow nod in return.

"Was it to stop Michael Lynch? A counter-spell that needed your blood?"

After a beat, she nodded again.

"But it didn't work?"

She shook her head. She reached a translucent hand out to me, and I felt the comforting chill of it as she brushed her fingers against my cheek. Cold against my face, already wet and warm with tears.

"Did he kill those men—Sam and Timothy Schneider, O'Hara?"

Another nod.

"How is he healing himself?"

She shook her head hard.

"He's not healing himself?"

She hesitated and shook her head again. Her lips moved but no words came out. Her form flickered in front of me. When it steadied, an image popped into my head.

Cora stood in a small room. Her hand held a white knife with a long blade, its edge darkened with blood. Michel Lynch lay on the ground at her feet, a stab wound in his chest. Blood leaked onto the floor around him.

She'd stabbed him?

I opened my mouth to speak, but the ghostly Cora in front of me raised a hand to stop me.

In my head, Lynch's blood stopped flowing—and reversed itself. Deep-crimson liquid slipped across the floor and poured back into the body. Surreal. Like liquid being spilled back into its glass.

The Cora standing above him turned and ran, bloody knife in hand.

This was so much worse than I'd thought. "He's

making himself immortal? How can he do that without killing both his parents?"

She closed her eyes again, and in my head I saw a single gravestone with no name. A second later, another nameless grave joined it. One by one, gravestone after gravestone appeared until they filled every corner of the image in my mind.

"He'd have to kill an infinite number of people," I said. "And then what's the point of immortality if you're alone."

The image in my head changed to the day I'd discovered Cassie's rash. I was sitting on the couch in Aunt Sara's living room, and in my lap sat the illegal book I'd stolen from Agent Tanner's library. Cassie bounded down the stairs to join me.

Cora had seen this moment?

"You watch me?"

Cora opened her eyes and smiled before closing them again.

In my mind, Cassie showed me her graphing home-work. She'd been studying asymptotes. I watched my lips move in response. I'd made a lame joke about the curve in her graph being close enough to the line it was approaching: *I mean, what's the real difference between 0 and 0.000001?*

"He doesn't have to kill an infinite number of people!" I said, finally understanding. "Just a lot of them."

She nodded.

"And you had his blood on your knife, so you tried to stop him with a spell of your own. But . . . you didn't stop the spell soon enough?"

She hesitated and shook her head. She rotated her shoulders to show me the small rash there, the one I'd seen when I found her body. I'd been right in thinking it was an intention, but it didn't exactly match the one Lynch was using. It had only one spiral, which represented life, and the arrows for banishment outside of it. Banishing life? The pentagram was there too, but nothing else. No symbol for good fortune and no second spiral.

Cora closed her eyes again, and I saw her in her ivory nightgown. She walked into my empty bedroom, blue letter in hand. My name appeared in her handwriting on the envelope. For a moment, she lay in the bed, staring at the ceiling, with tears wet on her face and her auburn hair spread across the pillow.

Eventually she stood, smoothed her hair, and placed the envelope on my nightstand. She spun a slow circle, taking it all in one last time, and then left the room.

The image faded away, and I blinked back tears.

"The rash is a death sentence," I whispered, my voice thin and hoarse. I didn't phrase it as a question because I knew the answer already. She'd known she had to die. She'd known that, if there was any way for her spell to succeed, it would take all of her blood. And she'd made that choice.

"He curses the people who get in his way—the ones he doesn't need for his immortality spell."

She nodded and mouthed something. This time I made out the words—*I'm sorry*.

My head spun, and my legs buckled beneath me. I hit

the floor of the bathroom, and Cora's form flickered again.

"I have to go," I said. "I will see you again."

Her lips moved. *Don't.*

"I miss you."

Her lips made another word.

I shook my head. I could make it out.

She made the word again, this time exaggerating the shapes of the sounds with her mouth: *Live.*

I released my connection, and her form faded away, leaving behind just the cold tile floor of the bathroom. The lights above shined too brightly. My stomach churned. My head ached. Tears covered my cheeks.

I wiped them aside.

A hand settled on my arm—a warm, living one. I looked up to find Lauren's worried face leaning over me.

"Did you get what you needed?" she asked.

I grabbed the piece of paper I'd used to write Cora's name and flipped it over. It smudged blood against the tile counter, but I didn't care. I snatched a pen from my bag and sketched the intention Cora had shown me on her back, while it remained fresh in my memory.

"This was on Cora?" Lauren asked. "What does it do?"

"Not sure. It's similar to the other intention—the one in the basement—except without the good fortune and the second spiral."

"So banishing life . . . ?"

I waited for her to finish. She was the brains of this operation, after all.

"The pentagram is protection, right?"

I nodded.

"With the other intention, the protection went into overdrive when we focused on Lynch with the knowledge spell, so this one may have some kind of trigger too. When it's triggered . . . it's a death sentence. Right? Simple."

I didn't get it. "Would you put a bow on it for those of us who are slower?"

Lauren pointed at the pentagram and then the arrows. "Protection. Banishing." Then she pointed at the spiral. "Life. When this intention is triggered, it protects Lynch by killing someone."

"So how's it triggered?"

She shrugged. "If it were my spell, and I was using this against someone who got in my way, I'd set it up to trigger whenever that person tried to tell someone what I was up to. But why not just kill them? Why curse them?" Her eyes went huge. "When did Rick Hale start seizing?"

"He was about to tell me everything he knew," I said, my tone grim and flat. "And Principal Spencer seized when he was about to say something to Ms. Louise—something bothering him."

"So that's it then. Talking about Lynch triggers the curse."

"But why? Why not just kill them?"

Lauren drummed her nails against the counter behind me. For a minute, the restroom was silent except for the rhythmic tap-tapping. "Maybe he can't kill them without using a trigger. All his victims were blood-magic users, right? Except Cassie? So their blood protects them to some degree—like that book in Marshall's library said." She gave me a smug look. "Told you learning was useful."

"Yeah, yeah, you're always right." I rolled my eyes. "There's more to it though. The people who are cursed feel sick. They have financial issues, malnutrition. They trip over manholes and get shot in muggings."

"Bad luck," Lauren said. She followed that with a nod, as if agreeing with herself. "It's part of the curse. A warning maybe, but it's as much as he can do to magic users before the trigger kicks in."

"When he kidnapped Hale, he said something about not being a killer. Maybe this is also his way of giving people a chance to live. An out. If they keep their mouths shut, they survive the curse."

"Cora knew better than to tell anyone what was going on," Lauren said. "It would have killed her. She tried to stop him instead."

"Then we'll have to be smarter about it." I swiped another hand across my face to brush aside the remaining tears. "I'm going to kill Michael Lynch."

CHAPTER THIRTY-THREE

"Try not to move." Lauren turned on the faucet and cupped her hands beneath it to catch a handful of water. She knelt beside me and tilted some into my mouth.

The summoning had left me hollowed out, and the cool liquid felt like acid against my raw throat. I sucked it down. "I'm going to take a quick power nap." I let my head fall against the base of the restroom counter.

When I opened my eyes again, Lauren was gone, and the room around me was mercifully quiet and empty. My chest ached from my short visit to the Deep. My throat burned. I tried to stand to reach the sink, but instead I doubled over in a coughing fit and landed hard back on my butt on the tile floor. Instead, I crawled into one of the two empty stalls, leaned against the wall, and closed my eyes again.

By the time the bell rang to end third period, my face

still felt cold and damp with sweat, but the clouds in my head had begun to part. I was still on the floor in a stall, leaning against the bathroom wall, when Lauren flung the door open and stared down at me.

"Feeling any better?"

I offered her a weak smile. "I'm not dead."

"You're not funny either. It's lunchtime, and you should eat. It'll make you feel better to walk around anyway. Can you stand?"

"I can. I don't want to."

Against my protests, Lauren nudged her shoulder under one of my arms and wrapped her arm around my waist. She dragged me to my feet and out of the stall.

"We need to call Agent Reyes." I pointed to the front pocket of my backpack, which sat on the floor under one of the sinks. When Lauren released me, I started to slump again.

"Don't sit. I'll just have to get you up again."

While I scowled at her, Lauren plucked my phone from my backpack and called. She set the call on speaker. The sound of ringing filled the restroom for only a couple seconds. The ringing stopped abruptly, and I sat up straighter, expecting to hear Reyes's voice.

"Your phone cut off," Lauren said. "Can you walk to the bridge?" Without waiting for a response, she grabbed my backpack and shoved my arms into the straps. Then she hooked an arm around my waist and led me to the door.

After a few steps, I shrugged her off and walked from

the building on my own. Lauren kept peering over, with arms at the ready to catch me. When we got outside, I squinted as the sunlight slapped me. But my head lightened, and the world sharpened. The grass and the trees and Lauren all looked less like a watercolor painting and more like actual, solid things. More importantly, my feet felt more like feet and less like giant cement blocks bolted to my ankles.

My stomach growled. I pretended not to notice, but Lauren gave me a smug look that left no doubt she'd heard it.

We crossed over the bridge and stopped under the shade of the tree where we usually ate lunch. I bent my knees to sit down. When Lauren glared at me, I leaned against the tree trunk instead.

She called Reyes on my phone again. This time, the ringing didn't stop—it went on forever. After the fifth ring, the call went to voicemail. Without my asking her, Lauren hung up and tried again. And again, we got his voicemail.

"Do you have Agent Tanner's number?" she asked.

"No. We have to go over there."

"To the Bureau." She stated it without any question in her tone. "Let's wait until after school, until you get your energy back." She dropped her backpack on the ground, dug inside it, and extracted a bag of chips. She passed them to me. "Eat. And remember our deal. I don't leave campus during school."

I'd been hoping she'd make an exception. After all, we

finally knew how Lynch had caused my stepmother's death. I felt . . . vindicated. It didn't bring her back, but I could get justice for her, and I could save Cassie. We couldn't waste any more time. "Text Marshall," I said. "He'll come with me."

"Only because he thinks you're less likely to get yourself killed when he's around."

I shrugged but didn't contradict her.

Lauren texted him from my phone. Less than ten seconds later, the phone beeped. "He's in. Meet at his car in the tech-side parking lot. He's on his way." She typed something else. "I let him know it'll take us five minutes to get there from the bridge."

"Will you grab that book from my bag—the one I took from Marshall's?"

"You mean *stole?*" She fished it out with the bag still on my back and passed it to me. My phone rang just as she was re-zipping my bag, and she checked the display. "It's Marshall." She connected the call. "Hey. I'm putting you on speaker." She kept a hold of the phone and gestured for me to follow her.

I pushed off the tree and followed her lead around the main school building and toward the parking lot.

"What's the plan?" Marshall asked.

I struggled to keep up with Lauren's pace, so that I could hear him through the speaker in her hand.

"I summoned Cora," I said in a loud hiss-whisper. That wasn't the sort of thing you could just shout in public.

"Maddy—"

"Can we jump to the end of the lecture, please? Or postpone it? This is important." My words came out in short pants. "Could you slow down, please?" I added to Lauren.

She slowed, but only by a fraction. "It's good for you to keep moving. You're feeling better, right?"

She was right, but I kept that to myself.

"Go on." Marshall's voice was too low, like how my dad's used to get before he sent me to my room to think about whatever I'd done. "What did you find out?"

I repeated for him everything I'd just told Lauren about my conversation with Cora.

"Holy shit," he said when I finished.

"My reaction exactly," Lauren said. "You guys are going to the Bureau because we can't reach Agent Reyes on the phone."

"And I want to read through this book a little more. I feel like it can help us understand Lynch's magic."

"What book? The one you stole from my mom?"

"I don't know why you guys are so focused on that part."

He didn't respond.

"You think it can help us figure out how to stop him?" Lauren asked.

"You mean *kill* him," I said.

"Cora already tried that. You saw the result. And she had a lot more experience than you do."

"She wasn't as motivated. He tried to kill you, Lauren. He *is* killing Cassie, and he might as well have killed my stepmother." I gritted my teeth. "I'll find a way."

"Even if you could," Marshall said, his voice still too low, "you can't just decide to kill someone. It's not right."

"You really want to talk to me about *right* right now?"

"Lynch is a murderer. You're not."

"We don't even know if we *can* kill him," Lauren said. "He's practically immortal at this point. If he can heal himself, he can heal himself indefinitely."

I gritted my teeth with the pain of moving as I flipped through the book's pages to find the section about healing spells.

Lauren snatched the book from me, passed me the phone, and found the page herself. She read it aloud as we walked. Thankfully, this required slowing her pace. "Practically speaking, spells to extend life are impossible. These include spells for youth, healing, resurrection, and the like. The price of these cannot be paid by the usual methods. For instance, to achieve youth, what does one give up in return? The obvious answer is: To extend one's life, another's life must be shortened. As one might imagine, this hypothesis has led to—"

"Wait." Despite the extreme weight of my hands—and my whole body—after that summoning, I held up one hand to stop her. "Read that back."

"To extend one's life, another's life must be shortened. As one might—"

"From the beginning."

Lauren flipped back a page to find the beginning of the

passage. "Practically speaking, spells to extend life are impossible. These include spells for youth, healing, resurrection, and the like. The price of these—"

"Resurrection," I said. "As far as blood magic is concerned, it's basically the same as healing, the same as immortality."

"Lynch isn't resurrecting anyone. How does that—"

I cut her off. "In the vision Cora gave me, Lynch was dead, but he woke up anyway. So it's the same. Right?" When no one answered right away, I added, "Marshall?"

"I guess," he said.

"Oh no," Lauren said, eyes wide. "No. No, no, no, no, no. Maddy, she's been dead for almost three months!"

"No!" Marshall shouted through the speaker once he caught on too. "You are not resurrecting Cora."

"Just hear me out. If we're going to kill Lynch anyway—"

"We're not killing Lynch," Marshall said.

"If we're going to kill him anyway," I continued, "then why not put that blood to good use? He's done all the hard work for us. We can use his blood to resurrect her."

"Assuming we could kill him," Lauren said.

"My mom worked on a case once, dealing with a supposed resurrectionist. He never succeeded. But I saw some of the photos of the bodies. Twisted stuff. It's playing with the dead, Maddy. It's a summoning and an immortality spell all bound up into a very sick ball."

"But if we already have an immortal, then it's really just a summoning. Right?"

Lauren shook her head, her mouth gaping open.

"The price of a life is an infinite number of other lives," I said, "or just one immortal. And we happen to have one of those handy."

Fifteen minutes later, Marshall and I arrived at the Bureau's headquarters in Marshall's car. He had spent the entirety of the car ride trying to talk me out of killing Lynch and resurrecting Cora, but I wasn't hearing him. It finally made sense.

I knew how to fix things, how to get my life back.

Even though the Bureau dealt with blood magic, their building stood outside the water line, right between a church and an office building. I'd asked my mom about that once, a long time ago. She said it had to do with the Practitioners Aid being a liaison organization. Non-magic folks didn't like crossing the water line, so it made sense for the Aid to be on the outside, where everyone could access it.

Since the Bureau had replaced the Aid, they kept the same building.

We slowed as we reached the guard station. Just like last time, they checked our faces against our IDs, took a note of our arrival, and waved us through the gate. We parked, and Marshall led the way through the front doors. Inside, we waited in line for one of the bored-looking receptionists.

My mother had taken me here on occasion when we had trouble with the neighbors or when she needed help with a blessing spell. Back when this was the Aid, there were no receptionists. Just an open room full of Aid representatives, who waved you over to them when they were available. And someone was always available—or apologetic that someone had been forced to wait a few minutes.

Now, I was nearly exploding with anticipation as we waited. We were so close to ending this, so close to returning my life to what it had been—before Michael Lynch.

Finally, a dark-haired receptionist waved us forward. "How can I help you?" She flashed us a painted smile.

"We'd like to see Agent Tanner. I'm her son, Marshall Tanner."

"Let's see." The woman typed something into her computer. "Hmm." She clicked something with the mouse and then looked back up at us. "It looks like she just wrapped up a meeting. I've notified her, and she'll be down in a moment." She gestured to the large waiting area behind us.

Five minutes later, a door opened in the white barrier separating the lobby from the secured area behind it. Agent Tanner stepped out, blond hair pulled into a tight ponytail as usual. Her face held a grim expression—also as usual.

Wordless, she led us through the security door and onto the elevator. She examined me with narrowed eyes throughout the entire elevator ride, and I found myself staring at the small television screen to the right of the elevator doors, just to look at anything except her disapproving face.

In her office, she gestured for Marshall and me to sit, and then closed the door behind us. She circled the desk and sat in her chair, her back rod straight. Although she hadn't been when we first met, today she wore a shoulder holster with a gun tucked in place.

"Shouldn't you two be in school?" Although she directed the question at both of us, her intense gaze stayed on Marshall.

He looked down at his hands.

"Let me rephrase. Why aren't you in school?"

"We have a lead in my stepmother's case," I said, even though she hadn't been looking at me.

"Your stepmother has no case. She killed herself. Her knife. Her hands. She even left a note and planned for someone else to find her body. I admit it's odd for a practitioner to slit her—"

I waved her words aside. "She killed herself."

Agent Tanner stopped talking and, for once, wore an expression of interest.

"Is Agent Reyes not joining us?" I shifted in my seat. Between the two of them, he'd always been the warmer one. And he talked more. Although slimmer and shorter, Tanner somehow came off more intimidating.

"No. Believe it or not, we have other things to do than

investigating what may or may not have happened to your aunt."

"Stepmother," I corrected.

She didn't apologize for the error. "What can I do for you, Miss Cooper?"

"My cousin has the same blood-magic illness that killed Sam Schneider, Jay O'Hara, Garrett Walker, and Principal Spencer. Michael Lynch cursed her. He cursed all of them."

She leaned forward in her seat, interested now. "What makes you say that?" She didn't ask who those men were or what made me think they were connected to one another—which meant she already knew that part.

I explained about Cassie's rash and tiredness, and how her symptoms matched those men's. I also told her about how Cora had the same rash, and that it looked a bit like Lynch's intention. And I reminded her that Lynch had attacked Lauren and me—although she still didn't know about the knowledge spell that prompted that.

"Reyes already told me your theory about your cousin's illness," Agent Tanner said when I finished. "You realize your cousin and those men have nothing in common?"

"But I just told you—"

She shook her head to cut me off. "Besides the symptoms. They are all magic users, all in social or work circles with Michael Lynch. For argument's sake, if Cassie has what they had, how did she get it? To curse her, Lynch would need her blood or bone, or at least a hair. Something naturally tied to her. And even then, why bother? She's no threat to him."

"A hair?" I asked.

"Yes, that would work in a pinch. Assuming the practitioner is superb."

"I was wearing Cassie's sweater the day he came after me and Lauren. He tackled me. He could have grabbed a hair off it. He probably thought it was mine."

Tanner leaned back in her chair and tipped her head back to contemplate the ceiling.

I held my breath while Marshall and I waited for her to react.

"And that's why you believe Michael Lynch is involved with your stepmother's death," Tanner stated as fact after a moment. "Not airtight, but I'm open to it." She drummed her fingers on the desk's surface. "The alleged healing-slash-immortality spell is problematic though. We'd need proof of it to build any kind of case against him."

"My cousin is dying. Can't you just arrest him? Or test his DNA against whatever you found in the park? I'm sure it'll match."

Marshall covered his eyes with his hand and groaned.

Agent Tanner leaned forward in her chair. "What do you know about the park?"

"I . . . uh . . . followed Agent Reyes because I figured he was looking for Lynch." It seemed as good a lie as any, and I was actually pretty proud of myself for coming up with it on the spot.

But the hard look on Agent Tanner's face stopped me

from celebrating for too long. "Outside of the men you mentioned, we're looking for Michael Lynch in connection with multiple murders. Believe me when I say the matter is at the top of our priority list. We will find him, and we will remove any active curses he has performed— one way or the other. Whether that will affect your cousin, I can't say."

"Multiple murders?" I asked. "Only two people died in the park."

Marshall let out a quiet groan.

Tanner eyed us in silence for a moment. I started to speak, but Marshall narrowed his eyes at me, and I changed my mind. My chair's wooden seat hurt my butt, and I squirmed to find a more comfortable position. There was *no* comfortable position in this room. Tanner reached for a large yellow envelope at the edge of her desk and turned it upside down.

A stack of page-sized photographs slid from the envelope and onto the desk. Most stayed on the stack, but a few kept going and spread across her desk. One fluttered to the floor by my feet.

In it, a small woman lay on her back on the floor of what looked like an alley. She lay in her own blood, and even the blood failed to hide the dark-red symbol beneath her. My stomach rebelled and tried to drop right out of me. I squeezed my eyes shut before I could see more.

"Thirty-two victims. All without a drop of magical blood. Each found bled to death on or near the same intention. We had no suspects until Agent Reyes insisted on tracking Michael Lynch, and we ended up at the park —where we found the most recent bodies in this case."

"Are you trying to scare us?" Marshall asked.

"Michael Lynch may have killed thirty-two people. Maybe more if your suspicions are true. We are handling this. Am I clear enough?"

I started to protest, but Marshall glared at me again.

"In the meantime, I suggest you both"—she looked at Marshall, who slumped further in his seat—"stay out of the Bureau's business before you get yourself killed. I suggest you forget everything you think you know." She pressed a button on her phone.

A second later, a male voice responded. "Everything okay in there?"

"Yes. I need an escort for two kids. They're leaving."

"Someone will be there in less than a minute."

"Thank you." Agent Tanner stood and walked around her desk. She stopped right next to my chair and leaned over until only a few inches separated her nose from mine. Her gaze landed briefly on my long sleeves and then locked onto my face.

I leaned back in my seat.

"My partner has a bigger heart than I do. He's a little soft because he has a daughter of his own, about your age. I have no such holdups. You will stay away from this, or I will bury your ass in the juvenile prison system—if Michael Lynch doesn't kill you himself. Am I clear?"

Marshall and I both nodded.

"Excuse my language." She sat on her desk and smiled a hard smile. "Get the hell out of my office."

We jumped to our feet. Marshall did it so quickly that his chair toppled over, and he didn't stop to pick it up. A guard met us in the hallway and escorted us out.

CHAPTER THIRTY-FOUR

I slept in on Saturday and woke in a great mood in the afternoon.

Something inside me felt settled, at peace. I whistled to myself as I showered and got dressed. Aunt Sara would be home today, and I'd managed four whole days without burning the house down or killing her kid.

"Cassie," I shouted as I ran down the stairs to the kitchen.

She sat at the kitchen table, her face pale and damp. "Stop shouting. I have a headache."

"Sorry," I said in an exaggerated whisper. "Your mom will be home around seven tonight. What do you say to making dinner for her?"

"Are you sick too?"

"Huh?" I opened the refrigerator and checked it for supplies. "We'll have to go shopping though. What do she and Ryan like to eat?"

"You're being weird."

"I'm in a good mood."

"That's being weird for you."

I stuck my tongue out at her. "Maybe I'm finally healing after Cora's suicide."

"That's good, I guess."

"And what's with you? You look like death."

"I *feel* like death. My head is pounding, and the room is spinning."

I walked over to her and felt her forehead. "You're burning up. Lie down until Aunt Sara gets home."

Cassie grabbed the edge of the table to push herself to her feet, and then wobbled for a second before righting herself.

"Whoa." I grabbed her elbow and led her to the couch in the family room.

"It's stress. Like Mrs. Evans said."

"When did you talk to Lauren's mom?"

"When you invited her here to check on me." Cassie reached up and felt my forehead. "Which one of us is sick here?"

"Right." I brushed her hand away and searched my mind for the moment she was talking about. Finally, it came to me. Tuesday, right after Aunt Sara left, Cassie complained about not sleeping well, and we . . . What did we do?

"You called her over Tuesday evening. Remember?"

"Yeah." Now that she mentioned it, I vaguely recalled

Mrs. Evans leaning over that couch, giving Cassie a full checkup. "She said it was nothing, right?"

"Stress. What's wrong with you?"

"Nothing." I pushed Cassie back down on the couch when she tried to stand. "Rest."

"I left my phone in the kitchen." With a grunt, she stood and took two steps in that direction. She swayed on her feet.

"I'll get it. Lie back down."

As she lay down, she reached for a small black book on the coffee table. "*The Theory of Life, Death, and Living*," she read from the cover. "What's this?"

"Not sure. Must be your mom's."

She opened it to a dog-eared page, and I retreated into the kitchen to find her phone.

"This can't be Mom's. It's blood-magic stuff," Cassie shouted from the next room. "Isn't this what you were reading the day I asked you about my math?"

"I don't know what you're talking about." I scanned the kitchen for her phone. There it was, next to the mini backpack I used on the weekends.

"This part's underlined: *Life is a unique entity, a combination of genetics and memory and soul that cannot be replicated by some arbitrary other life. By my calculations, a life-extension spell would take—*"

I'd barely laid my hand on the phone when Cassie abruptly stopped talking, and a thump sounded from back in the family room.

"Cassie?"

No answer. I turned and ran back the way I'd come, phone in hand.

Cassie lay on the floor in front of the couch, her body thrashing from side to side. Her mouth moved but no sound came out except for unintelligible grunts. Her wide eyes grew desperate.

"It's okay. I'm here. I'm here." I gripped her shoulder and rolled her onto her side.

Her face showed all the emotions I felt. Terror. Confusion. And most of all, panic. My chest ached with the need to do *something*, but I was helpless to stop this seizure. All the blood magic in the world, and my cousin was having a seizure right in front of me. I could touch her, I could speak to her, but I could not save her.

"Listen to me, Cassie. You're going to be fine. I promise." I kept one hand on Cassie and used the other to dial 9-1-1 on her phone. "My cousin is having a seizure. Please . . ." Cassie's thrashing became more vigorous and my breath caught in my throat. "Send someone!" I shouted.

I hit the speaker button and dropped the phone beside me.

"Paramedics are on the way."

I had a horrible, gut-wrenching flash of someone else lying on the floor. A sickening feeling of déjà vu as Cassie vibrated in my arms. Had we been here before?

The woman on the phone kept talking. Platitudes about everything being all right. I should stay calm. Help was on the way. Over and over. And on a soul level, I knew everything she said was wrong.

Minutes later, the paramedics burst into the house. Again, déjà vu hit me so hard it ripped my breath from my chest.

"If you're riding in the ambulance, you have to leave now," one of the paramedics said after they had lifted Cassie's writhing form onto the gurney and it bumped over the threshold and out the door.

I grabbed my phone and mini backpack from the kitchen, ran out the door, and scrambled into the ambulance behind them.

I called Aunt Sara three times from the hospital waiting room, but each time, the call went straight to voicemail. She was on a plane, on her way back to town. She would kill me when she got back. She'd tasked me with watching one of her kids, and I'd broken her.

I considered calling Mrs. Jacobs, the lady Ryan was staying with. But there was nothing he could do right now other than worry. Better to keep him out of the loop until I had good news to share with him.

I called Lauren and Marshall instead. Marshall stopped by Lauren's house to pick her up on his way to the hospital, and a half hour later, the two of them sat beside me in the waiting room.

"So you were right about the rash, huh?" Marshall asked, his face tilted back toward the sterile-white ceiling.

"Rash?" Today had the oddest feeling to it, like I was participating in a play without knowing any of the lines.

"I guess this means they haven't caught Lynch yet," Lauren said. "And we're out of ideas for catching him."

"What the hell are you guys talking about?"

They both turned to stare at me with that same odd look Cassie had given me before she hit the floor. They'd better not have seizures too.

"Seriously. I have no idea what's going on today. First, Cassie claims I called your mom to check on her on Tuesday. And then the seizure. And now this."

Lauren rotated in her seat to look me square in the face. "You're not screwing with us?"

"No!"

"Cassie had a rash on Tuesday, and she wasn't feeling well. Before that, Principal Spencer had the same rash and then a seizure just like Cassie's. When he died—"

"Principal Spencer died?" I hadn't known him well, but he'd always been kind to me.

"Why don't you remember any of this?" Marshall asked.

Lauren gasped and brought her hand up to her mouth. "The knowledge spell. You're paying the price for it."

"I don't know how to do a knowledge spell."

"No shit," Marshall muttered.

"That's not helping," Lauren said.

They filled me in on everything that happened in our investigation of Cora's death. With each word, it was like someone had hit the rewind button, and those moments replayed in my head with their narration. My memory was a puzzle with missing pieces, every one of which had to do with Cora. By the time they finished talking, I leaned back in the blue, plastic hospital chair, breathless.

I was officially retired from knowledge spells.

But I'd wasted an entire day without even knowing it. Cassie could die at any moment, and Lynch was walking around as a free man—a free immortal man.

I leaned forward and buried my face in my hands. "I don't know what to do anymore. It's too late."

Lauren rubbed my back. "It's not. They could still find him. Principal Spencer lasted over a week after his first seizure."

I nodded, but the motion was mechanical. Our principal had lasted over a week, but Jay O'Hara had died after his first seizure. So had Rick Hale, as far as I knew. We were out of time.

Marshall jumped to his feet. "Let's go find him."

"And do what?" I said. "Kick him in the shins? He's immortal."

"We'll call my mom and her partner. They'll take care of it."

"They're already looking for him," Lauren said.

"It's not going to hurt if we help out." He fixed his face into determination I'd never seen him wear before. It sparked hope in me. "We have to save Cassie. But no summoning and no reckless magic."

I jumped to my feet. "We could do a finding."

Lauren opened her mouth to say something, but I stopped her.

"Right," I said. "I remember. It won't work. What about . . ." Nothing else came to me.

"What if we make him come to us?" Marshall asked, his voice low and calm.

"How?" Lauren asked. Her tone made it clear she didn't actually want an answer.

"We do a finding!" I said.

"Maddy," Lauren said, her voice taking on that soothing quality that people get when the person they're talking to is being dense.

"I know. I know. We won't find him. But he has an active protection spell going. Any spell we do to him should alert him to our location. Right?"

"He didn't come after us when we did the last finding."

"Because we were headed to the park. He couldn't return to his crime scene. But he consistently attacks people who've figured out his game. Right? So if we do another finding, assuming we're not standing right next to Bureau agents, he should come after us."

Marshall nodded slowly. "So where do we want him to meet us?"

Suddenly, I saw one more chance to put everything right. "Cora's grave."

CHAPTER THIRTY-FIVE

We crossed the water line. A few minutes later, the car gave out, and we jogged the rest of the way to the church where Cora was buried. I took the lead, followed by Marshall, with Lauren barely keeping up behind us.

"This is a bad idea, Maddy," Lauren said when she caught up with us. "I mean, don't get me wrong—you have a lot of bad ideas. But this is on a new level." She stood right in front of me, blocking my path through the cemetery gate.

I squeezed her in a quick hug. When I released her, I looked her right in the eyes. "You should go home."

"We should all—"

"I have to do this. Cora's death has felt wrong since the moment I found her. Now I can make it right. I couldn't do anything for my mom and dad. I didn't know how back then. But this—this I can fix."

She laid a hand on my shoulder. "You can't fix it. Sometimes things aren't meant to be."

I shrugged off her hand. "Not this."

"Getting yourself killed isn't going to help Cora. She made her choice. You don't get to un-choose it for her. And think about what it would do to your aunt if this went wrong—especially if she loses Cassie too."

"No one's losing Cassie," I said.

"Then think of what it would do to me. Do you ever think of anyone but yourself?"

I stepped around her and hurried toward Cora's grave. It was only late afternoon, but cold wind whipped around us. Dark clouds cast the entire graveyard in shadow. I had to squint to make out the names on the gravestones.

On my way to Cora's body, I passed a shovel propped outside a small mausoleum. I grabbed it and kept moving until I located Cora's rose-colored gravestone. I dropped the shovel in front of it and shrugged out of my backpack.

Lauren and Marshall caught up with me. For once, Marshall was not objecting.

"I know you've made up your mind about this," he said. "I couldn't stop this if I wanted to—which I'm not sure I do."

"Why not?" Lauren said, her tone shrill. "She's going to get us killed."

"If it was my sister lying in that hospital bed, I would kill anyone who stood in the way of saving her." He looked me straight in the eye. "But I don't approve of the resurrection plan. Cora is gone, and if you try to change that, you'll be gone too. No resurrection has ever succeeded."

"No resurrection has had the blood of an immortal to help it along," I said.

"You're talking about undoing three months of deadness. The healing alone required to make her body fit for resurrection might take every bit of that immortality, and that's before you can even think about returning her spirit to the body."

"I can do it." I had to. There were no other options.

"I'm calling my mom," he said.

"No! We agreed to save Cassie."

"And if we're going to do that, we'll need my mom and her partner. We call her, then you do the finding spell. Hopefully, they'll show up before Lynch does, and they'll have no choice but to capture or kill him."

I gave him a quick hug. "Thanks."

Lauren crossed her arms over her chest.

"You can still leave," I told her.

"I'm your best friend. I always have your back—it's in the job description. But I'm here under protest."

"Noted."

The two of them stood nearby while I got to work shoveling. The graveyard sat in utter silence except for the leaves rustling in bursts of wind and the repeated stabs of my shovel into the dirt. Soon, Lauren's nervous humming joined with the shoveling. Together, they formed a rhythmic chorus that sounded more like a funeral march than I appreciated.

I'd seen a television show once where the two main characters dug up a grave. It took them about a minute of screen time to get it done, but in real life, it shocked me how long this would take. Five minutes later, the rub of the shovel irritated my hands, and I'd made barely a dent in the earth.

I threw the shovel aside. "Cassie's running out of time. There has to be a better way."

"Let's get Lynch here now," Marshall suggested. "Forget the resurrection."

I gave him a terse nod. I was *not* forgetting the resurrection, but I agreed with him that we had to get Lynch here as soon as possible.

He pulled out his phone and dialed. "Mom," he said after a moment. He paused and stared at the darkening sky while he talked. "Michael Lynch is on his way to Monroe Cemetery." He paused again. "We're already there." He disconnected without waiting for her response.

Two seconds later, his phone's display lit up as it rang with an incoming call. He turned the screen toward us, so we could see his mother's name on it. But after only one ring, the display flickered and went out. Once again, the graveyard went quiet.

"It's just as well," he said. "She'll be on her way now that she knows there's no way to reach us." He nodded toward me. "Now we call Lynch."

I didn't have a map on me, but I didn't need one. The visual wouldn't do me any good, since the point was to make him come to us.

From my backpack, I pulled out my knife and a notebook and ripped out a blank page. I sliced across my forearm and, with the side of the bone blade, swiped up some of the blood. I wrote Lynch's name on the page, closed my eyes, and focused on his location.

After a few seconds, the magical energy hit me in a shallow wave that smelled only vaguely of burnt rose petals. Light pinpricks scattered across my skin and disappeared. I opened my eyes. "That should do it. Either he's on his way, or my cousin is dead."

Lauren uncrossed her arms, apparently resigned to whatever fate we'd just set in motion. "How are you going to kill him once he gets here?"

"Reyes," I said. "He's been collecting blood from all Lynch's victims. He should be able to use that to reverse everything Lynch has done with the same blood. He was made strong by their deaths, so he can be weakened by their blood."

"Makes sense," she admitted. "How long do you think it'll take Lynch to get here?"

"Depends where he is," I said.

"What if he was already inside the water line? I mean, if he's still trying to solidify his immortality, wouldn't he stay inside the water where the magic is strongest?"

Marshall and I exchanged worried glances.

"I didn't think of that," I said.

The three of us went silent again. Overhead, the clouds had become even darker, and if I didn't know better, I would have thought it was nighttime. A sharp breeze hit my skin, and I shivered.

A noise toward the cemetery's entrance caught my attention, and I squinted into the gloom. The world sharpened, and for a moment, I could see the particles of magic floating upward like swirling dust in the darkness. No one was approaching. I let out a long breath of relief. No time for second thoughts, but I definitely preferred for Lynch to take his time getting here—just enough for Reyes and Tanner to beat him.

"She's going to ground me forever," Marshall said, laughing to himself.

"And I'll be in jail," I said. But at least Cora would be alive.

I heard the noise again, this time closer. I jumped, startled.

A person burst out from behind a tree and rushed toward us. The closer he got, the more I could make him out. He was alone—not the Bureau agents we were hoping for.

I held my bone knife in front of me.

Marshall shouted something I couldn't understand and grabbed the shovel from where I'd tossed it.

As the man came closer, there was no longer any doubt it was Michael Lynch, wearing that same cold expression he had each time we'd met before.

I shoved Lauren behind me.

Lynch slid a blade from his inside jacket pocket. Without so much as a hiccup in his step, he slashed across his forearm, drawing a thick line of blood. His eyes closed for only an instant.

"I can't move my arms," Marshall shouted. He had the shovel half-raised behind him, frozen in the act of hefting it onto his shoulder. "Or my legs!"

"Did he just do a spell?" Lauren asked.

Forty feet, thirty, twenty-five. With Marshall frozen, all that stood between a madman and me and Lauren was my puny knife. A weight slammed into me, and I flew backward away from Lynch. I crashed into Lauren, and the two of us hit the ground hard over twenty feet from where we'd started.

Pain vibrated up my spine, but I scrambled to my feet. "What the hell just happened?"

Lynch now stood beside Cora's grave, alone with Marshall, who still stood frozen in place. Marshall's head swiveled to look at me, and his eyes overflowed with pleading. I ran toward him—but smashed into something invisible and solid. I fell to the ground and landed hard on packed dirt and grass.

Lynch circled Marshall and took two steps toward me. Something invisible blasted into my chest again and shoved me backward.

Lynch tilted his head to one side. "That's interesting," he said in his flat voice. "You're protected." He gestured his blade toward Marshall. "But this one isn't." He showed me a mouth full of white teeth.

I expected someone like him—a murderer, a sociopath

—to be out of control, to yell, shout, curse. The fact that he wasn't terrified me even more.

I ran toward him and, once again, smashed into the invisible barrier. I pounded my fist against it.

Lynch moved closer to Marshall and drew in a long, loud breath through his nostrils. "Smells magic. Too bad. The blood is useless to me. Tainted."

"Why can't I get closer?" I shouted at Lauren.

"It's the blood promise," Lauren said, now on her feet as well. "Twenty feet away."

"Blood promise?" It took a moment for it to come back to me. Lauren had refused to help me find Lynch unless I promised to keep a distance between us. "Release me."

"It's protecting you."

"Lauren, *now!*"

"I won't—"

I spun toward her and sank every ounce of desperation I felt into my voice. "Release me now!"

She froze, her eyes wide like spotlights in the darkness. "I . . . I release you."

I ran toward the barrier again, and this time felt only a slight pressure as I passed through it.

Lynch smiled at me and, without breaking eye contact, drove his blade upward under Marshall's ribs.

I screamed. Behind me, Lauren screamed. And my whole world was screaming. This was not happening. It was a bad dream. It was a nightmare. I had come out here to save Cora. I had *not* come out here to fail.

I had not come out here to watch Marshall die.

Lauren was still screaming, but the pitch had changed. It was louder, higher. Was that a siren? Lynch turned and ran deeper into the graveyard.

Marshall lay at my feet, his eyes staring up at the dark sky, blood seeping from him and covering the toes of my shoes. I knelt and shook him, but he didn't move. He didn't blink.

CHAPTER THIRTY-SIX

No. No, no, no.

I took off after Lynch, but already I'd lost him in the dark cemetery. Agents Reyes and Tanner burst from the darkness and tore past me, searching the grounds for him.

I sank to the hard ground beneath me and dropped my head into my hands. Why couldn't I undo it? Why was I so goddamned stupid? Useless and stupid. Marshall and Cora were both dead. Cassie was dying.

I was a curse.

"I've got him over here," Tanner yelled somewhere in the darkness in front of me.

I stumbled to my feet and followed the voice. I still had a job to do.

Agent Tanner had Michael Lynch face down on the ground. She half knelt above him, yanking his arms behind him, her knee pressed into his back.

Her whole body trembled. "I can't fight his freezing spell for much longer," she said in short bursts of words.

Agent Reyes was pouring red liquid onto the edge of a long white blade.

"You can't kill me," Lynch said, teeth bared. "I'm immortal."

"You're only *nearly* immortal," Tanner corrected. She stopped talking to take a steadying breath as her body vibrated again. "And you killed thirty-two people to get there."

"I'm not a killer!" Lynch shouted. He struggled against her grip, but she held firm. "I've made them all immortal. They live inside me. It's a gift."

"And you're insane. Thirty-two deaths may be enough to beat your cancer, but thirty-two can be undone." She jerked her head toward Reyes. "Tell me you got all the victims in there."

Reyes turned the knife in his hand to catch the rest of the blood on the other side of the blade. "Every single one."

"Then kill him," she said through gritted teeth.

"Let him up," Reyes said.

"What?"

"Let him up. He has to have an intention on his body somewhere, and we need to destroy it."

Tanner released one of Lynch's arms and yanked the other to one side, forcing him to roll over. He screeched as he did.

Reyes jumped on top of the man and used his knees to

pin Lynch's arms to the ground. He sliced down the center of Lynch's shirt, revealing a set of thick scars in a distinct design. They matched the immortality intention he'd been using—the one from the basement. Life at the expense of life, as Sheryl had described it.

Reyes bared his teeth and angled the knife to one side of the symbol. He pushed the blade under Lynch's skin, and Lynch screamed. He twisted under Reyes's grip, but Reyes was bigger and stronger. He didn't budge.

I cringed but didn't look away as Reyes cut the symbol from Lynch's chest.

As he severed the last bit of skin connecting the intention from Lynch's body, thin scars appeared all over Lynch's left arm—his bicep, forearm, and both shoulders. More cuts popped up all over his torso—crisscrossing in every direction—until almost no patch of visible skin was spared. Hundreds of old cuts from old spells. Maybe thousands.

Three scabbed scratches darkened into existence on the left side of his face.

Reyes clutched the patch of destroyed flesh in his fist. In one smooth motion, with his other hand, he pulled down the collar of his own shirt and swiped the blade across his bare skin underneath. Then he slammed the blade into Lynch's chest.

Michael Lynch's eyes went wide, and then his body sagged.

A stinging-hot wind rushed past me toward the two men. I stumbled to one side as it shoved me off balance.

Instead of the relief I'd expected to feel at the sight of Lynch's corpse, my body felt twisted too tightly. Magic vibrated through the air, pulling the hair on my arms taut.

"That wasn't what we discussed." Agent Tanner's voice came out low and hard. As she spoke, her hand inched toward her sidearm. "What did you do?"

Reyes moved like a lion, fast and feral despite the sheer size of him. He backhanded Tanner before she could touch her weapon. She went down and lay limp.

"I became immortal," he said to her motionless back. He slipped her gun from its holster and tucked it into the back of his pants.

Reyes turned toward me, and once again, I recognized just how massive he was. A monster of a man with dark hair and dark eyes and a body that any weightlifter would envy. And here I stood with nothing between us. Even if I managed to stab him with my three-inch blade, he'd put a Band-Aid on it.

Reyes reached into his jacket pocket and withdrew a small bottle of water. He twisted off the top and emptied the water over the knife he'd just used to kill Lynch. "You need the blood of thirty-two victims to take what I have." He jerked his head toward Lynch's corpse. "Make that thirty-three." He wiped the last traces of blood from the knife on his light-blue T-shirt, leaving a dark stripe across it. "What a shame."

I backed up, patting my pockets for my knife. "I don't want any trouble."

"You always want trouble, Miss Cooper. And thanks for that, by the way." He grinned.

"You're welcome?" I kept moving backward.

"Your knowledge spell helped me connect Michael here to the murders he'd already committed. I wasn't sure at first. I thought Cora might know something, since she shared her suspicions about an immortality spell with me. She was vague though. Not enough details. I searched your house up and down, but any evidence she had—it died with her. I nearly gave up—until you convinced me he had a healing spell . . . Who am I to turn down immortality when it shows up on my doorstep wrapped in a pretty bow?"

"Yeah." I faked a laugh. "Can't blame you for that. I mean, who doesn't want to live forever?"

Reyes gestured at my hands. "Lost your knife?"

It figured that *now* would be the time one of those finding spells came back to haunt me.

Agent Tanner stirred on the ground behind him.

I tried not to look at her. "You mind if I borrow yours for a minute?" I said.

He chuckled. "You're a funny girl."

Agent Tanner rose to a sitting position and scanned the area. Her eyes met mine and then landed on Reyes's back.

"That's a good reason to let me live," I said.

Silently, Agent Tanner rose to her feet. She picked up an object from the ground and raised it. My knife!

She reached Reyes in two large strides and jammed the

blade into the side of his neck. He dropped to the ground with a sickening gurgle. I averted my gaze before I could see any more.

Reyes's knife dropped to the ground beside him. I snatched it up and wiped both sides of the blade in the blood pooling around him, careful not to look at his face.

"What are you doing?" Tanner asked, gripping my wrist. "No one's leaving this graveyard immortal."

"Don't worry. I don't want that," I said, shaking her off. "But he's going to resurrect since you didn't kill him with the victims' blood—unless we use up his immortality for something else."

I ran back toward Cora's grave, right past Lauren, still huddled over Marshall's body. My eyes stung, and my chest burned with the expanding hole occupied by all the dead people I loved. But there was nothing I could do about that. Like Lauren said earlier, some things weren't meant to be.

I knelt in front of my stepmother's gravestone. *Cora Cooper*, it read. *Beloved wife and stepmother.* She was so much more than that. She'd pulled me back from the darkness after my parents' death. She'd been the family I wanted, the family I needed.

But that didn't matter now. She would live for decades more, and when she died of old age, I'd make sure her gravestone said something more appropriate. I cut myself with my bloody blade and wrote Cora's name on the front of the rose-gold stone.

My body jolted as I accelerated toward the Deep in a

swirl of hot, floral air. The force hit me so hard that I lost my balance, and my shoulder banged into the hard gravestone. I gasped for breath, but the pressure pushed in all around me, dragging me under. The warm air turned cold as I slipped into the Deep.

I needed to stay focused. Just Cora. Nothing else. Not the pain. Not the suffocation. Only my stepmother. Finding her spirit, healing her body, bringing her back.

A shrill scream sounded nearby, followed by sobbing. Two women sobbing.

"Marshall. Marshall, baby, wake up." Tanner's voice was high-pitched, desperate.

Lauren sobbed more quietly.

Cora. Nothing but Cora.

Cold seeped into my skin and snaked across my bones. It tightened around them and squeezed. I trembled with the depth of it. My body weighed a ton. Heavy and freezing. I wanted so badly to just go to sleep.

"Cora," I whispered. "Where are you?"

I felt her just beyond my reach, smelled her scent. But when I reached for her, her spirit slithered out of reach. Too far away, but I would not leave without her. I would not fail her again.

"Marshall," a woman's voice whispered in the distance. "Please, baby."

Despite the chill, I focused on moving my consciousness deeper. Darkness crept in all around me. Dark and cold, and I was falling into it, drifting, floating. And it was amazing. Numb and peaceful and painless. I didn't want to fight it anymore. Beneath me, the darkness spread into void, into nothingness that promised peace and comfort.

No more pain in the Deep. No more pain if I gave myself over to it, if I let myself sink and sink and sink forever.

And Cora was there.

And my mom was there.

And . . . a familiar sandalwood scent that could only be my father's aftershave.

"Dad," I whispered. It had been so long. Years since I'd seen him. Years since I'd talked to him. Years since I'd laid my head on his shoulder and known that everything was fine. Everything was perfect.

I could stay here.

"Maddy." Someone was calling my name. My body shook. Was someone shaking me? "Maddy!"

I didn't want to go back. It was better here. It was better with Cora and Mom and Dad. I could let go here. I could stay.

I could get lost here.

"Maddy, come back to me." The voice sounded closer. Lauren?

I didn't want to come back. I liked it here. I wanted to see what lay beyond the darkness.

"Come back, Maddy."

In that faraway place, where someone was shaking me, my shoulder pressed against the hard gravestone. My knees ached against packed ground beneath me. My cheeks were wet. It hurt here.

Life *hurt*.

"Maddy!" Lauren shouted. Her face hovered near mine, wet with tears like mine. "Let Cora go."

"Marshall, baby. Please." More sobbing nearby.

I needed to maintain concentration on the resurrection, but I glanced over for only a second. Agent Tanner sat nearby with Marshall's head in her lap. She cradled his face against her bright-red one, her cheeks soaked with tears.

Souls floated around me in their forever dance. They urged me farther downward, into the depths. Tempting me toward the place where none of this mattered anymore. Each one unique. My mother, still as vibrant as when she lived. My father, his strong spirit wrapped around me, comforting. I felt their souls. I felt their peace.

And Cora, calm and earnest and peaceful too.

Live, she'd told me.

I could reach them all—if I just stretched a little. I could bring any one of them back.

A soul brushed against me, soft and familiar. I recognized it. I knew it. I reached out across the Deep and dragged it back with me.

CHAPTER THIRTY-SEVEN

The next day, I woke in Cassie's hospital room, curled in a plastic chair that was too hard and too small. Aunt Sara sat in a stuffed recliner right beside my cousin's hospital bed. She'd arrived home the night before and come straight here. I got back here from the graveyard shortly after she arrived.

"Has she woken up at all?" I asked, my voice heavy with sleep. I hadn't slept well. How could I in this plastic chair—and with everything that had happened the night before? I counted it a miracle I'd slept at all.

Despite the bruises developing on my arms, leg, and butt, my body felt numb. Heavy. I wanted to sleep for the whole weekend.

"Has she had any more seizures?" I asked, still blinking sleep out of my eyes.

Aunt Sara's eyes widened. "Did the doctors say she would?"

"No, no. Just curious."

"No more seizures. She slept through the night." Aunt Sara offered a weak smile. "Except for the snoring, of course."

"Of course."

Cassie's soft snoring ceased, and her eyes fluttered open. My aunt and I both went silent, and I held my breath while Cassie took in her surroundings. "Hey." Her voice came out low and hoarse, and she cringed as she spoke. "Don't look so serious."

Her mother laughed, and nervousness seeped away from her like air from a popped balloon. She sagged in place. I would have smiled too, but I had no energy for it.

"When did you get home?" Cassie asked her mom.

"Yesterday. I came straight here when I got Maddy's messages." Aunt Sara squeezed her hand. "Thank God you're okay. How did this happen?"

I opened my mouth to explain it all—that Cassie had been cursed by a madman who wanted to be immortal. That I was the real target for the curse because I was determined to figure out what happened to my stepmother.

Cassie reached a hand toward me. I was sitting too far away for her to touch me from her bed, but I took the gesture for a signal that she wanted me to come closer.

I hesitated.

I'd gotten Cassie into this mess. My meddling in Cora's life—or death—had put my cousin in this bed and almost killed her. I shook my head and curled tighter into a ball in my plastic chair. Cassie withdrew her hand, still looking at me.

"Thanks for bringing me here."

"Don't," I whispered.

"I couldn't talk while I was . . . I wanted to. I was so scared. But you—"

"Don't," I said again, louder this time. My eyes felt hot, wet. The last thing I deserved was her thanks.

Aunt Sara finished the thought for her daughter. "Thank God Maddy called the paramedics."

I directed my attention at my shoes. They had dirt—and maybe blood—caked in their soles from last night. Last night, when Lynch killed Marshall. And Marshall's mom killed Reyes. And I was so selfish and determined to bring Cora back that I endangered my best friends. I'd never forget it—regardless of how much I wanted to.

And here were my aunt and cousin congratulating me for my quick actions. Only they didn't know I'd had days of suspecting this would happen. For days, I was too focused to insist, to make Aunt Sara believe me, to get Cassie the care she needed.

I twisted my hands together in my lap.

Aunt Sara stood and pressed a hand against my forehead. "Are you feeling bad too?" Without waiting for my answer, she shouted into the hallway. "Could we get a doctor in here?"

"I'm fine." I brushed her hand away.

She glared at me and put her hand right back to my face. "Your temperature is normal."

"Seizures aren't contagious, Mom," Cassie said.

"I know. I just worry about my kids, okay? Is that so wrong?"

Her kids.

Before I knew it, I was up from the chair and had my arms wrapped around Aunt Sara's waist, my head buried in the crook of her shoulder. She squeezed me, her hand still locked with Cassie's.

Cassie's doctor swooped into the room. A short woman with wavy dark hair, she wore a white coat and a cheery expression. "You called for me?" She went straight to Cassie's bed and checked the machine beeping at her side. "Vitals look good. I'm happy to see you awake. How do you feel?"

"Weak," Cassie said. "Tired." She licked her lips. "Thirsty."

"I'll have someone bring more water," the doctor said. She glanced at Aunt Sara. "You called for me?"

"My niece looked a little clammy a moment ago." She pointed at me.

The doctor squinted as she scanned me from head to toe. "What hurts?"

"I feel fine," I said. "Everything's going to be fine."

CHAPTER THIRTY-EIGHT

"What do you think I should do with this?" I shouted across my old house.

I stood in Cora's bedroom, holding up an old photo of the two of us. It was taken shortly after her wedding to my dad, and in it, we were both laughing. My father had taken the picture that day, so in a way, the photo represented all three of us.

Heavy footsteps approached, and Marshall stepped into the bedroom. "Let me see."

He'd been moving slowly over the past week. Apparently, when someone died and came back to life, they didn't want to jump up and run a marathon a week later. Go figure. Still, even at low strength, his life for Reyes's immortality seemed a fair trade.

Marshall plucked the photo from my hand. "This is a great shot." He pointed at me in the picture. "What are you doing with your face?"

I squinted at it. "What?"

"Is that a smile?" He moved the photo closer to his eyes. "I didn't think your face did that."

"Shut up." I grabbed the picture back from him, careful not to bend it. "I'll take it home with me."

Lauren stepped into the room, her smile as tired as I felt. "*Home* to your aunt's?"

"That's where I live."

We'd finished packing up the things in my old bedroom, but I wanted to grab a few more things from Cora's room before we called it a day. We would drive these boxes over to my new home, and the movers would come to put the rest of it in storage.

I taped the last box shut and said my silent goodbyes to the home where I'd lived most of my life. Fortunately, I wouldn't have to say farewell to the memories that came with it.

When I finished taping, Marshall stacked the box in the corner with two others. Lauren straightened the stack as soon as he turned around.

"What about the rest of the house?" he asked. "The things you don't want."

"The movers will pack it up. How are you feeling?" I touched his arm. "You winced when you lifted that last box."

"You caught that? And I thought I was being subtle." He flashed me a crooked grin. "I'll be fine. Better every day."

I scanned the room to see if there was anything else I wanted to bring with me. "Where's my bone knife?" I pointed at the dresser, where I'd set it aside so I wouldn't accidentally pack it away.

"Not a clue."

"Oh, is it lost?" Lauren's tone was syrupy false. "So sad."

"Just because I'm ignoring you doesn't mean I don't sense your sarcasm." I peeked in the small crack between the dresser and the wall to see if it had fallen back there. No knife. I tore the tape off the last box I packed and checked inside. Still no knife.

I spun to face Marshall.

"I didn't take it this time," he said, arms up in surrender before I could even accuse him. "You'd just buy a new one."

I pulled out the top drawer of the dresser to search there, and then slammed it shut again. This was the price for my finding spells. It took two of them to follow Lynch to the park that day, and another to call him to the cemetery. I'd paid the price for only one of those so far.

"If it's gone, you're square with the universe now?" Lauren asked.

"Not exactly."

"In that case, have you considered maybe *not* buying a new knife right away?" Marshall gripped me by the sides of my shoulders and steered me away from my search.

I thought about it for a second. "It's not like I can afford one anyway."

A half hour later, the three of us finished loading my boxes into the car. While Marshall and Lauren waited outside, I walked through the house to make sure I hadn't forgotten anything. As a final check, I dropped to the floor to peer under Cora's bed, and there it was—my knife.

I snatched it up.

"Maddy," Lauren called. "You ready to go?"

I slipped the knife into my pocket and jumped to my feet. "Yeah. I have everything I need."

ACKNOWLEDGMENTS

This story was a journey.

I started writing it in 2013, completed it, scrapped it, completed it, scrapped it, and then finally made it happen as part of my MFA program with Seton Hill University.

To Shelley Adina and Barb Miller, thank you for your mentorship while I rewrote this novel a couple more times. Without you, Shelley, I would have given up on this concept. Without you, Barb, I wouldn't have explored the characters and relationships the way I eventually did.

Thanks also to Tambi Harwood, Kelly, Mary Boland-Doyle, and Melanie Bates. You are amazing critique partners who made me question my choices and improve with each chapter and each draft.

Thank you, to the SHU MFA program in Writing Popular Fiction and to everyone who touched this story while I was there.

And thank you for reading.

ABOUT THE AUTHOR

I decided to write books about ten minutes before graduating from law school.

Now, I'm an Atlanta attorney moonlighting as an author, electronics junkie, and secret superhero. With degrees in computer science and a healthy diet of fiction, I love all things high-tech and unreal.

I write fantasy and science fiction for young adults.

Now you know where to find me:
www.writeralicia.com

Sign up for my newsletter to keep in touch:
www.writeralicia.com/newsletter

amazon.com/author/writeralicia
goodreads.com/writeralicia
facebook.com/writeralicia
twitter.com/writeralicia
instagram.com/writeralicia